THE DEAD BORN

The Dead Born © Copyright Miranda Maples, 2022

All rights reserved. Published by OffBeat Publishing, LLC.

No part of this publication may be reproduced, distributed, or transmitted in any form or by any means, including photocopying, recording, or other electronic or mechanical methods, without the prior written permission of the publisher, except in the case of brief quotations embodied in critical reviews and certain other noncommercial uses permitted by copyright law.

For Information regarding permissions, write to: OffBeatReads@pm.me

This publication includes works of fiction. Any resemblance to actual events or persons, living or dead, is entirely coincidental, a product of the author's imagination, or used fictitiously.

ISBN (Print): 978-1-950464-25-8
ISBN (eBook): 978-1-950464-26-5

THE DEAD BORN

MIRANDA MAPLES

Dedicated to my family. To the ones still with me, to the ones who came before, and the ancient bloodline that ties all of us humans into a story ever unfolding.

The rule in the common law, is probably, the same, that a dead-born child is to be considered as if he had never been conceived or born in other words, it is presumed he never had life. It being a maxim of the common law, that mortuus exitus non est. exitus.

—*Adapted to the constitution and laws of the United States. – John Bouvier, 1856.*

PART 1

WHAT A LOVELY PARLOR

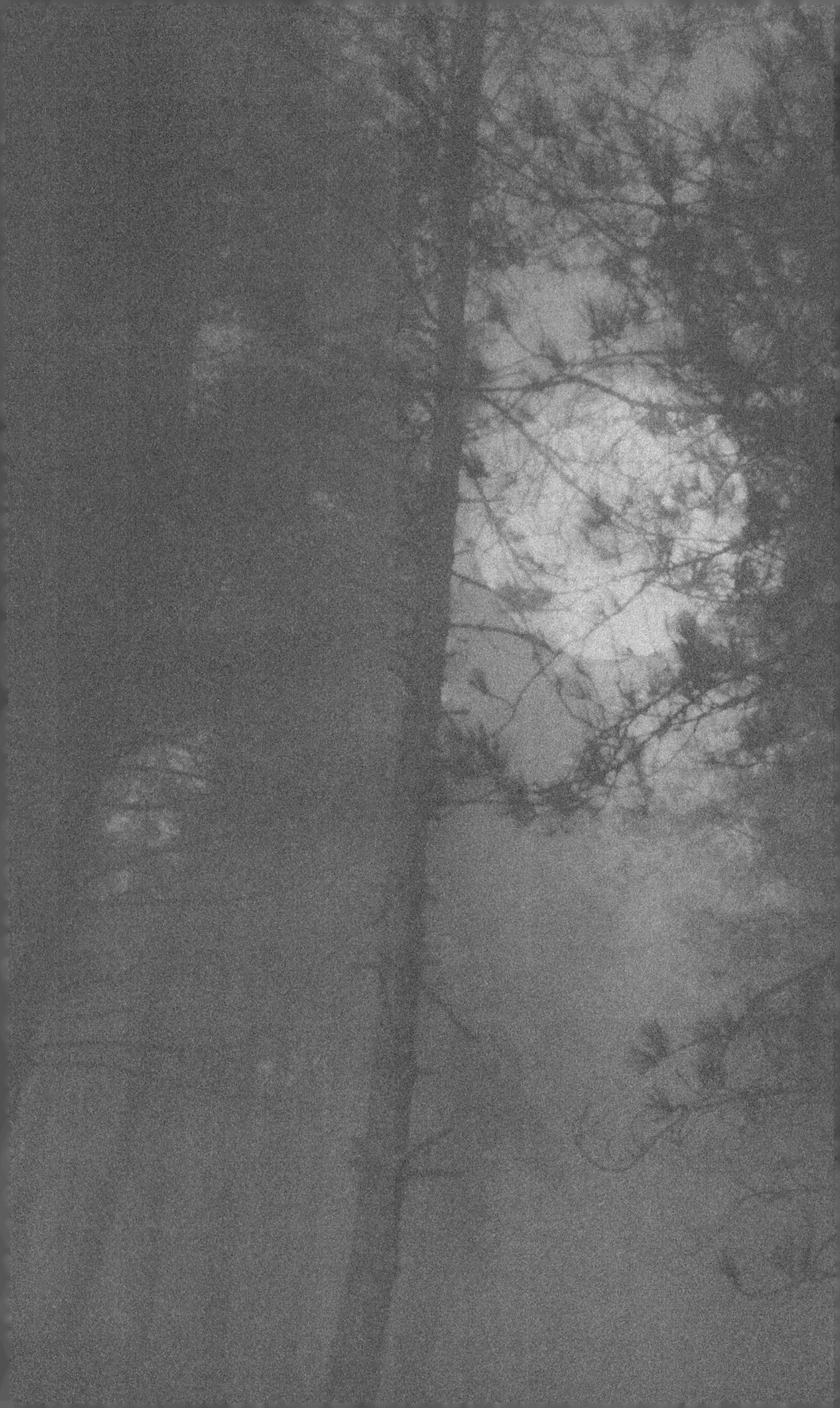

CHAPTER 1

Someone once asked her what her hometown was like. She described the appearance of the town: a rural farming community, one small grocery store, one bank, a diner, an ice cream stand that was better than good, no traffic lights, a small town in the American South. Then she was asked about the people. Farmers, she said, but an increasing number of the residents were transplants who worked in Knoxville, the closest city. She always stopped after a superficial description because it started to hurt.

It sounded idyllic to some, and boring to other personality types. But for Jacey Forestar, Poplar Hill was a place that brought up memories of shame and terror.

Jacey looked normal, many would say beautiful, and she was smart, funny, and always up for a good time. But speak of Poplar Hill and it would change her, would rouse the dormant wounded being that lived inside her, a most miserable soul who howled or hissed with pain and fury if forced to wake.

Jacey had tried to make it a fierce creature, but it was only a mewling, pathetic ball of fear and avoidance. It was like a child raised in darkness that someone had tried to disinfect with sunlight for a few minutes, only to scuttle back into the home of shadows, screeching and wailing with contempt and fear. What could one do with such a burdensome tenant that would not leave? You let it sleep, and so that's what Jacey did.

She passed the sign that read *Welcome to Poplar Hill, est. 1789*. She shivered and turned off the AC, lowered the driver's-side window, and let the hot air into the car. Jacey reflected on the events that led her to drive this highway, which led to the house she swore she would never revisit. It started in earnest yesterday morning, the dreams. ...

A VOICE SPOKE FROM BEYOND TIME AND SPACE: *MOMMA*.

The voice continued to speak to her as she ascended the levels of consciousness. *Dominion is decided and fate cannot be changed. From a poisoned womb, at the cellular level, you knew. On another plane beyond comprehension, your matter was altered, and now here you are, where you are meant to be.*

Jacey jerked awake, mentally swimming up to the surface from the fathoms of the nightmare, and was knocked back into reality with the sensations of a mild hangover.

Momma, the word tolled through her mind like a bell rang on empty streets. She was not a mother, just a divorced woman in an apartment alone with her nightmares. And this time the booze wasn't dulling them. Jacey waited as the dreams blew away like cobwebs in the breeze. She caught one last image of a man on top of her, so many shadows, and the outline of a cross hanging on the wall.

Then she went to make coffee. Such was the absurdity of her life as of late: nightmares, spending a few minutes doing something normal like making coffee and reading the paper, then work, then start drinking after her walk at dusk. Always at dusk, when the Savannah heat lifted a bit and she could walk a few blocks without sweating through her clothes.

Oh, and obsessing about a dead woman, don't forget that.

Jacey sat down with her coffee and opened her laptop on the small kitchen table and brought up an article about Crissy Freeman, Jacey's friend from childhood. The dead woman. Jacey had read the article countless times, and now she just stared at the headline. It was written in a grotesquely large font, as if the person who formatted it was trying to sensationalize the story: *LOCAL WOMAN FOUND MURDERED IN HER HOME.*

Jacey wished she had stopped reading the news from her hometown; then she would be free of any guilt about Crissy, and their unusual and painful friendship.

The smell of the river wafted in from the open kitchenette window, murky and fragrant with muddy earth and runoff from too many people, of creatures living and breeding and dying, with a slight trace of the ocean. The mighty Atlantic was close, and she often thought about walking into it at night, giving herself over to the will and power of the indifferent watery depths. She once read that the salt dissolved the skin of the ocean's victims, and when the bodies were finally fished out, the skin would slough off like the peel of persimmons she would pluck off the tree as a child. Jacey thought that was a humbling thing to know.

Jacey took her coffee and the laptop into her small office nook. She sipped more coffee, and the hangover mercifully subsided enough for her to write. She was drawn back into the world of ghost ships and a haunted family estate. Jacey's fierce, brave heroine, Adelaide, was saved from a demonic entity by her hero, the handsome and brave Asher, who swooped in and stopped

Adelaide from being thrown off the jagged cliffs into the cold, raging ocean below.

Jacey finished the last section and did some editing. She stood up and stretched. She had worked well into the afternoon, only taking breaks to get up and stretch and walk around, but she was done with this book. Jacey sat back down and changed the document file name from "Ghost Smut" to "Foolish Fire." Jacey always waited until she finished editing before she officially titled her books. It was mostly a habit but also a somewhat superstitious ritual on her part. She believed she should never name her children until she met them fully formed, freshly baked from the creative womb.

Jacey made a decent living as a romance/erotica writer. Her most popular books were angel erotica, but lately she had gone back to writing about spooky old crumbling houses with ghosts and witches; they had always been her favorite. Her sales were very good with these, but her bestsellers were the angel erotica fiction. But she always felt self-conscious about it, as if she wasn't a real writer.

Unable to stop herself, Jacey opened the article again. She had last seen Crissy after graduation, not long before Jacey left Poplar Hill. Crissy had been in an IGA, and Jacey had stopped in with a grocery list her mother had given her. Jacey's eyes had met hers, and Crissy had looked down and kept walking. Jacey never forgot the look on Crissy's face: It was one of the most sad and lonely expressions she had ever seen.

Of course she was sad; you left her there that night, ran away like you always do, Jacey thought. But what could Jacey have done? She was just a kid herself.

"I could have called the cops," Jacey said out loud. A therapist had told her she took on the guilt and shame of something that was out of her control, that the only ones responsible were the perpetrators, not Jacey. That sounded good, and it helped Jacey sleep at night – until now. Because it was a lie. We lie to ourselves all the time, and it usually works, unless the thing you lie about reaches out and knocks at your proverbial door almost twenty years later.

Jacey opened a new file in Word and typed: *The girl watched as she ascended out of her own body; her goal was to make it up to the moon, to merge with it and shine forever in the night creature's eyes, to illuminate the darkness with a pale, immovable glow.* Jacey stopped typing. She hovered over the save button, then clicked it. "Untitled Document." Jacey closed the laptop and looked out her window at the late-afternoon sunlight that dappled her apartment. In this light, everything looked magical.

Jacey took her walk at dusk, watching the soft night descend like a blanket put on by a loving cosmic mother. The majestic oaks caressed the velvet sky, and she stood under the tree where it was rumored a witch had been hanged in front of the townspeople. She reached up and gently swept her hand across the moss that draped from a branch like a sea witch's hair. A group of people passed by her, the ghost tour leader pointing out the tree under which Jacey stood. Jacey walked down the street, seeing the tip of the Cathedral Basilica of St. John the Baptist church. Jacey loved Savannah; it was genteel and lively, yet somehow bereft of any self-imposed vanity. It only wanted to be lovely and inviting. There was violence and ugliness attached to its past, but the city kept that part of itself hidden. Jacey could relate.

That night more dreams came, ruining any hope of bibulous repose.

In the dream, Jacey was standing on the hill. Behind her the woods, and in front of her the house. She saw the large kitchen window. She saw a pale face staring from the window. Suddenly, the woman was in front of her on the hill. She was speaking, but Jacey only caught certain words. The woman was ageless; she could have been fifty or one hundred years old.

"Through the trees," said the woman.

Jacey turned around, not knowing where to run. The woods were dark, and she felt danger coming for her. But the house was evil. Which was worse?

"The roots run deeper than you know," the voice said as it carried over the wind.

Jacey woke from the dream. She sat up and hugged her pillow, and she heard the voice in her mind still speaking: *Come home, it's the only way out for you.*

"Guess I'm going back home," she said aloud to the darkness. Anything to make this shit stop, or she would go insane. Time to run back instead of running away, and really, what choice did she have?

The next morning, Jacey began to pack. She realized now why all her belongings had never been properly stored: This was *tempore conversamini*, a temporary residence. That was about all she remembered from high school Latin. Most of her clothes and makeup and beauty products were kept in cardboard boxes. Some of her clothes had never been taken out of the storage boxes. Jacey now realized that it was a way station until she went back home. She wanted to pour a shot of liquor into her coffee, but she had a long drive. She would beat the rush-hour traffic, but it would still take about five hours to reach Tennessee.

Her ex had once commented that Jacey was like a ghost herself – she was never fully there, and sometimes, he would forget she was sitting next to him. Jacey excelled at blending in, at being invisible; a therapist had once told her it was a survival mechanism.

Jacey had mentioned that sometimes she truly believed she could become mist, not able to be seen, to hide. *Assigning magical abilities and meanings to coincidental or everyday things is a common belief amongst attachment-avoidant people and patients with PTSD*, the therapist told her. But Jacey still wasn't convinced. Anyway, it was her belief that perception shaped our worlds, so in a way, it was real.

Jacey zipped up her bag and dragged it to the front door. She made sure the gun was hidden but not too hard to get out quickly if needed.

Then she walked back into the bedroom and looked around one more time. Jacey noticed a small box in the closet. She opened it and saw there was some paperwork and framed pictures – her marriage license, pictures of her wedding day. Jacey stared at the picture. She remembered bits and pieces of that day. It was mostly a blur of pills and booze, and getting nice and high after the big nuptials at the courthouse. Later they had graduated to using needles, and Jacey wondered how she was still alive.

Because she had stories to tell, she answered herself. It was what had saved her. Even if they were banal or kitschy, they were her stories. Author was the perfect job for someone who loved nothing more than to detach from reality.

Jacey carried the box to the front door and set it down. Funny how our lives eventually become someone else's garbage, she thought.

You'll never come back here, the voice in her head spoke up. A coldness spread across her neck and she shivered in the muggy summer morning. She thought about Crissy, cold and still on the coroner's steel table. The murdered girl, who used to be Jacey's friend. Jacey closed her eyes and tried to picture Crissy, still and pristine. Jacey swiped a tear from her eye.

CHAPTER 2

Jacey saw the familiar black turrets of the house jutting into the genteel blue of the summer sky, and she came out of her malefic memories. She slowed down and pulled up to the top of the hill and got out of her car to look. Jacey marveled at the beauty the house possessed despite its neglected appearance.

She stood in between the wildly overgrown hedge bushes leading onto the porch. The porch was sagging and even had large holes in a couple of spots. As Jacey walked around the property, she became caught up in the foundational beauty of the house. She always had been a little awestruck at its elegance, and its architectural loveliness.

The house was a beautifully designed gothic revival: majestic and imposing in its heyday and exuding an undeniable elegance. Now it looked like a caricature of itself, ripe for the location of a horror movie. It was painted black and white and was centered between two huge sugar maple trees. The warped porch wrapped around a large section of the house. Underneath the chipping paint was some exposed brick.

Jacey walked around the yard to the side door, which led to the kitchen. The door was open, which was not uncommon in a small town. Then, for the first time in almost twenty years, she was back inside the house.

"Hello?" she called out. She looked up the property records before she left Savannah and saw that it was registered to someone named Ella Williams. The property transfer had happened not long after she moved away.

Jacey walked into the kitchen and stood looking out through the huge picture window. From here, she could see almost the whole property. She saw the garden, neglected and grown over with grass and weeds, and there was the barn, which Jacey figured was about to cave in on itself.

She felt a wave of dizziness come over her, and the temperature seemed to drop ten degrees. Jacey heard a sigh from behind her. She shivered but dared not turn around, her eyes tightly closed.

I'm getting out of here, she thought, *the hell with Crissy's funeral. I'm nuts if I stay here.* Jacey was about to hightail it out the door and never come back when she heard a voice in her mind, a sickeningly mocking female voice: "Go into the parlor, dear." Jacey opened her eyes, her body trembling. She peered out the window at the deep woods to calm herself. Go then; the parlor had always been her favorite room.

The heavy parlor door moaned in protest when she opened it. The room was dark; large, thick curtains covered the windows, and there was a small oil lamp burning a weak orange glow on one of the corner tables.

The light switch wasn't working, so Jacey walked carefully to the closest window. She pulled open the heavy curtains and squinted her eyes against the bright sunlight, then began to cough from the thick blast of dust that came off the curtains.

Jacey knew the body was there before her eyes adjusted to the light, and she felt her breath catch. This was Jacey's first time finding a dead stranger in a house, but she assumed it was something one could just feel before actually seeing. The woman appeared to be at least ninety years old.

Jacey studied the woman's face. She did not look like she had suffered; in fact, she looked like she was taking a nap, and there was even a slight smile on her lips. Just a sweet old lady, but Jacey felt repulsed by her. She stood up and went to the other window, opening more curtains so she could see better.

The fireplace had quite a lot of ashes and debris, which seemed odd considering it was June. She picked up the poker, lightly sifting the ashes. She stopped and gasped. There were bones in the soot and ashes. She bent closer. The bones were not human, she thought. They were small, probably from some animal.

She put the poker back in its stand. They could be from a child, she thought. But the place would reek of a burned body, wouldn't it? Unless it had happened a long time ago. Jacey wasn't sure how long it would take for that smell to leave the house. And from the looks of it, the house had not been aired out in years.

Just then she noticed two black candles sitting near the fireplace. They had been burned more than halfway, the black wax pooling around them.

She stood up, her knees popping loudly in the heavy silence of the house. She got out her phone and punched in 911, then stopped. She thought for a moment. She went into the kitchen and saw a card held by a large, magnetized cherry on the ancient refrigerator. It was the number for the Poplar Hill Sheriff's Department.

Jacey spoke to the dispatcher and calmly told the woman her name and address and that she had found a body in her grandparent's home. The dispatcher said someone would be over right away, an undeniable inflection of excitement in her voice.

Jacey hung up and went back into the parlor and opened the window, relishing the air that rushed in. It was hot, but it wasn't stale like the air in the parlor. She breathed deeply for a few minutes, then looked at the body again. She cocked her head. There was something in the woman's hand.

Jacey walked to her and bent down again. She gently pulled a book out of the woman's hand, careful not to brush the skin lest she scream in disgust. That serene grin on the woman's face was unnerving, creepy. Jacey took the book and sat in the windowpane.

It was a leather-bound book, not very thick, about fifty pages. Jacey opened the book, and on the first page was a picture that had been taped to the yellowed paper. It was a baby picture. She carefully worked the picture loose from the tape and turned it over and read the name written in spidery cursive writing: Jacinta Arabelle Forestar. This was Jacey's full name, and she was about five years old in the picture. She was sitting in front of the huge maple tree in the front yard, and she was petting a black cat.

Jacey skimmed the pages. It was filled with strange symbols and small verses written in small, painfully neat handwriting. They appeared to be spells.

"What is this, a Book of Shadows?" she asked the woman. This was insane, she thought.

Jacey had a flash of a memory. It was disjointed and jumpy, like a spliced-together reel of old film. Blood pooling in the dirt, a struggling animal.

Jacey heard a car pull up and almost jumped out of her skin. She looked outside and saw the sheriff's car. She shoved the picture back into the book and ran to the kitchen with it. She stashed it in her purse, then went out to meet the sheriff.

Two hours later, Jacey watched as two men put Ella into a white SUV. One of the men had introduced himself to Jacey upon arrival, his name was Bill, the owner of the funeral home, and he was quite polite and professional.

"Miss Forestar?" the sheriff said from behind Jacey.

Jacey turned around and again appraised Sheriff Josh Evans. He was about forty, tall and slightly lanky. He might have been handsome, but he had birdlike eyes that darted around when he talked, as if he was looking for another body Jacey might have hidden.

"Yes?" Jacey said. She felt dazed and tired. Evans had already questioned her about how she had come to be in the house, and evidently now he was back with more questions.

"Do you make a habit of trespassing?" he asked.

"No, sir," Jacey said. She figured the less she said, the better.

"You're staying to attend Miss Freeman's funeral?" he asked. He fixed his bright eyes on her for a moment, then flicked his gaze around the house again.

"Um, yes, I was planning on it. Why?" she asked.

"Are you moving back to Poplar Hill?" He looked at the sky as he spoke to her. Fine with her – the guy was annoying.

"What? No, I'm just in town for the funeral. Look, is anyone going to tell me who that woman was?" she asked testily.

Evans stopped looking at the sky. He put his hand on his hip. "So, you told me you didn't know her ... the dead woman?"

Jacey sighed, rubbing her eyes. "That's right, I didn't know her, or I would have told you I did."

Evans fixed his gaze on her, his eyes bright with suspicion. "She was a relative of yours. Your grandad's niece or something," he said, watching her reaction.

Jacey was stunned. She shook her head. "No, that can't be ..." she trailed off.

Can't be? Why not? She hadn't met most of her grandparent's relatives. She was certain her grandmother's immediate family was gone, but was her grandfather's?

"I thought they were all dead," Jacey said dumbly.

Evans' hand brushed the front pocket of his uniform pants. Jacey could see the outline of a dip can. He must be overdue for his fix. Jacey could relate.

"Well, looks like they are now," he said. "I only met her once or twice. She was a little strange, kept to herself."

"Strange how?" asked Jacey.

Evans shrugged. He handed Jacey a card. "This is the funeral home where she'll be taken. Apparently she made all the arrangements years ago. Sorry for your loss," he said and walked away.

"Wait!" Jacey called.

Evans turned, a look of impatience on his face. "What?"

"Well, what about all of her stuff … in there. I mean, what do I do with it?"

Evans finally looked her directly in her eyes. "You can call Blake Coffey, he has a moving and storage company. Or take all of it to the dump. All of it belongs to you now, so do whatever you want with it," he said.

"To me? What do you mean?" she asked him.

Evans finally gave up the polite front. He took out his dip and plugged a glob in his gums. It made Jacey's nerves sizzle; she wanted a cigarette and a beer like no one's business.

"She left a copy of her will on the kitchen table, and it clearly names you as the heir. That's why I couldn't bust you for trespassing," he said and spit a brown glob in the grass.

Jacey stared at Evans, her mouth open in disbelief. She was about to launch into a series of questions when a large black truck pulled up in the driveway. The truck was new but dusty.

"Morgan!" Evans shouted. Evans raised his hand in a wave and walked to the truck. A man got out, and as Evans shook hands with him, Jacey examined him. He was tall and probably not much older than her. And he was extremely handsome. Jacey had never seen such a good-looking man before. He looked like he should be in Hollywood, not in the driveway of her childhood home, where a possible witch, who was a relative, had just been found dead in the parlor. As he came closer, Jacey saw he had intense eyes, and he flashed a smile of perfect white teeth.

Jacey looked away as she felt her face redden.

"How have you been, Josh?" asked Morgan. He kept glancing at Jacey as he spoke to the sheriff.

"I'm good, man, how's your pop?" Evans asked.

"He's doing great. He's in Atlanta right now," Morgan said.

"Does your pop know how to do anything besides work?"

"Hell no, he don't," Morgan said and walked over to Jacey, who Evans evidently had forgotten about.

"Hi, I'm Morgan DeArmond. You really gotta excuse Josh, he doesn't mean to be rude." Jacey shook his hand. She fancied she felt a crackle of electricity in the touch of his warm skin.

"He was literally born in a barn," Morgan said cheerily.

"Jacey Forestar," she said.

"Is everything okay here?" He took his eyes off Jacey for a split second to look up at the house, then his eyes locked on hers again.

"Fine, fine, I have to get going," Evans said. He shot Morgan an "I'll tell you about it later" look.

Morgan smiled again. Jacey felt embarrassed. She must look frightful, and they probably would laugh about her predicament later over a beer.

"See ya, Morgan. Don't go too far, Miss Forestar," Evans said as he sauntered to his car.

"Asshole," Jacey said under her breath.

Morgan laughed. "He can come off that way, but he's not a bad guy," he said.

"Seems to me y'all are old friends," Jacey said.

"Not really. Are you okay, Miss Forestar? Is there anything I can help you with?" he asked. He seemed earnest enough.

"What are you, my neighbor?" She didn't care how rude she was being. She was tired and needed a drink.

Morgan seemed unphased. "I am, as a matter of fact. I live over there," he said and pointed across the road to the sprawling farm.

"That's your place? I thought the Richards family owned that," she said.

"They moved about ten years ago and my father bought it. He's from here originally," Morgan said.

"How wonderful. Well, I have to go now, so ..."

"Will you go out with me?" asked Morgan.

Jacey stared. "What?" she asked.

"I asked if you would go out with me, have dinner, maybe see a movie?"

"I ... no, what, why?" she stammered.

"How about tonight?" he asked.

"I never heard of such bad taste – I just lost a relative," said Jacey, her heart racing.

"I'm sorry, I don't mean to be so forward, but *carpe vitam* and all that," he said. Jacey was dumbstruck for a moment, remembering she had used a Latin phrase earlier. Merely a coincidence, she told herself, calm down.

"I can't, I have stuff to do," she said.

He stepped a little closer to her. "Stuff?" he asked. Jacey studied his face to see if he was playing with her. He seemed sincere. She found she wanted to keep staring at his eyes, which were light hazel with flecks of gold.

"Listen, Morgan, I'm only in town for a few days for my friend's funeral, then I'm leaving," she told him.

"Crissy Freeman – yeah, I met her a few times, she seemed like a sweet girl. It's sad what happened to her," he said.

"You knew Crissy?" she asked, suddenly alert.

"Not very well. Listen, I have to go, but I'll give you my number." He held out his hand for her phone. She sighed and got it out of her pocket and unlocked it for him. He typed in his number and handed her phone back to her.

"Call me any time. It was nice to meet you, Jacey," he said. He began to walk away, then paused, looking back at her. "If you're leaving, what's gonna happen to this place?" he asked her.

Jacey shrugged. "Burn it," she muttered under her breath.

"What's that?" he asked. He was looking at her strangely.

"I said better just sell it, all of it," she said.

"Shame," he said. He looked around at the property. "You call me, any time, or just yell across the road." He smiled and walked to his truck.

She watched him drive away, then went and sat on the porch. She lit a cigarette.

She realized the man, Bill was his name, was walking over to her. Jacey had forgotten he was there.

Jacey stood up. "Bill, right?" asked Jacey.

"Yes, hello again, I am going to take Mrs. Williams to the home, and we will handle it from here. I believe the sheriff gave you the card, so if you have any questions, just call," said Bill.

"Thank you, I appreciate it," said Jacey. She watched as they finally drove off with the woman, and Jacey breathed a sigh of relief.

Jacey walked around the side of the house and looked around. The sun was beginning to set, and the sky was a ferocious display of red, violet, and deep orange. She took a deep breath, inhaling the green and dirt and the evening air.

Jacey smoked, put her head in her left hand, and wondered what she was going to do now. She finished her cigarette, then made herself get up and go inside.

She walked into the parlor. Jacey looked again at the ashes and small bones in the fireplace. The sheriff had not noticed them, and Jacey had not mentioned that to him. She told herself it was because she didn't want any trouble, but the truth was, *secretive* was

Jacey's default state. That was mixed with an odd sense of familial loyalty.

Jacey went to her car and got her bag. *Might as well stay here and not at a hotel in town,* she thought. She went into the guest bathroom downstairs and used the bathroom. She brushed her teeth and splashed cold water on her face. She leaned over the sink, looking at herself in the dirty mirror. She looked awful. She desperately wanted a hot shower, but she also needed a drink. Suddenly she felt lightheaded and the room turned cold. She gripped the sink and looked out the window, but she felt like she was falling away from herself. She closed her eyes and tried to steady herself against the sink. She saw images in her mind's eye and could do nothing to stop them; she was hurtling through the past, as if someone had taken over.

It was the height of summer, like it was now, and the heat was glorious and sweet. Dust and bits of hay clung to Jacey's skin. She had been jumping from the top of the rafter to the hay pile below. When she got bored of this, she raced out of the barn and down the hill to her house. The grass made crunching sounds under her bare feet, and she looked up at the sky; the sun was high and magnificent, and the sky was clear blue, completely free of clouds. They would need rain soon – the ground and the trees and grass cried out for rain. She leaped off the grass onto the gravel driveway. It was so hot it would have burned her friend Shawnee's feet. The last time she had spent the night, she couldn't walk around barefoot. "It's too hot!" Shawnee had yelled and put on her shoes.

Jacey smiled, remembering that when she told her mother about it, her mother had stated that even though they were from the same county, Shawnee wasn't a country girl like Jacey. She lived in a subdivision, with neighbors and cable and even a pool.

Jacey went to the backyard and found the hose. A rush of cold water came out, and Jacey stripped down to her undies and held the hose above her head, letting the icy water cascade down her body. She squealed with delight. After a few minutes, she turned off the spigot and stood in the shade. She was wild to go swimming in Shawnee's pool, but Shawnee was out of town for the week. At the beach with her mom and stepdad.

Jacey was never sure if she really wanted to be Shawnee's friend. Shawnee got to go on vacations, she always had new clothes, she had a pool, and she had her own phone. Jacey liked Shawnee but always felt like she would never be as good as Shawnee because her family didn't have as much money as Shawnee's family.

Jacey was almost dry, so she put on her shirt and shorts. She decided to ride her bike around the huge gravel loop that went around her grandparents' home. There were two dips in the drive, and she loved to pedal as hard as she could, all the time gaining momentum, and when the dip started, she let her feet come off the pedals and coasted, closing her eyes as the wind blew her hair back.

No, don't do that! Jacey thought now. She knew what was going to happen but could do nothing to stop the events, nor could she stop the vision. There was no detour, only a one-way street with no foreseeable way out. She was a wild animal running in the woods, fast and free, unaware that she was about to encounter a trap that some hunter had laid for her. She would not be killed, but she would be wounded. She would be able to work her way out of the trap and find a cool, quiet place to tend to her injuries. And perhaps heal. Oh, but the scars. ... And how long until she can run free again, if ever?

As Jacey rode her bike around the gravel loop, the man watched her from the wide window above the same sink where Jacey now stood.

He waited for the child to come around into his sightline, her white-blond hair blowing as she sped across the road, dust trailing behind her.

He looked at his hands gripping the sink and frowned at the number of wrinkles. He was in his sixties, but sometimes – like now – he momentarily forgot that he was old, and he marveled that it had happened to him.

He held up his hands: steady. Then he rubbed them over his bald head. There used to be a mass of dark brown hair on top. He remembered all the women that his hands had touched in Memphis, where he had grown up strong and handsome, all the parties that were held in houses in the good part of town.

He got his fedora and walked outside into the blazing heat.

All alone, the child Jacey slowed down when she saw him come out of the house. He had admonished her before about riding her bike so fast. He waved at her and she stopped her bike, waiting for him.

He felt outside himself as he walked toward her.

Jacey was looking at him, and he could tell she sensed something was wrong, but he was her grandfather, and so she waited, her head tilted slightly to the side, her small hands still holding the handlebars of her bicycle. Her legs were spread slightly, her feet planted on the ground while she held up the bike.

He touched her shoulder and began to rub, soon moving to her neck. He picked up some of her hair in his fingers; it looked like spun gold. He put both hands on her shoulders, holding her still. Jacey tried to bolt, as if she sensed his intentions, but he held her in place. She struggled for a few seconds, then stopped. Something appeared in the road in front of her. It looked like a large cloud of mist, like steam had been released from inside the ground and come to the surface, but it had the consistency of a thick smog. It hung in front of her, and she saw a face come out of the smoke. It was something she couldn't comprehend or reference, but there was a primal, unconscious knowing, and Jacey fell away from herself. She didn't move; she seemed frozen or stuck somehow, like a statue.

Her grandfather moved one hand down inside her shirt. She tensed. "Don't move," he said. He felt enormous, like a deity brought into human form for a little while, and he was unnerved that his voice came out in a barely audible whisper. Everything was still; only the heat was alive and pulsing. He gently tugged her off the bike. He held her by her small shoulders in front of him, her back to him. They stood in the middle of the gravel road in the baking heat. No one was home. He felt like the forces in the earth were standing guard over him. Like a spell had been cast and everything and everyone had been paused for a few moments.

He unzipped his pants. It was as hard as he could ever remember. He put his hands down her pants and rubbed her. He undid her shorts and put his hand between her spread legs. There was no hair, and he slipped his finger inside her. He moaned loudly and closed his eyes as he came.

THE DEAD BORN

When he took his hands off of Jacey, she was panting, her eyes wild and scared. She yanked up her shorts and ran away, her bicycle forgotten in the gravel.

He moved the bike off the drive and leaned it next to the chicken shed. She would come back for it later.

Jacey came back to herself and unclenched her sweaty hands from the sink. Jacey turned on the faucet and splashed cold water on her face.

The room was no longer cold but had returned to its normal temperature, which was oppressively muggy. Jacey leaned on the counter and named the states, a trick she learned to make herself calm down quickly. She forced herself to take long, deep breaths, and held them and repeated until she felt calmer. She had been taken over by something. She could still feel the presence and see the horrible memory. Not only had she lived it, but she had now been forced to relive it from inside *his* mind, too.

Jacey finished counting the states. She felt her chest begin to loosen, her guts began to unwind; the thing inside had raised up its head, sniffing and beginning to pant. Jacey decided to go somewhere to have a drink. Scratch that – several drinks. The thing inside quieted, satisfied she was going to damage herself, satiated for now. Jacey splashed more cold water on her face and patted herself dry with a dingy hand towel that was as dusty as the parlor. Jacey got a flash of an image of a woman with long golden hair and eyes the color of garnets. She was standing and smiling, then she faded. Jacey almost had it, a memory from childhood, but an actual good memory. But she couldn't comprehend what it was.

"Enough," Jacey said.

She changed into fresh shorts and a tank top and walked to her car. She pulled out and sat for a minute thinking. "*Carpe noctem,*" she said to herself. She made a right and headed to the highway.

CHAPTER 3

Poplar Hill was a dry county, so Jacey had to drive fifteen minutes to reach her destination. A few feet from the county line sign, she turned left into the bar's gravel lot and found a parking spot in the back. The place was packed, and music thumped from inside, and raucous laughter mixed and echoed with the music. This place had been around as long as Jacey could remember, although it had many incarnations under many different owners: The Roundup, County Line, Dee Dee's. On this muggy Friday night, it was called The End of the Line.

Jacey walked across the gravel, her flip-flops sinking into the rocks as she made her way to the entrance.

A group of huge, gleaming motorcycles lined the front of the bar. Jacey stood and looked at the bikes. They were all Harleys. None of the other vehicles in the lot were anything extraordinary. Most of the cars or trucks were older and dusty. A few large, shiny Hemis were parked on the other side.

The door opened and a couple, about mid-fifties, sauntered out, the man with his arm slung around the giggling woman's shoulders. They didn't notice Jacey, and the woman leaned against a truck as they made out. Their kiss was loud and sloppy enough to be heard over the thump of the music. The man held on to the woman's large can, probably for balance.

Jacey looked again at the lineup of Harleys; there were about six of them parked with uniform neatness. Could be some older men who were out riding and wanted a drink before they went home to their wife and kids. Jacey glanced back at the couple. They weren't paying any attention to her. Jacey bent down and looked at one of the saddle bags. The symbol for *The Outlaws* was stitched on the leather.

She walked inside the bar clutching her purse, which held a gun and a taser. The place was so crowded, she had to rub against a group of men as she made her way to the bar. They gave her a quick once-over and then tipped their bottles to their mouths. They smelled like soap and cologne, and wore jeans with boots and either plaid button-down shirts or T-shirts. She noticed their tanned arms in short-sleeved shirts, muscles bulging as they lifted their beers. Jacey felt an urge to take one of them to the parking lot and press her body against his.

There was a pool table and a few dart boards toward the back of the bar. The bikers were there, shooting pool and laughing and talking in booming voices. There were three women with them. Jacey almost made it to the bar when someone yelled, "Jacey Forestar!"

She turned and saw a familiar male face. The guy waved his arm wildly at her, and she waved back, smiling despite herself. Someone grabbed her ass as she waded through the crowd to the guy's booth.

"Corey?" she asked when she finally made it. Jacey couldn't believe it: Corey Fawver. Corey and Jacey had known each other since kindergarten, when they were both tickled by the fact that their last names began with the same letter.

Corey stood up and hugged her. "How are you? Glad you came out. Damn, it's been what, fifteen years?"

Jacey smiled and nodded. "Yeah, at least that," she said.

"Sit down, we've got room," he said and gestured to the large booth, where a man and woman were sitting.

"Definitely, I'm just gonna grab a drink," Jacey said.

"I'll come with – we need another pitcher anyway," Corey said.

"And a couple of shots to go with that pitcher," she replied.

"Absolutely!" Corey said with a laugh. He stopped and squinted his eyes at her. "You okay?" he asked her.

Jacey made herself smile. "Yeah, yeah, I'm fine, just a little tired," she said.

Corey put his arm around her neck and kissed her head. "Come on, let's get a drink," he said.

Corey and Jacey inched their way to the bar. A man and a woman were filling pitchers and opening cold beer bottles, their hands and arms flying and somehow not knocking into each other or spilling a drop of alcohol.

"Sherrie!" Corey yelled over the chatter and music. "Another pitcher, and?"

"Two shots of Jack, and get another pitcher, I'll buy this round," Jacey said.

Corey shook his head, "Like hell you will. Sherrie, two more pitchers and four shots of Jack!"

Jacey looked around trying to see if she recognized anyone else. Corey hugged her again. "Damn, I can't believe you're here, Jacey," he yelled in her ear.

"I'm really glad to see you, Corey. Hey, cheers," she said as Sherrie brought out the drinks. She and Corey toasted, and they threw back their shots. Jacey downed her second one, and Corey signaled Sherrie for two more shots, then they headed to the booth. Corey introduced her to the couple, Joe and Cynthia. Corey explained that he worked with Joe and usually came here every Friday after work.

Corey introduced her by saying, "This is Jacey, I've known her since kindergarten!" Jacey giggled. Corey was definitely buzzed, which made him more loud and animated, but he was so good-natured and fun that he wasn't annoying.

"Damn, Jacey, I can't believe you're here! And you're a famous writer, too," Corey said. He leaned over and hugged her again.

"I ain't famous," Jacey said. Her accent was back in full force now.

"Yeah, you are, I saw your books in the bookstore. I tell people working there, that girl, I used to pull her braids, and we would give each other wedgies!" He laughed raucously. Jacey laughed, too.

"Yeah, you're due for another one, it's been almost twenty years," said Jacey. She went for his boxers peeking over his jeans, and Corey snickered and squirmed away. He goosed her in her side, and she slapped his hand away.

Jacey and Corey toasted and drank another shot. Corey and Joe started talking about work, and Jacey tried to make small talk with Cynthia but only got nods and shrugs in response to her questions. Jacey looked at the bikers playing pool and shooting darts. "I'm going to go to the bathroom. Be right back," she said.

Jacey slowly walked past the bikers and tried to get a good look at them without being obvious. Most of them watched her walk in return. When she got to the bathroom, which had a wooden door that looked like it had almost been kicked in, Jacey tried the door handle. Occupied. She took out her phone and pretended to look at something important while stealing glances at the bikers. Jacey's gut twitched when she spotted a tall man in his early forties. Somehow she knew Crissy had dated this man.

He had dark hair and a full beard, and his arms were riddled with tattoos. He was good-looking, and he knew it. But he was

THE DEAD BORN

also one of those people who reaches their prime early in life, she thought.

He looked up and saw Jacey staring at him. Jacey looked down at her phone, and the bathroom door finally opened. A woman with dark hair almost knocked Jacey over as she made her way to the pool table. She clapped her hands and yelled it was her turn. Jacey looked back once more before closing the bathroom door, and she saw the woman stand next to the tall guy. Jacey figured she was with him – or at least leaving with him.

Jacey peed and washed her hands as best as she could; the dispenser barely spat out any soap. Jacey looked in the mirror, put on some lip gloss, and spritzed some body spray on her wrists and neck. She looked a bit haggard, but thankfully the neon in the bar made everyone look better.

Jacey walked by the pool tables, and the tall guy leaned in her direction. "Hey," he said.

"Hey," Jacey said.

"Can I buy you a drink?" he asked.

Jacey looked at him and then at the woman, who was giving Jacey a death stare.

"I don't think your girlfriend would be okay with that," Jacey said.

"Her? She's not my girlfriend." He grinned.

"Then why is she looking at me like she wants to rip out my throat and bathe in the blood?" Jacey asked him.

Tall guy's laugh boomed over the music thumping from the jukebox and the loud clacks of the balls on the pool table.

"Pretty *and* funny. Must be my lucky night," he said as he looked her up and down.

Jacey failed to see what was funny, but she smiled at him and said, "Excuse me, I gotta get back to my friend."

"Randy! It's your shot!" one of the guys yelled at him. The dark-haired girl was talking to a biker with a long, red beard and still staring at Jacey.

"Better go, it's never a good idea to leave your balls on the table," Jacey said and squeezed by him. She knew he was watching her walk away.

Corey had ordered another pitcher and two more shots.

"Corey, who are those guys shooting pool?" Jacey asked as she sat down.

He glanced toward the pool table and shook his head. "The bikers?" Jacey nodded as Corey took a shot and wiped his hand across his mouth.

"I sorta know one of them, but not too well. He was in the same grade as my older brother."

"Which one?" she prodded.

"Randy Ellis, the steroid king with the dark hair." He looked at her. "Word of advice, stay clear of them."

Joe and Cynthia were nodding their heads vigorously. Jacey leaned forward, "Why?" she asked.

"Bad guys. Well, not all bad, they do some good stuff, like charity for the community, but … they are involved in a lot of illegal shit."

"Like what?" asked Jacey.

He shrugged. "Prostitution, drugs, you name it." He filled everyone's mugs with beer.

"Murder?" Jacey asked. Her question was accidentally timed perfectly with a break in the song and came out louder than she had anticipated.

"I don't think the whole bar heard you, Jace, say it louder," he said with a laugh. The couple laughed nervously, but Jacey noticed the woman's eyes flicked in the direction of the pool players.

Jacey looked toward the back room, where there was a small dance floor with a large disco bulb overhead. Some couples were drunkenly swaying on the dance floor, and Jacey suddenly wanted to dance and began moving to the beat.

"You like this song?" Corey asked.

"I love it," said Jacey, smiling. She was feeling great. The events of the afternoon seemed far away and unimportant.

"Wanna dance?" Corey asked, grinning at her.

"Yes," Jacey said without thinking.

Corey led her to the small dance floor, and he took her hand in his and put his arm around her waist. He moved easily with her; he was good. His movements were smooth and intimate without being uncomfortable and clumsy or territorial. He twirled her and dipped her, perfectly keeping pace with the song.

Other couples joined them, and two drunk scantily clad young women danced together, drawing much attention from the men. Jacey held on to Corey as they moved in a small, fluid circle on the dance floor. They swayed back and forth, and she closed her eyes as he dipped her again, and Jacey laughed, swaying her hair and her hips. She felt light and free. She only felt the vibration of the music and the sensation of other bodies around her. She was lost in the music, like she used to be when she was a kid. Then she got an image of her and Crissy dancing in her bedroom. They were so young. Jacey and Crissy stood in front of the mirror pouting and posing in time to the beats of a sugary pop song.

Jacey told Crissy that she was going to save up her money and move to Hollywood or New York City to be an actress and a screenwriter. Crissy told her she wanted to be a showgirl in Las Vegas and meet a rich man who would love her forever. Jacey said they would visit each other in their big homes, and sit outside by the pool and drink fancy drinks.

Morgan DeArmond, who had just come in with his friend, stood and watched Jacey and Corey dancing. Morgan couldn't stop staring at her, admiring her muscular legs in cut-off shorts, the swell of her breasts filling out the ratty tank top, and the curly hair that hung almost to her waist and seemed to glow under the lights, making her look magical. She looked like a goddess who had been plucked from days of yore. Morgan felt a twinge of jealousy at the man's hand around her waist, and the closeness between them, but he could tell by Jacey's friendly smile that there was no way in hell anything would happen for the poor guy. Morgan watched her body move, and he felt a deep pang of lust and awe and familiarity.

He had not stopped thinking about her since they met. She was ... stunning. She looked so free and sexy and care-free. She closed her eyes when the guy dipped her, then raised her arms above her head and circled back around her partner. She was totally locked into the song and the moment.

He had asked Josh about her and found out that she had grown up here and left almost as soon as she graduated high school. And that she was back not only for her old friend's funeral, but to look into the murder.

This would be tricky, he thought – she had been stubborn and aloof toward him, and seemed to have no interest in him. *Well, I'll make her interested.*

Morgan watched as Jacey and Corey finished their dance and walked to their booth, laughing, their arms slung across each other's shoulders.

"Corey, I think you're a better dancer than you used to be," Jacey said.

Corey bowed dramatically. "My pleasure, my lady. Save another dance for me," he said.

The bartender appeared at their booth, balancing two shot glasses in her hand. "From Randy," she said and nodded her head toward the biker standing at the pool table. "Sorry, Corey, he said these are for your lady friend here."

Jacey handed Corey one of the shot glasses.

"Since they are mine, I can do what I want with them," she said and clinked her glass against Corey's and downed it. Jacey thought now was as good a time as any to speak to the biker. Corey and his friends were talking, and Jacey excused herself.

Randy stepped in front of her as she walked to the pool table.

"Play a game with me, and I'll get us some more drinks," he said, looking her up and down.

"Maybe later. I'm with my friend right now," she said.

"Come on, one game," he said, leaning forward with a predatory grin. They were interrupted by someone putting money on the edge of the pool table. Jacey looked behind her and saw a smiling Morgan.

"Me and you against Randy and one of his friends," he said with a laugh.

He walked around and shook Randy's hand, then slapped him on the shoulder a tad too hard.

"Morgan, when did you get back?" Randy suddenly seemed like a neutered dog. It was subtle, but his shoulders hunched slightly and his voice was less booming.

"Couple days ago," he said. He looked at Jacey, and she felt her face redden.

The woman who had given Jacey the stank eye earlier walked up to Morgan and introduced herself as Kelly. She stood close to him, obviously smitten with him. She flipped her hair as Morgan said hello to her.

"One game. Everyone in?" he said and then addressed Jacey. "It looks like Corey's busy anyway." Jacey turned and saw Corey dancing with a pornographically curvy girl with a pretty face and hair the color of a ripe peach.

Randy racked the balls while Morgan grabbed a cue stick for Jacey and began to chalk his own.

"You know what? Jacey, you and Randy versus me and Kelly."

Kelly giggled and blushed. Jacey figured this was probably the only time in Kelly's life she had ever blushed. Or giggled.

Jacey shrugged, walked to Randy's side of the table, and looked at Morgan. He was ignoring her.

"You break, Morgan," Kelly said.

"Yes, ma'am," he said and took a swallow of beer and sat his bottle on the edge of the table. He broke, and Jacey sighed. *If nothing else, he's a great pool player,* she thought.

Morgan proceeded to wipe the table with them, which pleased Kelly, who jumped up and down so much her boobs almost bounced out of her top. Jacey wanted to break her cue stick over their heads, but she made herself place it lightly back in its holder.

"Good game," she said.

She walked away before anyone could say anything to her. She went to the booth, but new people were sitting in it. She looked for Corey. He was standing at the bar, deep in conversation with the peach-haired girl.

Jacey walked outside, lit a cigarette, and looked up at the sky. She decided it was time to go home. She doubted she would get anything out of Randy or any of his crew tonight.

The door opened before she finished her smoke, and Morgan came out.

"So, this is what was so important that you canceled our date?" he said. "You had to shoot pool with some bikers?"

"I guess," she said.

He looked up at the sky, then back at her. "You guess, huh?"

"Look, I just don't see the point. I'm leaving after Crissy's funeral. I thought I would come here and find out—" She stopped herself from saying more and threw her cigarette butt in the gravel and stomped on it with her flip-flop.

"What? Find out who killed her?" asked Morgan.

"I don't know, yes, maybe. I mean, she was my friend. No one else is going to do it, are they?"

"Funny, I thought that's what the police get paid for."

"She had a kid. Did you know that?" Jacey asked.

"No, I didn't."

"Doesn't matter. I never should have come back here, it was stupid." She turned away.

Morgan touched her shoulder. "Let me drive you home," he said.

Jacey looked up at him. "I'm fine," she said.

"No, I don't think you are," he said.

Jacey got in his face. "I'm not drunk, and I can take care of myself, thank you."

"Yeah, you seem like you have it all together," Morgan said.

The door opened, and a group of girls walked out. One of them squealed when she saw Morgan, and she hugged him, pressing her body close to his. She began to chatter about how she was so glad to see him.

Jacey walked off and heard the girl ask Morgan who she was. She couldn't hear Morgan's answer, but it was met with laughter. Jacey felt tears welling up in her eyes. She hoped she was walking in the direction of her car.

Morgan began to walk after her, but the brunette grabbed his hand. "Whoa, where do you think you are going?" she said with a laugh. She and her friend pressed close to him.

Morgan smiled and put his arms around them. "Back inside, ladies?"

The brunette put her arms around his neck and kissed him. Her tongue danced against his for a second, and when she pulled away, she smiled up at him. The other girl, a bleached blonde, wrapped her arms around his waist.

"We were thinking your place," the brunette said.

Morgan looked at her cleavage and the swell of her hips in the short skirt. And the blonde had nice lips. "Let's go," he said. He opened the door, and a blast of air conditioning and raucous bar noises and cigarette smoke barreled out.

Jacey had found her car and was digging for her keys when a voice said, "Where's your friend?" Jacey jumped and whirled around. Randy walked toward her, smoking a cigarette.

"Who, Corey?" She shrugged. "Went home with a redhead."

"No, not Corey, the big guy, Morgan." Randy walked close to her and put his arm out to lean against her car. His face was too close to hers, and Jacey leaned back. She took out a cigarette, and Randy lit it for her.

"On the verge of a threesome would be my guess," she said.

"How long have you known Morgan?" he asked.

"I don't, I only met him today," she said.

Randy looked her up and down, then tossed his cigarette butt.

"How do you know him? Is he a friend of yours?" asked Jacey.

"Morgan ain't a friend, he's an acquaintance. Guys like Morgan don't have friends like me," Randy said.

Jacey looked at the row of bikes. They gleamed sleek and devilish in the neon light. Jacey marveled at the beauty of them and wondered what it would feel like to ride one.

"Which one is yours?" she asked him.

Randy put his hand on her shoulder and guided her to his Harley. It was flashy and huge, painted a deep-blood red with silver chrome gleaming atop of it. Jacey wanted to touch it, but she held her hand back. She saw the neon sign reflected red in the chrome, and lowered her face over it and smiled at her reflection. Finally, she put her hand on the leather seat – it had the texture of oily beef jerky.

"Come on, I'll take you for a ride," he told her.

Jacey shook her head and backed away a few steps.

"You'll like it, promise," he told her.

"No helmet," she said, shrugging her shoulders.

Just then a couple of Randy's friends came out. "Coming to the barn?" a heavyset guy asked.

"Yeah, right behind you," he replied, then grinned at Jacey. "Come on, I bet Jason has an extra helmet."

"The barn?" she asked.

"Their clubhouse," a voice said from behind her. Jacey turned and saw Morgan.

He walked over and stood in front of Randy's bike, looking it over. "I don't think that's her kind of place, Randy," Morgan said.

"Well, it's just our clubhouse, ain't it, Morgan? I know it's been a while since you've been up there, but you're always welcome," Randy said, smiling. Just then, two of Randy's buddies came over.

Jacey's mouth fell open a little. She looked at Morgan, an expression of disbelief on her face. "You're an Outlaw?" she asked.

Morgan wouldn't look at her, instead shifting his gaze from the bike to Randy.

"Sure, he is," said Randy, "him and his daddy both, huh, Morgan?"

"You're brave with your friends around," Morgan walked closer to Randy, and they stared each other down.

One of Randy's friends tried to break the tension. Jake, the larger of the two men, chuckled and walked to Morgan with his hand extended. "Morgan, you should come up, we'll play some cards, smoke some cigars, catch up?"

Morgan shook his hand. "Another time, Jake, thanks," he said.

"I'd like to catch up with you, so come up anytime," he said and then looked at Randy. "Come on, let's go, boys, I'm ready for my stogie!" He laughed and walked to his bike. Randy squeezed past Morgan and got on his, and the bikes rumbled to life.

"Go home, Jacey," Morgan said quietly to her. "Don't follow them up there. Trust me, you don't want to get involved with them."

Jacey looked at him. He seemed earnest, but she wasn't going to let him off the hook.

"Do you think I'm some dumb skank? You think that's the type of thing I'm into?" she asked him and then walked away without waiting for an answer.

When she pulled into her driveway, she was struck by how dark it was. She remembered she had missed being able to see the stars when she moved away, and she had never gotten used to the light pollution. She stood outside for a few minutes, marveling at the stars crowding the night sky. They were brilliant. She watched a shooting star streak across the sky, leaving a bright trail of light in her vision. She wanted to make a wish, but she was afraid. Nothing good ever came from her wishes.

JACEY WALKED INSIDE, STANDING IN THE DARKNESS OF THE HOUSE.

The house seemed to be breathing, seemed to be alive. It enveloped her, and she had to sit down. She sat at the bottom of the staircase, which creaked and groaned as she settled in. She closed her eyes and rubbed her hands on the hardwood steps, feeling the heat from the day stored up in the wood. It was oppressively hot in the house, and Jacey didn't know if the air conditioning even worked. Jacey moved her hands to her breasts and slid them down her waist. She squirmed, pressing her thighs together, suddenly feeling horny.

She opened her eyes and looked at the parlor, and a shadow stood in the parlor doorway.

It'll take more than that to scare me after today, she thought, but she wasn't quite brave enough to say these words out loud. The shadow disappeared, and Jacey quickly went upstairs and took a shower. The water was lukewarm, but it felt amazing to be clean after a long day.

After the shower, Jacey looked around the bedroom once occupied by her grandmother, and more recently by a relative she had never met. Jacey only now remembered her grandparents had separate bedrooms. Jacey paused and stopped brushing her wet hair. Had her grandmother known about her husband's tendencies? How could she not? It could be one reason for the separate bedrooms. Now that Jacey was an adult, she realized that people could only hide so much from each other in an intimate relationship. Jacey sighed. She was so tired she couldn't handle thinking about this anymore.

Jacey pawed through her bags and picked out a sheer chemise and clean undies; it was simply too hot for much else. Jacey switched off the small lamp and walked to the large window across the room.

She looked at the windowpane and saw a face looking back at her. She stood completely still. Then she closed her eyes and counted to ten. The face was still there when she opened her eyes.

It was her grandfather.

"No," Jacey whispered. "No, you're dead ..."

The face grinned a chilling smile. Jacey walked closer to the window. She saw his skin had a greenish tint. His eyes were sunken, yet they shone with a sickly glow.

The image slowly faded, and Jacey slid the window up. The soft night air – fragrant with honeysuckle and dewy grass – rushed into the room and over her body. Jacey sat down on the bed. How could she stay here? There were literally ghosts here. Well, one ghost that she knew of. Oh, yeah, and a demon or some other spirit. And she couldn't talk to anyone about it. Who would believe her? *But haven't I always been alone?* Jacey relished the sense of freedom that filled her right now. She was scared, but more than anything, she was curious. She felt some strange destiny was being offered to her from beyond the grave.

Jacey settled into the bed and stared out the window, listening to the light breeze rustling the thick green leaves of the trees, the crickets humming, and the frogs croaking in a chaotic synchronization. She fell asleep a few minutes later.

Jacey woke up suddenly in the dark and looked at her phone. She had slept three hours; it was almost three. She turned over, closed her eyes, and tried to go back to sleep but couldn't get comfortable. After a few more fitful tries, she threw back the sheets and got up. She sat by the open window, lit a cigarette, and looked out at the night. She heard a bobcat scream in the distance.

She had been dreaming of Morgan, but she couldn't remember details. She closed her eyes for a second and saw him smiling at her.

Jacey heard something, a scratching sound. She opened her eyes and peered out the window. She heard rustling and then something being knocked over.

She took the gun out of her purse and walked down the stairs. They squealed with every step, and she tried to will them to stop making so much noise.

She stood looking out the back door, leaving all the lights off. She spotted a white cat and opened the door. The cat looked at Jacey and ran a couple of feet away, then stopped, watching. Jacey could see its eyes glowing in the dark.

"Kitty, kitty," Jacey said. She knelt, laying the gun next to her. "Come here, it's okay," she said. The cat stared at her but didn't move.

Jacey went inside, set the gun on the table, and rummaged in the fridge. She found some deli meat that hadn't expired and tore it into chunks and put it in a small bowl. She brought it outside and set it at the bottom of the steps.

The cat walked over cautiously, sniffed the bowl, and began to eat. Jacey slowly reached out and petted the cat, which looked at her. "It's okay," said Jacey.

The cat – Jacey thought it was a she — kept eating. She was skinny, but she had beautiful soft white fur, and in the moonlight, she seemed to glow. "You're made of moonlight," Jacey said.

THE DEAD BORN

The cat finished eating, and Jacey rubbed the top of her silky head. The cat purred and turned her head, looking up with eyes that shone like peridot jewels, then sat down, staring at Jacey. Just then the bobcat screamed. The cat immediately got up, looking in the direction of the noise. Off in another direction, Jacey heard a pack of coyotes howl. The cat was poised for action: front legs straight, back straight, fur standing on end. Her little nose twitched in the night air, her head high and alert.

"Want to come in with me?" she asked.

Jacey got up slowly and stood at the open door. "Come on," she said.

The cat walked up the steps, stopped on the last one, then looked up at Jacey.

"Come on, Moon," she said. The cat walked inside, as if she had been waiting to be properly invited inside the house.

In the kitchen, Jacey poured some water in a bowl and watched Moon drink, then bent down and picked her up. Her white fur was a little matted, but it could easily be brushed out, and Jacey didn't see any wounds or fleas. Moon squirmed, and Jacey put her down.

"Let's go to bed," Jacey said. She grabbed the gun and waited patiently while Moon followed her upstairs, stopping to sniff every few seconds.

Jacey put the gun in the small nightstand drawer next to the bed, laid down, and waited for the cat to look around the room. Jacey gently patted the bed, and Moon jumped up, settled next to Jacey, and curled into a ball. Jacey petted the cat's head and dropped off to sleep almost immediately.

While Jacey slept, shadows crept in from the open window, spreading out across the ceiling like probing tentacles, and swirled in the space above her bed.

Moon looked up, her eyes gleaming like yellow-green fire in the darkness. She arched her back and gave a low growl, her eyes following the shadows.

Jacey turned over, murmuring something in her sleep. Moon looked at her, then back at the ceiling. The shadows were gone. Moon leaped onto the windowsill, looking out into the yard, and saw a man. She growled again as he looked up and smiled an icy grin.

Moon kept watch until the first pink streaks of dawn began to paint the navy-blue canvas of the morning sky, finally settling back down beside Jacey. Moon had been waiting a long time for Jacey, her mother, and she was ready, her purpose was finally aligned with her mother's. It was good to have a purpose, Moon thought.

CHAPTER 4

Jacey woke up several hours later, the sun shining brightly through the windows. It was already hot; Jacey would have to buy a fan. She sat up and examined the room. The furniture was nice but old and dusty, only needing some polish. But the paint was chipping off the walls, the windows were extremely dirty, the curtains were a cheap fabric that was shiny and thin with age, and the floor was covered with something that looked like a cross between linoleum and plastic.

Jacey used the bathroom, washed her hands, and brushed her teeth. She sat back on the bed, checking her phone. It was Friday, and Crissy's funeral was at noon. Moon leaped off the bed and ran down the stairs, which Jacey took as a hint to not waste any more of the day.

She grabbed her purse to get her cigarettes, then stopped, picking up the book that she found on the dead woman. In all the chaos of the previous day, Jacey had forgotten to read it. She put it on the nightstand, not wanting to look at it right now.

She threw on some shorts and went downstairs, carefully walking down the steps and speed-walking past the parlor. Jacey let Moon outside to do her business, and looked out at the land. She couldn't help but marvel at its beauty. Unless some other relative came out of the woodwork to challenge her, she supposed it was hers.

Thankfully, there was some coffee and a coffee maker in the kitchen. While the coffee brewed, she searched the fridge and found some turkey bacon and eggs. She fried the bacon and cooked the eggs and wolfed them down, too hungry to think about the fact that she was eating a dead woman's food.

Jacey had left the door cracked, and Moon came back in. Jacey scooped her up, and Moon clamped her teeth on Jacey's arm but didn't break the skin. "Still not used to being picked up, huh?" she said. Jacey put her down and plopped more deli meat into her bowl, along with leftovers from breakfast, and refilled her water bowl.

Jacey showered, then decided on a black maxi dress for the funeral. It was long, but the material was cool. Jacey pinned her hair in a twisty low bun and put on some earrings and dressy sandals. It was just too damn hot to wear much more. Jacey decided she looked okay. She had slept well last night, so the circles under her eyes had faded. She grabbed her purse and headed out.

Moon was lounging on the front porch, and Jacey bent down and patted her silky fur. She smiled at her tilted head and her brilliant eyes that were slightly crossed.

"I'll be gone for a while, but I'll be back," Jacey said to her. Moon looked at her and stretched her head forward, and Jacey pressed her face to the cat's, giving her a kiss on her pink nose.

"Don't go in the road, and if you see any animals bigger than you, run and hide," she said.

THE DEAD BORN

Jacey drove to the cemetery in silence. She cranked up the AC, but it only blew out warm air. Men in suits with sunburned faces directed cars into rows alongside the curb of the gravesite. Jacey parked and walked up a slight hill to Crissy's grave.

Jacey stood behind the chairs reserved for family, which consisted of Crissy's aunt and uncle. A child of about five or six years old sat in the chair next to Crissy's aunt. Whenever he started to fidget, the aunt put her hand upon his arm. He looked neither sad nor bored, and Jacey realized that the kid probably hardly ever saw his mother.

The aunt and uncle turned and looked at Jacey. They knew her but said nothing, only turned back around. The pastor stood and waited for the small crowd to settle, and Jacey was directed to a seat in the back row. Crissy's family was under the shaded canopy.

The aunt – Marla, Jacey remembered – held a small box of tissues in her lap. She was already crying, even though the pastor hadn't started. It was the fakest weeping Jacey had ever seen and heard. The child looked at his aunt, his mouth open, then he turned and looked at Jacey. She smiled and waved at him. He was a beautiful child, and he had inherited his dark-brown hair and huge brown eyes from his mother. Not for the first time, Jacey wondered who his father was. The boy grinned back at her, then hid his face behind the chair, but he looked back up. Jacey smiled, and the aunt looked at Jacey, her mouth set tightly. "Sit still," she hissed at the boy.

Someone took a seat near Jacey, and she looked up. It was Morgan. Jacey stared at him, and Morgan smiled at her.

Jacey shifted in her seat. Why was Morgan here? He didn't know Crissy that well. At least, that's what he had told her. Jacey made herself face forward and sit still. She felt her eyes start to water and cursed herself. *Do not cry in front of these assholes*, she thought. Well, Morgan was not an asshole; he was here, even if it was just for Jacey.

The pastor mopped his red face with a handkerchief, then opened the Bible in his hands. Jacey noticed that his hands were short and stubby, and his nails looked manicured.

Jacey wiped her face with her handkerchief and glanced at Morgan. He was sitting stiffly in his dark suit. He glanced over, and for a moment, she looked into his bright yet deep greenish-gold eyes. His eyes reminded Jacey of dawn's sunlight reflecting on water, glistening and penetrating and magical. Jacey shifted in the hard, plastic seat, then glanced at his biceps outlined in the fabric. Jacey shifted again, crossing her legs and pressing them tightly together for half a second.

"Friends, the Bible says that we are all God's children," the preacher said and paused with his plump hand in the air. He wiped sweat off his brow and continued. "And God will welcome this child into His kingdom, and from that promise, given to us by His only son's sacrifice, we can take comfort."

Marla wailed, and Crissy's son began to whimper and cover his face with his hands. Jacey wondered why the aunt had brought the poor kid to this circus. "Lord help," she said in a whisper.

"In Jesus' Christ's name we commit to the ground the body of Cristina Diane Simmons ..."

The aunt pitched herself forward, crawling toward the casket. She raised a fist against her head, weeping in theatrical fashion. Morgan sat forward a little, his instincts to help a hysterical woman kicking in, but Jacey put her hand on his arm and he sat back. She kept her hand there, feeling the muscles through the expensive fabric of the jacket.

As Marla crawled around, Jacey noticed her bare legs and feet and was immediately offended. Her grandmother would never wear a dress without pantyhose and a girdle. A woman ran to Marla and pulled her back into her chair, but she continued to wail.

Jacey frowned and looked away, scanning the group of people standing adjacent to her. She saw Corey had showed up, with the redhead, and she and Corey smiled at each other. Jacey suddenly recognized the guy standing next to them: It was Jesse Vineyard. He was smoking a cigarette, and his shoulders were hunched. He had put on a wrinkled dress shirt and tucked them into a pair of dark-brown cargo pants. His shoes were scuffed, and to Jacey he looked miserable, and not just from the heat and his ex-girlfriend's funeral. He looked pale and on the verge of passing out. She decided to talk to him after this spectacle wrapped up.

Suddenly, as if he had read her thoughts, he looked at her. He stared for a moment, looked down, then looked back up at her. He took a long drag off his cigarette and tossed it in the grass, then whispered something to a young woman and walked off, not waiting for her response. She followed him, and so did an older woman.

Jacey sat up like she had been pinched. She looked at Morgan, who was staring at Crissy's aunt, seemingly lulled into a trance by the heat and the droning preacher. She nudged him, and he blinked and looked at her. She motioned with her head and stood up. He nodded and they walked out toward their cars.

"What?" he asked.

"Jesse," she said, then stopped and looked around for him.

"He was here?" Morgan asked.

"You didn't see him?" Behind them, she heard the service come to an end.

"No, but I wasn't looking for him to be here," he said, wiping sweat off his forehead.

"Dammit, did they run to the car? How could they get out of here so quickly?"

People were walking to their cars. Jacey looked behind her and saw Crissy's coffin and stopped. The woman inside used to be her friend, who bore a child, who had survived ... awful things, awful people from the moment she took her first breath.

Jacey felt dizzy, and she closed her eyes.

"Do you want to go back, take a minute?" asked Morgan.

"I have to get out of here," she whispered. Her body was soaked with sweat, and she felt like she might pass out.

Morgan nodded and gently took the crook of her arm, guiding her to his truck. He opened the passenger door and practically lifted Jacey into the seat. He got in and cranked up the A.C. Jacey let out a sigh, leaning back.

"You okay?" he asked.

Jacey shook her head, eyes closed. "No, I need a drink."

"Yeah, me, too," he said.

Jacey opened her eyes and looked out the window. She had bailed on Crissy again. Couldn't even make it through her funeral.

Morgan got on the interstate. Jacey didn't ask where they were going, and Morgan seemed to know she didn't want to talk.

He pulled into a little bar that sat right outside of a small downtown. The air conditioning was blasting, and Jacey smelled beer and liquor. She and Morgan sat at a table near the back, and he ordered them double shots of bourbon. Jacey downed hers right away.

"I'm a terrible friend," Jacey told him. "I was never there for her."

"From what I heard about her, she was ... troubled, so it may not have been easy to be a friend to her."

Jacey laughed. "More like damaged – she never had a chance." Jacey looked at him. "Did you ever talk to her?"

"Yeah, like I said, I saw her when she was at work. I would go in, make small talk, tell a joke. She was always friendly and nice," Morgan said.

THE DEAD BORN

"So, Morgan, what do you do? When you're not, you know, running with the Outlaws?" Jacey asked.

Morgan chuckled. "I think you have the wrong impression of me," he said and downed his bourbon, then signaled the waitress for another round.

"Maybe," Jacey said.

"I'm sort of a consultant," he said.

"With whom do you consult?"

"Different entities. I do security consultation for companies."

"Sounds mysterious."

"No, it's not really," Morgan said.

"Not much need for that in Poplar Hill," Jacey said.

"True, which is why I'm out of town a lot."

"Oh, well, that must be exciting."

Morgan looked down; he was remembering something, Jacey could tell. She studied him and tried to read what was going on, but the moment passed and he said, "Not as exciting as being a writer."

Jacey shrugged. "It's pretty … solitary," she said. She almost said lonely.

Morgan nodded. "Lonely?"

Jacey stared at him, suddenly a little angry. The thing inside her peeped its blind face out from behind a corner, sniffing.

"I'm not lonely," she said.

"I meant no offense," he replied.

Jacey sat back, crossing her arms.

Morgan did the same and said, "You're not an easy person to know."

"Look who's talking," Jacey said.

"All I meant was, I admire what you do, that's all. I wish I could write books," he said.

"You all say that, but you wouldn't if you attempted such a feat. Try sitting in a room for hours on end, metaphorically gutting yourself and putting it out there for the world to enjoy or criticize," she said.

Morgan leaned forward. "You just proved my point – lonely. Believe me, I know what you mean," he said.

The waitress brought over their drinks. "Thank you," Morgan said to her, and she smiled and brushed the hair out of her eyes. She was pretty, and she was obviously smitten with Morgan.

"I'll be back to check on you," she said to him.

"Thank you," Jacey said. The waitress never even looked at her. Jacey rolled her eyes. Morgan raised his eyebrows and grinned an aw-shucks smile.

"You're very … grating," Jacey said.

Morgan's glass paused midair. He furrowed his brow, then shook his head, and downed his shot.

"No, I don't think so," he said.

"Did Crissy ever date one of those bikers?" asked Jacey.

"I don't think she dated them, but she ran around with a couple of them, Randy and another. He owns a strip club, and she stayed with him before she moved into her trailer," said Morgan.

"Was she a stripper?"

"Yeah." He offered up no details.

"Did you ever go see her there?" Jacey asked.

"She was not working there when I went."

"So, you go there a lot?" she asked.

"No, not really my thing," he said.

"Why's that?"

Morgan shrugged. "I don't know, too old for that type of thing. And besides, I just don't get off on seeing women dance for money, not that there's anything wrong if that's what they want to do."

"That's a very politically correct answer," Jacey said.

"There is no right answer to your question," he replied. "But I don't think most of them like doing it, so it's not fun for me."

THE DEAD BORN

"So, if they enjoyed it, you wouldn't mind them dancing naked in front of you?" she asked.

"I would be bothered less by it, but …" He trailed off.

"But what?" asked Jacey.

He shrugged. "Well, I think sex, it's all about one thing, and we mess it up, we just complicate the hell out of it," he said.

"One thing?" asked Jacey.

"In the end, it's about reproducing, about carrying on your genes. When I see a beautiful woman, I'm looking at her physical attributes. Does she have nice … um, you know. Is she healthy, does she look fertile, can she bear offspring? When women see a man, they kind of look for the same things, but also is he a good provider, will he keep her safe, will he keep her offspring safe?" he said. He looked at Jacey and shook his head. "I mean, when you strip everything else away, no pun intended, that's all it is."

"Okay, that was not politically correct at all," she said, laughing. "What about love? Is that just the higher brain's response to biological imperatives of reproducing?"

"I don't know, I've never been in love," he said.

"Yeah, me neither."

They sat in silence for a minute, but it felt oddly comfortable.

"I need to smoke," she said and got up. Morgan's phone rang.

"Excuse me," he said and took a step away and answered the phone.

Jacey pretended to look for her lighter while she listened.

"Yeah, I'll take care of it," he said abruptly and hung up. He turned to Jacey and said, "Listen, I have to go, but let me drop you off first. Talk later? You go home, try to relax. I should be done by then."

"Sure," she said.

Morgan dropped her off at her car, and after she got home, Jacey took an hour long nap. She woke up feeling better, and she was determined to at least clean up a little. She couldn't find cleaning materials, so she ran to the small grocery store nearby and bought supplies and some food.

She cleaned the upstairs bathroom, scrubbing and disinfecting until it gleamed and smelled sharply sterile. She swept the bedroom and mopped, then made her bed and took down the torn and dusty bedroom curtains. Moon jumped up and lounged on the bed in a ray of sunlight.

During her cleaning, Jacey found the card Evans had given her and decided to call and get any updates, but just then her phone rang. It was Corey. They chatted about the funeral for a few minutes, and he asked if Jacey was okay.

"Yeah, no, I don't know," she said. Jacey shook her head and decided she couldn't think about it right now. "So, how's the redhead?"

"Ariel? Oh, she's great, I'm seeing her tonight," he said. "Why, are you jealous?" She could tell he was smiling.

"You wish," she said.

"No need to be jealous, there's plenty of me to go around," he said.

"Mmhm, you'll have a regular harem before too long," she said. She put him on speaker and got up and walked to the window, looking outside.

"Hey, you saw Jesse Vineyard there, didn't you?" she asked.

"Yeah, I saw him," he said.

"Did you all talk?"

"Yeah, he said he was going to the Tomato Festival tonight, asked if I would be there."

"Will you be?" she asked.

"Yep. You want to go? I'll pick you up," he said.

"And piss off that redhead? I don't think so, Cor," she said. "But I'll meet up with you there."

"All right, see you there," he said, and they hung up.

THE DEAD BORN

The festival could be fun, she thought. It had already started, but the good stuff happened after dark when the bands played and a fireworks show took place. Maybe Morgan would want to come with her.

Jacey suddenly felt the need to walk around the property. Just a short hike for now, she thought. She changed into jeans and a long but sheer shirt, and put on tennis shoes. It was blazing hot, but she wanted to be protected from the weeds and bushes.

She downed some water, then filled up a bottle to take with. She grabbed her gun, as well, tucking it into her jeans. *Need to get a holster*, she thought. She walked out the back and noticed a hat hanging on a nail on the porch. It looked like a fishing hat, but it had breathable material and a wide brim, just what she needed.

Jacey walked to the edge of the property where the ground sloped down. She saw the abandoned barn and a small wooden building that used to house chickens. She walked past them and made her way to the barbed wire fence that looked over the old cemetery. She had forgotten it was this close to the property. Jacey wanted to walk around it, but she felt she was being led to find something else.

Jacey gazed up at the huge trees. She remembered how they blazed with color in the fall: red and orange and yellow, almost neon in their brilliance.

The late afternoon was eerily quiet, and Jacey broke out in goosebumps despite the horrible heat. She walked on, occasionally looking behind her to make sure she wasn't being followed.

She made her way to the upslope of the field that led into deep woods. The grass was getting tall, but it wasn't as bad as she thought it might be. There had been no rain, and the grass was beginning to get crunchy, but it was still green. She dodged piles of cow manure and wondered when cows had last been there. Quite recently, she guessed, as the piles didn't seem completely dry.

Jacey stopped and wiped sweat from her face and behind her neck. She was thankful for the hat, and she took a swig of water.

She trudged on until she reached a gate. The hinges squeaked loudly when she opened it, and flecks of rust fell off onto the ground. This was where the pond was, she remembered, but it now was almost dried up; only toward the middle was there some water. Jacey wondered if snapping turtles still lived there. She walked around the perimeter, then stopped. She squatted down, peering at the remnants of a campfire. She shook her head. It was dangerous to have a fire out here – the surrounding vegetation could ignite quickly.

She walked around to an old tree, thankful for the shade. She stopped to rest and noticed the grass was dotted with drops of blood. *You don't know if that's blood,* Jacey scolded herself. *But what else would it be? Paint?*

"Not likely," Jacey said out loud.

Her phone beeped, startling her. It was a message from Corey. He said he was heading to the festival. Jacey decided to head back.

She jogged to the house, sweating and breathing hard, her heart pounding in her ears. She got a glass and filled it with ice and stood in front of the open freezer for a while. Then she stood over the sink and drank two glasses of water. She took a cold shower and drank another glass of water, and finally felt normal again. She was hungry but decided to eat at the festival.

Just then she got a text from Morgan, apologizing that he was delayed, but could they meet up later? Jacey texted about the festival, and Morgan said he would call her when he was done and agreed to watch the fireworks with her.

Jacey changed into shorts and put some food and water out for Moon and left. Jacey soon realized she was headed to her old high school, and that she had not been on this stretch of highway for years. It was a beautiful drive, and it was rumored that Hank Williams had driven that same highway long ago, to his last concert in Asheville, and that his car had passed by her house and farm. Jacey remembered sitting out at night, *Lost Highway* playing on her portable CD player, hoping to see his ghost motorcade pass by. Now, she hoped she never saw a ghost again.

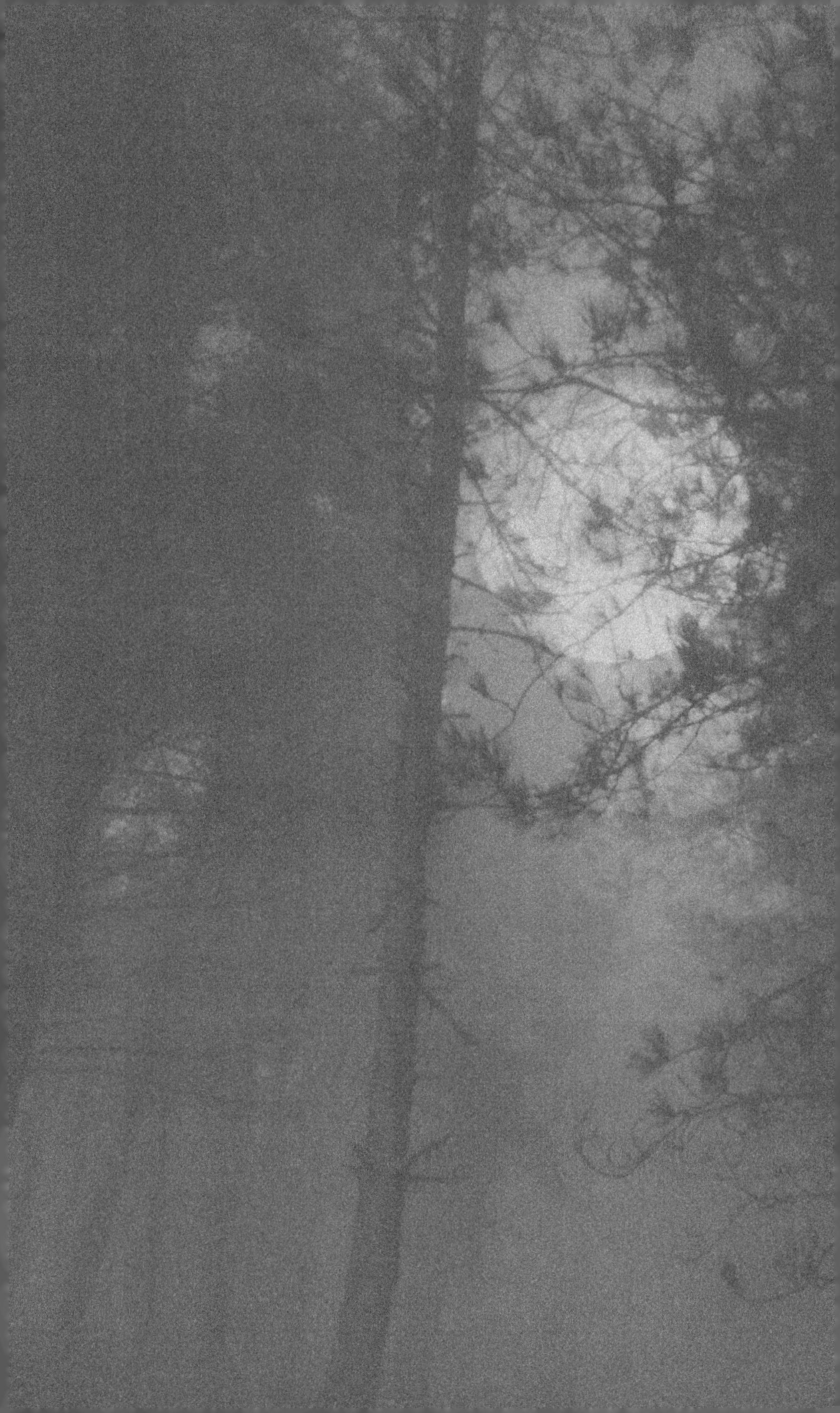

CHAPTER 5

The Tomato Festival had been a local tradition for the past thirty years or so, depending on the person you asked. Jacey tried to remember the last time she had gone, but all she could remember was walking around bored and hot, and wanting nothing more than to leave home for good.

Jacey tried to ignore the excitement she felt when she got into the city limits of Rutledge and saw the festival in full swing. She saw tents lining the right side, and she rolled down her window and breathed in the fragrance of grilled hamburgers and hotdogs; she could even smell the sharp tang of the mustard and sautéed onions and green peppers. She saw kids riding horses and ponies. The place was packed with people of all ages.

She maneuvered through the crowd and busted a U-turn and finally found a parking spot on the street. She locked her car and began to walk toward the festival grounds.

At the entrance, as Jacey dug in her pocket for some cash to pay the admission, she was surprised by a woman who yelled, "Jacey, oh my gosh, I can't believe it!" People turned and stared, she was so loud. Jacey grinned, but she couldn't place the woman. She saw she had a nametag, which read *Volunteer: Ashley King*. Jacey knew she had a couple of classes with Ashley, but they had not been friends. Ashley came from money, and she was a popular kid. She had always been nice but a little icy.

"How are you, Ashley?" Jacey asked, moving off to the side. Another volunteer continued to take money while Jacey and Ashley chatted.

"I'm great! I'm volunteering. Well, obviously," she said and laughed as she looked down at her nametag.

"That's cool. I remember you were always volunteering in school, too," Jacey said. "Did you end up going to Tulane?"

"I did, I went to Tulane." Ashley's face lit up, and she smiled brightly. Jacey smiled, too; Ashley looked genuinely happy.

"Law, right?" asked Jacey.

"Yes, criminal law. I don't practice anymore, but I met my husband in law school, and we have two children," she said.

"Oh, wow, that's wonderful, Ashley," Jacey said. "Criminal law, huh?"

"Yeah, it was quite an experience, but not what I thought it would be," she said and looked off into the distance for a second.

"Mommy!" A girl of about five with long auburn hair and huge emerald-green eyes ran up to Ashley. She had her face painted like a butterfly and was holding cotton candy. "Mommy I want to ride the pony, Daddy said to ask you."

"We will do that later, Mommy has to finish up here first," she said. "That's my husband, Chris over there." Ashley waved, and Jacey saw a man wave back quickly, then wipe a young boy's face with a napkin. The boy squirmed and bolted, and his father ran after him. Ashley's husband was bookish, with glasses, and a crop of the same beautiful auburn hair he had passed on to his daughter.

"And this is Emily. Say hi, Emily," Ashley said.

"Hi," she said, peeping up from her mother's side.

Jacey waved at the little girl and said hi. "She's beautiful, Ashley," Jacey said.

"Thank you. I would love for you to meet my whole family. Actually, do you want to have lunch? I mean, will you be staying here a little longer?"

"Um, yeah, I will, at least for the time being," Jacey replied.

Ashley looked at her, eyebrows raised.

"Oh! Yes, I would love to have lunch with you," Jacey said, hoping her face didn't look annoyed.

"Well, how about Monday? We can meet at Ruby's Café downtown. Say, one o'clock?"

Jacey decided to just go with it. "Sure, that sounds just fine."

"Great, well let me give you my number," Ashley said. "You know, Jacey, I've read all your books. I really like them!"

Jacey felt her face redden, and she looked down at her phone. "Ah, thanks," she said. She looked at Ashley. "I never would have thought you'd be a fan of ... well, that genre of writing." She meant *smut*, but there were kids around.

"They're very good. You have a way of writing characters that is so compelling, especially the villains, I just love it," Ashley said. Jacey searched her facial expressions for any hint of sarcasm or insincerity. She detected neither.

Ashley leaned in conspiratorially and asked, "Are you working on a new one?" She seemed genuinely excited.

"I am, actually. I'll tell you about it at lunch," Jacey said.

"Great! I can't wait."

"Me, too."

"See you then!" Ashley said and walked back to the admissions table.

Jacey walked through the entrance into the fairgrounds, realizing Ashley had not charged her to get in. Jacey texted Corey, then saw a stand that sold iced tea, lemonade, and funnel cakes, and immediately went over and ordered a lemonade.

"It's a sin to drink my lemonade without one of my funnel cakes, young lady," the vendor said with a boisterous laugh. His face was red from the sun, and he had sparkling blue eyes, gray hair, and a handsome face.

She drank half of her lemonade while she watched him take a funnel cake out of the deep fryer and coat it with powdered sugar. White powder flew up around his face, and he twitched his nose and chuckled with satisfaction. A grim-faced teenager was making another batch of lemonade, and Jacey noticed a line had formed behind her. The man handed her the funnel cake and refilled her lemonade.

"Here you go, doll. Now, if you want to run away with me, I shut down after the fireworks." He winked at her and flashed a smile that probably charmed the panties of many a lady back in his day.

"I don't think your wife would let me run off with you," Jacey responded.

He leaned forward and whispered, "She's a devil woman. I need an angel in my old age."

Jacey stuffed some bills in the tip jar, shaking her head and laughing with him.

"No offense, but you don't seem to know women very well – I'm definitely no angel," she said.

"Psshhh, I know an angel when I see one. Don't keep me waiting too long," he said.

"It's a date," Jacey said and blew him a kiss, and she walked off with her funnel cake and lemonade. She took a bite and seriously considered running off with the mischievous man who made such wonderful sweets.

"Wow, that's good," she said and crammed more of the funnel cake into her mouth. It burned the roof of her mouth, but she didn't care. She closed her eyes for a second, relishing the delicious fried dough.

"Jacey!"

She looked to the side and saw Corey and Ariel waving at her. She waved back and walked in their direction.

As she got close to them, Corey doubled over with laughter. Ariel elbowed him and told him to stop, but Jacey could tell she was struggling not to laugh, too. Jacey looked down at herself and saw her tank top was covered in powdered sugar. She realized her face probably looked just as bad.

"Oh, Lord, help," Jacey said and laughed. She shook the powder off her shirt and wiped her face as good as she could with a tiny paper napkin.

"You missed a spot, Spacey," Corey said and pointed to her shirt. Jacey looked down and he playfully thumbed her nose lightly and laughed.

Jacey shoved him. "You suck so bad," she said.

"Come on, we're going to my cousin's food stand – they have the best hotdogs in the state," he said.

The three of them sat and ate their hotdogs and drank more lemonade. Jacey spilled chili and mustard on her shirt, and Ariel dropped her hotdog on the asphalt. "I can't take you all anywhere," Corey said and went off to fetch another hotdog for his lady.

While Corey was gone, Jacey got to know Ariel. She was going to school to be a veterinarian and was madly in love with Corey. She never came out and said it, but Jacey could tell from the way her eyes sparkled when she mentioned him. Jacey was happy for them, but she felt a little sad, too. She suddenly wished Morgan were here with her, the four of them laughing together.

After Corey got back and Ariel finished her hotdog, they wandered around looking at the horses and cows until they heard the band performing a sound check. It was dusk, but still incredibly hot, so they walked to the tent to wait for the band to start.

Jacey excused herself to find a bathroom before the music began. She soon found herself in front of her old high school. The front doors were open, so she walked in. It had been almost twenty years since she had last done that.

She looked to her right. The cafeteria. She walked in and looked around, amazed. Aside from a few coats of paint, it looked the same. It was so quiet, she could hear her own breathing. Then she went into the gymnasium. It was just as preserved from her time there. How could everything look the same? A group of kids saw her and lowered their voices. Jacey was the adult now.

She walked into the hall, looking into the classrooms. She opened one of the doors and walked inside the dark classroom. This was where she had civics class. She remembered she had a crush on a boy who sat across from her. That triggered a memory of algebra class where her guy friend Jody would draw her grotesque but hilarious dirty pictures, and she tried to find the classroom but got turned around. Jacey stopped by a row of lockers, wondering which one had been hers. All of the sudden, her heart started beating fast and she felt dizzy and clammy.

She found the girls' bathroom and went inside. She had smoked cigarettes in here sometimes with … what was her name? She couldn't remember. She felt like she was going to pass out. Jacey splashed cold water on her face until she felt better, then patted herself dry with paper towels.

She found the back door and walked outside and breathed in the night air deeply. What the hell was that in the school? she wondered.

Her phone buzzed.

"Hey, did you fall in?" Corey asked with a chuckle.

"Sorry, I was just being nostalgic looking around the alma mater," Jacey said.

"If you're in the main hallway, make sure to check out all my trophies," he said.

Jacey laughed and heard the band playing *The Closer You Get* by Alabama. "I'll be right there," she said.

While they were listening to the band, Jacey looked at a group standing just outside the tent and recognized Randy among them. He was staring at her. He motioned for her to come over, but she turned away.

Corey and Ariel stood up, and Corey leaned in to talk into Jacey's ear. "Hey, I'm taking Ariel home, she has to work in the morning," he said.

"You all aren't staying for the fireworks?" Jacey asked.

"Nah, we'll come back tomorrow night, that's when they have the good ones. We're gonna head home and, you know ..."

"Yeah, well, drive safe," said Jacey, and she hugged them goodbye.

"I will. And, hey, cookout at my place next weekend!" he said over his shoulder.

Jacey watched them walk away, Ariel leaning against Corey as he put his arm protectively around her waist. Jacey then walked down to the football field to watch the fireworks. She sat in the back of the bleachers and lit a cigarette. Still no word from Morgan – she supposed he wasn't going to make it for the fireworks.

She heard a loud group walking her way and saw that it was Randy with three other guys and a woman. They were being rowdy, and one of the men was smoking weed openly.

"Havin' fun?" Randy asked as he took a seat beside Jacey. When he spoke, he leaned too close to her ear. She realized he was buzzed.

Jacey took a drag off her cigarette and blew it in his face.

He grabbed her elbow and pulled her close to him, then put his arm around her shoulders and plucked the cigarette from between her fingers. He laughed and puffed on it, then threw it down on the bleachers. An older couple sitting below Jacey got up and walked away.

"I like you, blondie, but I think you have the wrong idea about me," he said with a chuckle.

"What idea is that?" she asked.

"That I am not a nice guy," he said.

"I don't care."

Randy pulled her closer. She tried to squirm away, but he grabbed her face and made her look at him.

"I care. See, I hear you're asking questions about me, assuming things about me that maybe I am not so nice. Like maybe I was involved in your friend's death," he said.

"Were you?" She stared at him.

Randy stared back in disbelief.

"You got spirit, blondie, and I gotta say it drives me nuts; I am into it," he said. One of his lackeys brayed like a donkey.

"Take your hands off of me," Jacey said.

"Who else likes blondie, huh?" he turned and asked his minions.

None of them responded, not even donkey guy. As Jacey scanned the faces, she realized one was Jesse. He hadn't given any indication that he knew her, and now he just stared at his phone. He finally looked up, lit a cigarette, and glanced around, but still he didn't make eye contact. He was very skinny, and his pants were slightly sagging, but Jacey suspected it wasn't a fashion statement. He seemed unhealthy and malnourished, he kept itching his nose, and his eyes looked glazed.

Randy tightened his grip on Jacey's arm. One of his friends – a huge, muscled bald guy – came and sat on the other side of Jacey, and she realized too late that they had surrounded her.

She felt a crazy sense of calm come over her. "What do you want?"

"I want you to go for a ride with me, Jacey," Randy said. "We never got to go for a ride."

He smiled at her, and she winced at the gleam in his eyes.

"I need to get my tomatoes, asshole," she said.

"Later," he said. Jesse smirked.

"Fine. Let's go then," she said and stood up. Randy paused and then stood up and nodded his head.

"After you," he said and swept his arm forward. Jacey walked down the bleachers, and Randy's goons fell in line behind her.

Just then the first booms and hisses and crackles of the fireworks started. Jacey stopped and looked up, and despite her situation, she smiled. She remembered being little and watching the fireworks here with her parents.

Randy gave her a shove, and she continued walking.

When they got to the motorcycles, Randy handed her a helmet. After a couple of attempts, she finally got the strap buckled. Randy got on, and Jacey sat behind him. She felt a thrill when the engine started and the seat shook underneath her. He throttled it and the bike bolted forward, startling her. She tightened her grip around his waist and held on.

He opened it up once they were on the highway, and Jacey gasped and closed her eyes. The bike seemed to fall out from under her, and she wasn't prepared for the sensations. It felt like she was flying, and the wind and the sound of the engine growling made her want to cry or scream with delight – it was such an assault on the senses, she couldn't tell if she was feeling fear or pleasure.

She felt a shift in the speed and finally opened her eyes. She saw the moon and stars in the skies around them, and then looked down and saw her feet propped up on the stand, the asphalt flying by. Randy was driving right on the yellow line, and there wasn't another car in sight, only bikes on either side of them. Wondering if the whole group had followed, she carefully turned to look behind her and saw the headlights of the other two.

They pulled off onto Ridge Road and went for about a mile on the tiny road. They turned into a driveway and parked in the small gravel drive, and Jacey got off the bike. Her legs were already sore.

She figured they were about five miles from the fairgrounds. She could walk if she had to, but hopefully someone would take her back to get her car.

Jacey took off the helmet and handed it to Randy, then followed the others into the clubhouse.

The place was crowded; she figured about thirty people were crammed in. Randy handed her a beer.

"I need a shot, too," Jacey said, and in a minute, he came back with a bottle of Jack Daniels. He took her wrist and led her to a back room that seemed to be an office/bedroom. There was a small bed, a small couch, and a large wooden desk, and on the walls were neon beer signs and posters of bikes. She noticed a nice laptop on the desk.

Randy poured her a shot and she downed it immediately. She held out her glass, and he refilled it, and she drained it again just as fast. Jacey exhaled loudly, sat down on the couch, and lit a cigarette. She watched as Randy walked over and sat next to her. Someone knocked on the door.

"Come in," Randy said. He took a sip of his beer.

Jesse came into the room and sat at the desk. He lit a cigarette and leaned back in the chair, staring at Jacey.

"You have five minutes," Randy said to Jacey. Then he walked out the door.

Jacey got up and sat across the desk from Jesse. His eyes looked small and watery, and they were such a light bluish gray that they almost appeared colorless.

"You wanna ask me something? About Crissy?" He dug in his pocket and pulled out a baggie of pills. He began to crush up a pill on the dirty desktop.

"Did you kill her?" she asked.

He looked up for a second, then bent back down to his work. "No," he said. He split the pill into two lines.

"Do you know who did?" She was mesmerized by his pill-crushing skills; there were no gritty lumps in the lines.

"Nah, I don't, but I wish I did," he said. Jacey didn't quite believe him. But she did believe he was telling the truth about not killing her. Jesse pulled a straw out of his pocket, bent forward, and snorted a line.

He sniffed and shook his head. "Fuck!" He smiled and handed Jacey the straw.

"No thanks," she said.

Jesse stared at her. His eyes looked less dead now.

"Sure, why not." She snorted a line and held her head back and snorted the residue back up into her nostril. "Oh, shit," she said. She held back the urge to sneeze. Then she felt a warmth spread from her head down to the rest of her body. Her face flushed with heat, and she felt nauseated.

Jesse lit a cigarette. He lit the wrong end, realized it, and put it in the ashtray. Jacey watched, her mouth slightly open, her eyes watering. Then she lit a cigarette and took a drag to calm the queasy feeling in her stomach.

"You don't remember me, do you?" Jesse asked.

"What do you mean?" Jacey held up the cigarette in front of her and looked at him through the smoke.

"I was with you the night you lost your virginity," he said with no inflection in his voice. "The night you let Darrell fuck you. In high school. At his house. I was there."

"I didn't have sex with Darrell," Jacey said. She was too high to be angry. She started giggling.

"Oh, my God, is that what he told you?" she asked.

Jesse smirked. "Well, yeah, he did," he said.

"You're both stupid. I would never sleep with him," she said and giggled again.

"Crissy said you did."

Jacey paused and looked at his face. His watery eyes looked amused.

"Bullshit," Jacey said.

"It's true, she said you let him fuck you because you were jealous that she had lost her virginity before you," he said.

"You're a liar," Jacey said.

"I ain't the one who killed her. They even questioned me, but I was with my girlfriend at the time. So why are you wasting your time if the cops ain't?"

"Oh, yeah, you were just an innocent bystander?" Jacey stood up and got in his face. "You may not have killed her. In fact, I know you don't have the balls to do anything like that. But you know something. That's why Randy brought you in here, right?"

He shoved Jacey and she stumbled back a bit.

"Too bad she ain't around, she could show you the scars and bruises I gave her. She was a worthless slut, and apparently she wasn't even a real friend to you," he said.

"Fuck you!" Jacey shrieked and hit him in the side of his head, right on his ear. He yelled in pain and fell to the floor.

After a moment, he said, "You read my palm one time, do you remember?" He didn't sound angry, only sad, and tears sprang to Jacey's eyes.

"What did you say?" But suddenly she remembered. She had read his palm on the bus home from school one day.

Randy came in, and Jesse stood up and smiled at him.

"You remember what you said?" Jesse asked Jacey and slapped her across the face. She barely reacted, she was so caught up in the memory.

"All right, Jesse, time to get back to work," Randy said.

Jesse grabbed Jacey's hand and twisted it to show her palm. "Yours looks a lot like mine," he said.

THE DEAD BORN

"I won't tell you again," Randy said and Jesse let go of Jacey's hand and walked out, sparing one final glance at her. It was a look that was both pitiful and full of menace. He was like a dog that had been kicked and beaten but still proudly remembered its wolf ancestry. It broke Jacey's heart. Maybe because it was similar to a look Crissy had given her years ago, in the IGA.

"Sit down," Randy told her.

"I wanna leave." She hated the way her voice sounded – whiny and weak. She blamed the pill she had snorted.

She got a flash of a memory: her and her ex, high on pills, listening to music, her crying because he cheated on her. She was crying and saying she didn't want to live without him. In reality, she wanted to keep him around because he supplied a steady stream of pills.

Randy guided her to the couch, sat down, and patted the spot next to him like she was a pet. Jacey sat down, and he put his hand on her leg, and began to rub. She looked at him.

He kissed her, and she leaned back to get away. He then scooped her legs up and laid her down on the couch so she was underneath him. He pulled up her shirt and kissed her neck and tried to pull down her bra. She squirmed to get away, but she also felt her body responding, and she began to cry. Jacey tried to push him away, but he was too strong. She closed her eyes. She was so sleepy. *Just go to sleep and let it happen*, she thought. *Just like before. Just let it happen.*

"No!" Jacey yelled. "Stop it, Randy, let me up."

He got up and she crawled out from under him. She stood up and was trying to pull down her tank top when the door opened. It was a woman, and right behind her was Morgan.

Jacey looked down at herself: barefoot, shorts unbuttoned, shirt barely on. She looked like a drugged-up whore. Which was half right, she thought wryly.

Randy got up from the couch. Somehow his shirt was off, and he had an obvious erection. The woman took in the scene and left, but Morgan just stared at Jacey. She looked down; his gaze was like a sharp knife through her guts.

Then she turned and threw up her hotdog and the delicious funnel cake into the small garbage can next to the desk.

"No offense, Morgan, but what are you doing in here?" Randy asked. He lit a cigarette, but he kept his shirt off.

"I'm going to go," Jacey said.

"Sit down in that chair," Morgan said.

"Morgan, I–" she began.

Morgan took her wrist, gentle but firm, like she was a child. "Don't move," he said.

He walked closer to Randy.

"You don't want to do this, man," Randy threatened. Morgan said nothing.

Randy held up his hand. "Come on, man, just calm down. I don't want to have to fuck you up," he said.

"I am calm," Morgan said and took off his belt. Randy backed away. Morgan closed in, and Randy took a swing, but Morgan dodged it and punched Randy in the face. Randy fell, and Morgan began to whack Randy with the belt. Randy could only hold up an arm to protect his face as the belt repeatedly slapped against his skin.

Jacey was horrified.

Finally, Morgan stopped and stood over Randy, who was in a heap on the floor. He kept his head down and didn't look up.

Morgan looked at Jacey. "Get in the truck," he said. He sounded eerily calm, and Jacey got up and went with him.

She was so ashamed she didn't dare speak or even look at Morgan. She knew he thought she had fucked Randy, and she was angry at herself, and at for Morgan for assuming that.

Morgan had wanted to kill Randy with his bare hands. He wasn't sure how he had restrained himself. He glanced at Jacey and felt disgust, anger, and desire. He was afraid of what he might do to her. He wouldn't hurt her, not physically, but he might say some terrible things, and when he thought of her standing in the office half-naked, he had to fight the urge to pull the truck over and fuck her right then and there.

Morgan pulled up to Jacey's house and shut off the engine.

"My car, I left it at the festival, I need to get it," she said.

"You don't need to be driving," Morgan said.

Jacey nodded and opened the door. She got out and looked at him. "Will you look at me for a minute?" she asked.

Morgan stared straight ahead.

"Nothing happened with … with him," she said.

Silence.

"Fuck it," Jacey said with a chuckle. "Better this way, because I don't know how to be anyone but this person anymore." She swayed a little, then she slammed the door. She walked toward her house.

Morgan watched her walk away. She looked so small against the huge trees and the maw of the front porch. He got out of his truck and jogged to her. Jacey turned. She looked lost. He knew the look; he saw it in the mirror daily.

"You said anymore," he said.

"What?" she asked.

"You said you didn't know how to be anyone else anymore, which implies at one time you did, so you can again. You just have to decide it's what you will do," he said. "Grow up, and quit being selfish."

He turned and walked back to his truck. He seemed to vanish into the darkness.

She closed her eyes and remembered reading Jesse's palm. She had received a vision of him lying in a pool of blood. She had assured him his lifeline was fragmented, "or it could mean past lives, like you were a cowboy and died in a gunfight," she had told him. He had seemed pleased with that. Then she let him read her palm, and he said, "Looks a lot like mine."

CHAPTER 6

On Sunday, Jacey tried to do some writing, but as she sat staring at her laptop, her thoughts kept drifting off to Crissy, Randy, her house ... but mostly Morgan. She slammed the laptop closed, then began to furiously sweep, mop, and clean windows. She wondered if she should call Corey to take her to get her car when she walked outside and saw it sitting in the driveway. The keys were laying on the dashboard. She knew Morgan had the car brought back for her. She wasn't sure why, though. Jacey kept checking her phone, hoping Morgan would call or text, but he didn't.

When Jacey went back into the house, she saw the funeral home's business card laying on an end table. She decided to give them a call, half hoping they wouldn't answer.

"Hello, Bill speaking," a very professional deep voice said over the line.

"Yes, hi, hello," Jacey began but had to pause to clear her throat. "I'm not sure if I have the right number."

"This is Bill Montgomery of Montgomery Funeral Home. Am I the person you were trying to reach?" he asked.

"Yes, sir. My name is Jacey Forestar, and um, well, my distant aunt was brought there," she said awkwardly.

"Yes, of course, Miss Forestar, I've been waiting for your call," he said.

"I wasn't sure if anyone would answer today, since it's Sunday."

"We are always here." He paused, then said, "Would you like to come down and collect your relative's remains?" He sounded as if that was the most normal question in the world.

"Now?" asked Jacey.

"Unless, of course, this is an inconvenient time for you," Bill said.

"No," Jacey said.

"You have our address?"

"Yes, it's on the card—" began Jacey, but she stopped short of telling him she didn't want the ashes.

"Wonderful, I will be here in the office until three today. I hope to see you, Miss Forestar, and if you can't make it, we will hold remains for up to one month, until they will be relegated to a special section of our appointed final place of rest. Good day, Miss Forestar," Bill said and hung up.

Jacey sat and pondered. He could throw the ashes out the back door, for all she cared. But she liked his voice, so she decided to go meet Bill Montgomery.

Three hours later, Jacey was sitting with Bill at a low-key but hip bar in downtown Knoxville. She and Bill were laughing and chatting like old friends.

"I can't believe you've never had a gin rickey. Didn't you just tell me you lived in Savannah?" asked Bill, shaking his head. He had dark blond hair and wore glasses. He looked like a college literature or classics professor, cute and bookish, nothing like the Bram Stoker character he came across as over the phone. Bill was thirty, with a sweet smile, and huge blue eyes with the lushest eyelashes Jacey had ever seen.

"Well, honestly, I didn't go out that much when I lived in Savannah," Jacey replied. She had a moment of shock – why had she said that? It was a leading statement, opening up another part of Jacey's life she did not want to revisit. But Bill was so kind, it was hard not to open up to him. She supposed that was part of his job, to make people feel comfortable.

Not long after Jacey walked into the funeral home and shook hands with Bill, she had a panic attack.

"Miss Forestar, I think you should sit down. Please come to my office," Bill said and led her to a cozy but professional office. Jacey sat on the small couch and sipped the ice-cold water Bill handed her and used her state-naming technique to calm down. Bill sat opposite Jacey, close, but giving her plenty of room. He must have seen more than a few panic attacks in his line of work, she thought.

When her heart rate returned to normal and she stopped sweating, she looked up at Bill, who was looking at some paperwork, waiting for Jacey to calm down.

"I'm sorry, I don't know why that happened, I haven't had one of those since—" Jacey stopped herself and took a drink of water. She had almost said since she had the vision in the house.

"No need to be sorry. It's not the first time someone has had a reaction to being here; it's a lot to deal with," he said smiling amiably at Jacey. "Miss Forestar, why don't we do this another time, when you feel more up to discussing this. I realize now I should not have rushed you, and I apologize for that."

Jacey shook her head. "No, I want to get this over with, if you don't mind." Jacey took another sip and tapped her fingers against the water bottle, trying to decide if she should ask the question she wanted to. Then she blurted out, "Mr. Montgomery, was there anything unusual about my great-aunt when you brought her here?"

Bill sat back and placed his hands in his lap. "No, nothing unusual, which is why an autopsy was not done on Ms. Williams. She was ninety-two years old, and all signs pointed to natural causes," he said.

"I don't mean that, I mean … was there anything you noticed about her? Anything … odd?" asked Jacey.

Bill leaned forward and placed his hands between his knees. He looked vaguely troubled for a moment, but he cleared his throat and regained his composure.

"Yes, as a matter of fact, there was something I noticed that was strange," he said. He looked down at his hands.

"What?" asked Jacey.

Bill sat in silence for a beat, then he got up and went to his desk. He opened a drawer and took something out and came and sat back down. Bill handed it to Jacey, and she saw it was a printed copy of a picture. She saw a strange design she didn't recognize, but she felt like she had seen it somewhere before. She looked more closely.

"Is this a tattoo?" she asked.

"It's a brand," Bill said.

"Excuse me?"

"A brand, she was branded. Look here. It's pink, so the scar is quite old. I would say from when she was a young child."

"What is the symbol?" Jacey asked.

"I don't know. I haven't had time to really research it, but an internet search didn't find anything that resembled this," he said.

Jacey stared at the symbol. It looked Celtic or pagan, but she felt it was something else. Jacey looked at Bill. "Were you going to tell me about it if I hadn't asked?"

"No, probably not," he replied truthfully.

Jacey studied him. "You want to say something else," she prodded.

"What do you plan on doing with her remains?" Bill asked.

Jacey shrugged. "I don't want them, but now I feel like I should have them with me."

Bill nodded. He looked at Jacey. He trusted his instincts about her, even though he knew her history and felt her chaotic energy. He felt the same presence he had felt around her great-aunt Ella, an almost oppressive engulfing feeling.

"What is it?" Jacey said.

"I have been doing this for about five years now, but I've really been in this business my whole life – my father owns this place, and I have assisted him since I was young. I spend my time comforting people by telling them their loved ones are in a better place. But I never believed it; I always believed death was the end. I'm not religious, I believe in what I can see and touch. I never had any experiences to change my mind. Until your relative came through my doors," said Bill. He stared at the wall for a few seconds, then continued.

"When I was preparing her, I felt … something. Which was strange, because I've never felt that before. I felt watched, as if she was there in the room with me. And when I found the mark on her neck, I swear I felt heat rise off her. I haven't been sleeping well since she got here either. I want you to take her ashes out of here. Today."

Jacey nodded and stared at the picture of the symbol, absorbing what Bill had just told her. "Can I keep this?" she asked.

Bill nodded. "Are you sure you want to keep her ashes?" he asked, clearly hoping Jacey would say no. When she said yes, Bill grew self-conscious, as if he couldn't believe he had told her what he had.

Jacey looked at Bill, and he felt his stomach do a somersault; her eyes seemed to bore into his soul.

"I appreciate you telling me that, and I promise I will keep it between us," she said.

Bill nodded and stood up. "That would be much appreciated, I can't have everyone thinking I spook easily. If you're ready to take her, we can go."

Jacey nodded and put the picture in her purse.

"Bill," she said. "Did you tend to Crissy? Was she brought here?"

"No, she was taken to the medical examiner in Knoxville, and when her body was released, she was taken to another funeral home," he said. "I found that odd, since she was buried here in town; usually the family would use our services for local burial. My father also knows Marla, Crissy's aunt who raised her, so we were surprised."

"Oh," Jacey said.

Bill found himself wanting to tell Jacey something to make her feel better, but he kept quiet. He knew the folks who ran the funeral home where her friend was taken, but this was a pending murder case, and he could not risk losing his license, much less be charged with interfering with an investigation. Bill decided he would ask his buddy Mitchell, off the record, if he had noticed anything unusual.

"If I hear anything, I will let you know," was all Bill said.

"Thank you," Jacey said.

Bill led her into another room and invited her to sit down. Then he placed what looked like a large cake box on the table in front of her. The box was stamped with the Montgomery Funeral Home emblem.

Jacey opened it and saw a large black velvet bag with a drawstring. She opened that and saw a large slate-gray urn with dates and her aunt's name engraved on it.

"She had ordered it years ago with what she wanted inscribed, the lettering, the color," Bill said.

Jacey didn't look inside, only stared at the urn. "This is a person in here," she said.

"Yes."

Jacey placed the urn back inside the bag and set it in the cake box. She saw Bill looking at her and felt like he wanted to tell her something else.

"You know about me, about what happened with my brother," she said.

Bill nodded. At the time, he thought he might go into pathology instead of working with his father in the family business. He was doing an internship at the medical examiner's office when they brought in Jacey's brother and his family.

Bill drifted off for a second, replaying the grisly scenes in his mind, remembering the horror of seeing the dead family. In addition to Jacey's brother, there had been two young girls and his wife.

He was shaken out of his reverie when he saw Jacey sink to the floor and hold her head in her hands. She began to cry, her body shaking with the force of her grief.

Bill stood in shock, not understanding what had happened. She must have been overcome by the memory of her brother and the tragedy, but she was acting like she had plucked images out of his mind and seen them herself. Bill refused to believe that she had just read his mind. At least he pretended he didn't believe it.

He sat with her on the soft carpet and held her as she cried, saying nothing, knowing that she just needed to be comforted. She soon calmed down, and Bill reached up and grabbed a box of tissues and handed it to Jacey. She pushed the box away and leaned in and hugged Bill. He was surprised, but he hugged her back. She moved her hands to his head and held him while she kissed him, but then suddenly pulled back, her eyes wide.

"I shouldn't have done that," Jacey said.

"It's okay, it's a normal response to grief," Bill said. He was vaguely troubled to realize he was turned on, and he half-hoped she would tell him it hadn't been just a grief response.

"I'm sorry, it was a mistake and inappropriate," she apologized again.

Bill sighed and stood up and offered his hand to Jacey and helped her up.

"I think we could both use a drink. Interested?" he said.

CHAPTER 7

At the dimly lit but cozy bar, Bill forced himself to focus on the flowing conversation and cheery atmosphere instead of the hug and kiss. Her reaction was just the result of a stressful situation, he told himself.

"I love Savannah, it's such a lively city. Good energy," Bill said.

"Definitely. It has a charm, as if it only wants to be beautiful and welcoming. And the food is amazing," she said.

Bill nodded in agreement. "Have you lived anywhere else?" he asked.

"No, it's strange, I always thought I would, I always wanted to, but I never did," she said.

"Why not?"

She hesitated and said, "I think the real reason is I'm scared, scared to stray too far from home." As soon as she said it, she realized how silly it was, and how so much of her life was lived in fear.

"Well, there's nothing stopping you from doing it, if it's what you want. Plus, you seem like a brave person," Bill said.

"The longer I stay here, the more leaving seems like a good idea," Jacey said. She finished her gin, appreciating the new experience but really wanting a whisky with a large ice cube. "Well, I should really get back. My cat has gotten quite used to her feeding schedule."

Bill nodded and signaled the waitress for the check, and Jacey grabbed her purse. "Let me get this," she said.

"No way," said Bill.

He paid and they walked out of the bar. The area used to be empty, save for warehouses and the bus station and train depot, but now it was home to apartments and restaurants and bars. The air was hot and thick with the smells of baked bread, grilled meats, and the faint aroma of garbage.

"Probably changed a bit since you were down here last," Bill said as if reading her mind. They strolled on the sidewalk, the heat rising from the old concrete.

"Yes, it's much livelier than before. I never thought people would live down here. It used to be kind of rough, and now it's wealthy couples with dogs. Don't take this the wrong way, but I picture someone like you living here," she said.

"I've visited a lot of different places, and after I graduated I traveled around, but I guess I always knew I would go back to Poplar Hill. It's where the family business is, and I like it there," he said.

On the drive back, they both were quiet. It suddenly felt uncomfortable, and Jacey was ashamed she had kissed him. He probably didn't get a lot of that because of his profession, she thought. She wondered if he was lonely.

"Bill, have you ever been married or in a serious relationship?" she asked.

"No, never married. Only one semi-serious relationship, with a woman who was a pathologist. She was ambitious and couldn't understand why I wanted to be a mortician. She thought I was too smart, as if being a mortician is a job for a person who lacked will or intelligence," he said. "It's okay, though. I have friends, my family, and I love what I do even though a lot of people don't understand it or think I must be a weirdo for doing it. I think most people don't like it because it frightens them."

Jacey nodded but kept quiet.

Soon they passed the white sign with black lettering that read, *Welcome to Poplar Hill*. She realized the shape of the sign was almost like the shape of her house – sloped downward on the sides, with a large almost jagged curve that jutted up in the middle.

Back at the funeral home, Bill parked next to Jacey's car and went inside to get the box. She opened her passenger-side door, and he placed the box on the floor of the seat.

Jacey stood in front of Bill, and she extended her hand. Bill shook it. "Thank you for everything," Jacey said.

"Of course," Bill said. "Maybe one night we could go out to dinner, if you like."

Jacey opened her mouth to tell him no, she was seeing someone. But she realized she was not. She didn't know what the hell Morgan was to her, or what she was to him.

"Yes, I would like that," Jacey said and realized she really did.

"Great, how about next Friday night? Eight o'clock?" he asked, his eyes sparkling.

"Sure," she replied.

He smiled. "Okay then, it's a date." He turned to walk to his car, then paused. "One thing you may not know, I'm always on call. I don't anticipate having to tend to anything, but you should know it's a possibility."

Jacey nodded. "That's not a problem," she said.

"Well then, see you Friday around eight, Miss Forestar," he said.

Jacey watched him drive off, then got in her car, wondering what the hell she was doing. When she got home, she put the box in the parlor on a table in the corner. She fed Moon, then got the picture of the symbol and went outside to sit on the porch. Jacey lit the flame on the citronella oil lamp and sat down in the chair. She studied the symbol, hoping she would recognize it from somewhere. Jacey tapped the image with her finger.

She got up and fetched the Book of Shadows from the bedroom. Moon sauntered onto the porch and laid near Jacey. She hissed at her, swishing her tail back and forth.

"I'm trying to find out what this symbol is, that's all," Jacey said to Moon. Her cat continued to side-eye her.

Jacey flipped past the spells and recipes, then paused and brought the book closer. She saw a symbol on the top of a page that looked similar to what she was looking for. She examined it closely, comparing it to the picture. It was slightly different, but it was incredibly similar; it had to be the same symbol, she thought. The name written under the symbol was Moloch, and near it was a drawing of an androgynous goat-headed figure that said Baphomet. Below this was an incantation:

"Thee I do invoke, the Bornless One. From deep below, from the mud and the filth, from the rocks and the trees, awake from your imposed sleep to serve the daughter of earth, the witch of this dwelling place."

Jacey thought for a moment, then quickly looked up the alchemical symbol for earth. It matched the brand on Ella. So she was earth. But who were fire, water, and air?

Jacey recognized the incantation as a jumbled form of an Alister Crowley one, probably borrowed from the freemasons; low magic for sure. But still, it was magic, and she knew Crowley had been the leader of a self-proclaimed satanic cult called the

Ordo Templi Orientis. Jacey remembered from what she had read about him that the cult was mainly focused on sex magick. Jacey knew there was power in the incorporation of sex magick, but how much she wasn't sure.

Her aunt clearly was a practitioner of this stuff, and she was branded, which Jacey thought meant there were more practitioners. But how many, and where were they? And why would she leave this book for Jacey?

She decided to visit the library or courthouse the next day and do some digging; there had to be tax records, and marriage and birth certificates. Then she planned to call Bill to get him to ask around if the brand had been seen by anyone else in his business. Oh, and she wanted to get a book on astrology. She knew very little about astrology – all she knew was that she was a Scorpio sun – and thought it might help.

Jacey closed the book. She stretched and watched the fireflies blink in and out in the darkness; they reminded her of when she was a girl and would catch them. Jacey looked up and saw an owl silently glide past. She felt comforted. Even in the face of evil and heartache, all of these things still went on, the world still turned no matter what she did. This thought used to frighten her, but now she happily clung to it because it showed there was something more above it all. It did not matter if it was random or planned, the world still turned in the vast universe.

Jacey picked up Moon and took her inside. They slept peacefully that night in the velvety summer air that seeped in through the open window.

CHAPTER 8

On Monday, Jacey visited the library as soon as it opened. She got a library card and perused the shelves and found some books on astrology and witchcraft. Out of habit, she looked to see if her books were kept at the library. They carried four of them.

Jacey also went through the local genealogy records, but she only found birth, marriage, and death certificates for Ella Williams, née Corbitt.

Next, Jacey perused the property records. She made notes for about an hour, then noticed the time and checked out her books. It was time to meet Ashley for lunch.

WHILE JACEY WAS AT THE LIBRARY, JESSE VINEYARD WAS DRIVING UP the bumpy road to Morgan's house.

Jesse parked his car down the hill and walked until he was stopped by a gated entrance. He lit a cigarette and walked around looking for a way in, but in addition to the fence, the property was overgrown with trees and bushes and weeds. He decided this was more trouble than he had bargained for. Besides, Randy probably deserved what Morgan gave him, Jesse thought. I'll just tell Randy there were other people here and that security is too tight.

He looked at the property again. The security *was* too tight. But why? Jesse decided he didn't really want to know.

Jesse walked back to his car and took off. He passed Jacey's house on his way out and decided to snoop around there. He parked in the lot of a little store that was only a short climb up the hill in the back of her property, then trudged up the hill and walked around the side of the house next to a huge tree. He looked through the screened-in area above the stairs and saw a white cat sitting on the steps. She stood up and arched her back and hissed at him.

Jesse picked up a small rock and chucked it at the cat. She leaped down the steps, dodging the rock, and ran off the porch, hidden by the untrimmed hedges.

There was a light breeze, and a cloud drifted over the sun, darkening the land. He heard a low growl near him and jumped in fear. He heard it again and realized it was the cat.

Jesse walked to the front of the house. He saw no cars, and the inside of the house was dark. The place was really in need of work: the porch sagged in spots, and he could see paint chipped away in huge chunks. It reminded him of the Addams family house, except legitimately sinister.

In fact, Jesse was downright scared right now, and it wasn't just the house's spooky appearance. There was something here, and Jesse felt it. He wasn't one for anything that was not of this world; he hated haunted houses and scary movies.

He was about to leave when he thought of Randy. He might be happy if Jesse did something to Jacey. Hell, he probably would be so happy he would promote Jesse. If he was still even able to do that after the smackdown by Morgan. Or it might be time for Jesse to take Randy's place at the table anyway.

Jesse walked to the front door. The cat streaked in front of him, and Jesse jumped back, almost screaming. The fearless cat ran behind him and came back around in front of the door, guarding it. Jesse kicked out with his foot, but the cat was like greased lightning, so fast he couldn't even see where she went. He heard her hiss and growl. It sounded like she was above him now.

"Fuck you, cat," he whispered.

Jesse tried the doorknob. It was open. The cat growled again and he was amazed by the intensity of it; if he hadn't seen the cat already, he would have thought it was some demonic mountain lion. Jesse walked in and shut the door. The only light was at the top of the stairs. But it was a strange, soft light. Almost like the glow of a candle flame.

Jesse looked to his right, which was an empty room, and to the left he could see the shape of an old-timey couch and a large rug. It was what fancy people called a parlor. He looked up the stairs and saw the light was still there.

He started up the stairs but stopped when they groaned and wheezed like an old man. He took his hand off the banister. It felt dusty but also somehow oily, like the skin of a snake.

He took a deep breath and continued up. At the top of the stairs he turned to look down and saw the cat sitting at the foot of the stairs, looking at him. How had it gotten inside? He ignored it and went towards the soft, witchy glow.

When he got to the bedroom, he peeked around the corner and saw a woman lying on the bed. She was naked, her legs slightly spread and one of her arms above her head. She saw him and smiled. Jesse stared at her, his mouth hanging open in an expression locked in an odd mixture of lust and terror.

She resembled Jacey, except this woman had dark hair and almond-shaped eyes. Jesse walked in the room toward her. She spread her legs wider, then put her hand between her legs. She whispered something and Jesse stepped closer, trying to hear what she was saying.

She sat up and reached out her arms, inviting him to the bed. Her lips were parted in a red pout. Jesse sat next to her, and she closed her eyes and turned her head away from him, cupping her breasts and arching her back slightly.

The house was silent. A breeze blew in through the open window, and the thin curtains fluttered like torn angel wings in the soft wind. Jesse could smell rain in the air, and he heard tree branches rubbing together and leaves rustling softly. He took off his pants and marveled at how hard he was. He didn't understand what was happening, he just knew he wanted this woman, needed her.

He climbed on the bed slowly and hesitantly, and she spread her legs wider. Jesse looked at her, then put his hand between her legs. She kept her eyes closed, but she turned her head shyly away from him. She was wet, and he rubbed up and down. She arched her back higher and sighed, and he climbed on top of her and moved inside of her. He moaned and increased his speed, pausing to suck on her perfect breasts. He wanted to pull out and do it all over her face. He looked at her.

Her eyes were open, gazing blankly up at him, and now her hair was not black, but a bright blond. It was Crissy. There was blood on her face, and her head was caved in on one side. He cried out and tried to move off her, but she held him inside her and continued to move her hips. He cried out as he came, and involuntarily closed his eyes, and when he opened them again, he saw tiny bugs crawling all over her sallow skin.

He screamed and jerked backward and fell off the bed. He crawled away and scrambled to his feet, trying to pull up his jeans and boxers at the same time, but he tripped on a rug and scurried away on his hands and knees until he got to the door. He saw Crissy get off the bed, her stomach swollen and scarred with the stretch marks that freaked him out, and blood poured from her head. He made it to the stairs, crying and maybe still screaming, he wasn't sure. He was about to go down the steps, but he saw a figure standing at the entrance to the stairwell.

It was an old man. His eyes glowed as he smiled at Jesse. It was him, Jesse realized, Jacey's grandfather, the man who had raped him when he was a teenager. Jesse screamed. The man's smile spread into a cavernous maw that opened to the black pits of hell, and he was advancing on Jesse.

"Please, stop, please, no not again." Jesse was crying.

You can stop it, the man's grating voice said in Jesse's mind.

Jesse looked at the huge picture window in the stairwell. Without thinking, he squirmed out of his pants and ran toward the window and plunged through the glass. He only made it halfway through when his midsection got snagged on the splintered wooden frame. Jesse was hanging by his abdomen, and his body folded like a shirt. He gasped and pushed up with his arms and coughed out blood. His hands dug into splinters and broken glass trying to find purchase.

He was so crazed he didn't feel any of this. His only thought was he had to get out of this house, away from them, away from this hell. He managed to wrench himself out of the window frame and stood up on the gable. He looked at his abdomen. Blood poured from his body as it had from the demon Crissy's head. He pulled a huge shard of glass out of his side.

As Jacey pulled into her driveway, she saw something on her house. She squinted, not quite believing what she was seeing. "What the hell?" she whispered.

Jacey quickly parked and fumbled with her seatbelt as she hurried to get out of the car. She finally got out and walked closer to the house and recognized the figure as Jesse Vineyard. He was standing on her gable, the window broken behind him, and blood seemed to cover his entire front. He was looking behind him like he was listening to someone. Lightning streaked across the sky, and a huge thundercrack boomed over them.

"Jesse, hey, look at me, look at me, I'm calling an ambulance," she said. She scoffed as she said it – it was obvious that an ambulance couldn't help him at this point.

Jesse hadn't seen or heard her, and when he turned around, Jacey saw a look of terror on his face. He looked down at the stone sidewalk and let himself fall forward, as if he was diving into a pool. He landed headfirst on the sidewalk with a sickening sound.

Jacey looked away when Jesse fell. She held her hands over her mouth and dropped to her knees. She felt something brush against her leg and almost leaped away in fright until she saw it was Moon. She meowed loudly and butted her face into Jacey's hand. Jacey picked her up, and she meowed again, pressing her face into Jacey's cheek.

Jacey saw a blackish-gray mist hover above Jesse's body, then rise a few feet, stop, and swell in size until it looked like a storm cloud. Then the mist rose and floated off into the sky, mixing with the real storm clouds that were rolling across the sky.

Moon squirmed out of her grasp and walked around Jesse, then looked up at the house.

Jacey followed and looked at Jesse for a few seconds, then turned around and bent over, fighting the urge to vomit. She closed her eyes and took a deep breath, and it passed. She started to walk back down to her car, but her legs began shaking and she had to sit down in the grass. She squeezed her eyes shut, but she couldn't get rid of the image of Jesse's head caved in, blood spattered on her walkway.

She opened her eyes and put her hands over her mouth and screamed into her hands. She should run, now, she thought. Take the cat and leave, go back to Savannah. But Jacey saw Morgan in her mind. *Be honest, he is the reason you want to stay*, she thought. Also, if she fled now, they would accuse her of … something. Maybe they would say she killed him, that murder ran in the family.

Jacey grabbed her phone and called Evans.

"Hello?" He sounded like he had been asleep.

"It's Jacey Forestar. Jesse Vineyard is dead in my front yard. I came home and found him," she said. Her voice shook as she spoke, and she screamed when a lightning bolt struck nearby.

"Don't touch anything," Evans said and hung up. Then the rain came.

CHAPTER 9

Jacey watched from a window inside the parlor as crime scene technicians and policemen walked around her yard. At least they had finished in the house. She lit a cigarette and opened the window halfway.

Her phone buzzed and she saw it was Corey. Jacey quickly texted him, *I'm fine. Will talk later.*

Moon jumped onto the windowsill. Jacey jumped, startled but glad to see her. Moon opened her little mouth in a silent meow, then yawned, her pink tongue visible. She jumped onto the couch with Jacey.

Jacey finished her cigarette and carried Moon into the kitchen to feed her, then carried her upstairs and laid her on the bed.

"Rest, I'll stand guard for now," Jacey told her. Her cat curled up in a ball, closed her fierce little eyes, and went to sleep.

Jacey walked out of the room, leaving the door open a crack so Moon could get out. She stood with her hands on her hips, took a deep breath and closed her eyes. She held it for a few seconds, then exhaled. She opened her eyes and looked to the right, where her picture window used to be. Now there was a giant hole. Then she noticed the door to the bedroom in front of hers was open. She slowly walked over and peered inside. She hadn't been in here since she was young. She turned on the light and saw a bed frame with a bare mattress, boxes on the floor, and an empty wooden bookshelf. She walked in and went to look in the closet.

There was a loud knock on the front door. She paused, then tried the closet door. It was locked. She would get the skeleton key later and look inside. Jacey went to answer the door.

"Hello, ma'am," the guy said. "Are you Miss" … he looked down at his phone … "Jacinta Forestar?"

"Who are you?" asked Jacey, too tired to be polite.

"I'm Chris Bryant." They shook hands. "Nice to meet you. I apologize for the late visit, but I figured you would want me to at least cover that broken window," he said, pointing at it.

Jacey blinked. "How did you get past the police? It's a crime scene."

"Oh, well, I think they are pretty much done, ma'am," he said, looking behind him for a second.

"The police are paying you to cover my window?" she asked.

"No, ma'am, Mr. DeArmand is the one who hired me," he said.

"Morgan?" Jacey asked.

"Yes, ma'am. Um, may I come in?"

Jacey sensed he wanted to be done with the job as soon as possible. She stepped back and opened the door for him. He walked past her, looking around. "How old is this house?" he asked.

"More than two hundred years old. I think it was built in 1820," she said.

"And it's still standing," he said.

He had a toolbox with him and pointed upstairs. "Mind if I go up and get started? I'll measure, then cover it with some plywood, then come back tomorrow and put in a new window for you," he said.

"Do you always come out on calls at this hour?" she asked.

"It's unusual, ma'am, but I know Morgan's dad, and his whole family, so I don't mind doing him a favor. They're nice people," he said.

"Important people, too, I take it," Jacey said.

"Nice people," he said. He seemed to be getting impatient.

"May I get you anything, Mr. Bryant? Something to drink, perhaps?"

"No, thank you, ma'am," he said and went upstairs.

Jacey looked outside to see if Evans was still there and saw Bill Montgomery talking to him. She had forgotten about Bill. But of course they would call him. She was suddenly embarrassed and wanted to scream. Bill here again, to clean up someone else she knew.

There was a knock on the door. "Jacey, it's Bill," his familiar voice was the same calm and professional one she had immediately liked on the phone not so long ago.

Jacey opened the door, and Bill came inside. "How are you doing?" he asked.

"What are they saying out there?" asked Jacey.

"They are saying it looks like suicide, but they will be performing an autopsy. It's normal for a man his age, they have to rule out anything else as being the cause of death," he said.

"I found him like that Bill, I don't know what happened."

"Of course," said Bill. He took a card out of his back pocket and handed it to Jacey. "It's free, if you need it."

"What?" asked Jacey

"A grief and crisis counselor," he said.

Jacey didn't say anything. She put the card in her pocket. A man walked up to the open door. "Miss Forestar, I'm Detective Harris with the Knoxville Police Department," he said and shook Jacey's hand.

"How are you, Jack," Bill said, and the two men shook hands.

"Can we sit down and go over a couple of things, Miss Forestar?" Harris said.

"Sure, let's go into the parlor," Jacey said. "Is it all right if Bill stays?"

"Of course," he said, and she led them to the parlor.

Harris immediately started back up. "Now, if you could tell me how you found Jesse. From the time you saw him to when you called the police."

"Do I need to have a lawyer?" asked Jacey.

"If you wish, but you are not under arrest, nor are you suspected. I just need to get the details of how you came to find Mr. Vineyard in your yard," he said.

Jacey looked at Bill, and he nodded at her as if to say it was fine.

Jacey told her story, beginning with how she had met Ashley for lunch and up until she saw Jesse in her front yard. The only part she left out was the mist entity she had seen.

"So the door was open?" asked Harris.

"Yes, I didn't lock it," she said.

"Honestly, Ms. Forestar, you need to get some kind of security system for your home and property," he said.

"I will, although I don't know if I will be staying here much longer. I might go back to Savannah."

The detective blinked at her. "Ms. Forestar, you can't leave, at least not any time soon. A man died on your property, and we have to wait on the medical examiner to confirm exactly what happened. And, as I said, you're not suspected, but this is the second person who knew you that's died horribly recently. It just so happens, too, that those two people used to date each other. We have a lot of questions."

"I had nothing to do with this, or with Crissy. She was my friend, for God's sake," she said emphatically.

"And Jesse Vineyard? Why would he throw himself out of your top-floor window?" Harris asked.

"I don't know. I asked him about Crissy, so I suppose he was angry at me," she said. Jacey left out the part about the palm reading and Morgan beating his hero Randy. And the drugs they had done together.

"You saw him before this happened?" asked Harris.

"Yes, I saw him from a distance at Crissy's funeral, and then at the festival. I asked him if he had anything to do with Crissy's murder."

"And?" asked Harris.

"He said he had nothing to do with her being killed, and that he had already been questioned by the police and was cleared," she said.

"And that was the end of the conversation?"

"Yes, and I never saw him again. Well, until tonight."

Detective Harris studied Jacey for a second, then wrote some more in his small notepad. Harris stood up and put the notepad in his back pocket. "I can have a patrol car stay here overnight if you're worried about being alone, Ms. Forestar," he said.

"No, don't do that, I think it would make me more uneasy. And I won't go anywhere – I'm just shocked and upset, I spoke in haste," she said.

Harris smiled. "Well, that's understandable." He shook Jacey's hand and handed her his card. "Call me if you have any more questions or need to talk about anything," he said.

Harris shook hands with Bill, and they walked outside together. Evans then came inside and stood in the parlor. He looked at the spot where her aunt had been found.

"We're all finished. Harris said you may want a patrol car to stay outside with you tonight?" he said.

"No, I don't want that, I just want to be left alone," Jacey said.

Evans put on his hat and walked closer to Jacey. "Ever since you came back here, there's been nothing but trouble, and I want you out of my town. I always thought those whispers about you and your family being witches were just small-town gossip, but either way, I don't want you here. So, when this gets cleared up, I hope you leave."

"Damn, Josh, take it easy," Bill said. He had come back in unnoticed.

Evans looked at Bill, then back at Jacey. Evans shook his head and chuckled. "Don't waste any time, do you, Forestar?" Evans said. "Excuse me, I have to notify Vineyard's next of kin that her grandson is dead. You two have a great rest of your night." He walked out without closing the door.

Bill sat next to Jacey. "He didn't mean that, he's just upset; he knew Jesse pretty well," Bill said.

Jacey said nothing. She felt as if she were slipping off the edge of reality, and it felt familiar. She had done it before, and this time, she might not come back. But did it really matter?

Jacey heard footsteps on the stairs. It was Bryant. He popped his head into the parlor and said, "Goodnight, ma'am, I'll be back around ten tomorrow, if that's okay?"

Jacey stood up and walked to the door. "Yes, that's fine, thank you," then showed him out.

Bill got up. "I have to take Jesse to the medical examiner, but I could come back after, keep you company."

Jacey shook her head. "No, I want to be alone, but thank you, Bill," she said.

Bill was disappointed. He felt like a giant wall had come between them.

On his way out, Bill stopped to talk to Evans.

"You know, Josh, you don't have to be such an asshole to her – she had nothing to do with Jesse's death, and then you tell her she's town gossip again. It's unprofessional and just a damn mean thing to do," Bill said. He wasn't a confrontational person, but he felt it was the least he could do for Jacey.

"Bill, you're a good guy, so let me give you some advice: You need to stay away from her. She's nothing but trouble, and she's been stepping out with Morgan, and I don't think he would appreciate you coming around his girl," Evans said.

"Morgan DeArmond?" Bill had met him a couple of times. Bill remembered the guy was standoffish and a bit mysterious, although nice enough, and the subject of plenty of gossip himself.

Evans nodded. "He was the one who sent Bryant out to fix her window, so he knows what's happened, and he probably knows you are here."

"She never mentioned she was dating anyone," Bill said.

"Like I said, she's not a good person, so be warned. Goodnight, Bill," Evans said.

Bill suddenly felt foolish. He looked at his vehicle and realized how crazy he was for thinking someone as beautiful as Jacey would be into someone like him. She probably was using him as inspiration for a new character in an upcoming book. It wasn't the first time Bill had been in a relationship where he was let down after the woman realized she would be married to someone in a dark profession. Bill sighed and left, determined to put Jacey out of his mind.

CHAPTER 10

Evans pulled into Gwen Mynatt's tiny driveway, hating to visit late, but he was in a hurry to get home, and he always tried to do unpleasant things as quickly as possible. His mother referred to it as quickly ripping off the bandage.

Evans didn't think she would be too upset; she and Jesse had not been close, and Evans knew that Jesse had caused Gwen nothing but grief. Evans had been called to their place several times. Gwen would report Jesse for stealing her car or stealing money. Evans would track down Jesse, usually at the ballfield, or when he got older, at the End of the Line, and send him home.

The final straw was the time Jesse stole all Gwen's pain medication and sixty dollars from her purse. Evans told her he would look for Jesse, but he knew it was pointless and hadn't done so. About a month later, he saw Gwen at the IGA and said hello. She sniffed and said if he spent as much time patrolling as he did lollygagging, people like her grandson would be behind bars.

She had said it loudly, and some people had snickered. Evans was furious at the time, but he soon forgot about it. He was not one to hold grudges, and besides, she was an old lady who lived alone and had no family or friends to speak of.

Evans knocked on Gwen's door loudly, as she was hard of hearing. He heard her cane thump as she made her way to the door. "It's Sheriff Evans, Ms. Mynatt," he announced.

She peeked out from the little window in the door before opening it.

"It's Mrs. I still consider myself a married woman, sheriff," she said.

"Yes, ma'am. May I come in?" he asked.

"Of course," she said.

Evans walked in and stood in front of her. She looked tiny and frail, and he suddenly wished he had let Mike or Benny do this.

"Well, Gwen, I'm sorry to have to be here, but, well, it's just a damn shame." He couldn't quite get it out.

Gwen waved her hand and walked to the couch and sat down. She pointed to a chair, and Evans sat.

"Is he in prison this time?" she asked. Her eyes were tired, but they were still sharp.

"No, ma'am, he, um, he ..." *Dammit, man, don't make her say it for you, just tell her*, he told himself. Gwen looked at him and then at the floor. She knew but was waiting for him to tell her.

"He um, he passed away today. I'm so sorry, Gwen, Mrs. Mynatt," he said.

Gwen nodded. "Well, probably for the best. What happened? Did he overdose?"

"No, he ... we think it may have been suicide," he said. He took off his hat and ran his hand across the brim.

"Think it was?" she asked.

"Why don't we talk tomorrow, Gwen, and I'll fill you in on what I can," he said.

"Did it happen at that house?"

Evans knew she was talking about Jacey's place. "How did you know?"

"Dreamed it about a month ago. That place is evil. Don't worry, Evans, it's for the best. I hate that he died like that, but maybe he's at peace now," she said. She stood up, indicating she wanted him to go.

He walked to the door. "Gwen, I ... listen, I'm sorry I acted like an ass—"

"Stop it, Evans, you aren't so bad. You actually care, you just need to learn not to be so offended. You're a halfway decent man who could be a good man, just stop worrying about what other people think," she said.

Josh felt awful – he was the one who was supposed to be doing the comforting. He gently touched her shoulder and cleared his throat. "I'll be by tomorrow, Gwen. Lock up and try to rest," he said.

Gwen closed the door. She sat on the couch, sighed, and looked at the picture on her wall. It was of her only child, Michelle, her husband, Keith, and their baby, Jesse, Gwen's only grandchild. Jesse had always been troubled; from the moment he came out of the womb, he struggled with what life threw at him. Michelle had endometriosis, so the baby was a surprise, but she had a hard pregnancy and had to stay in the hospital a couple of times while she was pregnant. But the baby had made it, and they named him Jesse, after Jesse James the outlaw, because Keith thought he would be tough.

Then Michelle died in a car accident. She went to a concert with a group of girlfriends, and on the way home, a tire had blown out and the car had gone off the road. Back then no one wore seatbelts. Gwen always wondered if that would have saved her girl.

Gwen felt like she might die herself when that happened. But she hung on for Jesse, who needed her more than ever because

Keith went downhill fast after Michelle died. He was weak, a man who needed someone to pet him, and he was completely broken. She was his whole world, and he simply never recovered. When Keith turned thirty, his behavior became more and more erratic, and he began to claim he heard voices – aliens – and sometimes he would stay outside at night with his telescope and his radio and CB, claiming they were trying to contact him.

Gwen tried to keep Keith away from Jesse, but one day she had some appointments and had to leave the boy with his father. That was the day Keith killed himself in front of Jesse, and Gwen knew that Jesse would never be the same, that he would never be a normal, well-adjusted kid or a functioning adult. But Gwen always tried to make a normal life for him.

Gwen wondered what she should do. She was truly alone now, even though she hadn't had Jesse to cut the loneliness in a long time. She wiped tears from her eyes.

"I'm glad you're not around to hurt yourself or anyone else anymore, child," she said out loud. Even after all the hurt he had caused, she couldn't help but love him. It was what mothers did.

She made herself a cup of chamomile tea and sat on her bed while she drank it. Her thoughts drifted to the house where Jesse died. She knew that after that evil woman died, the girl whose family had lived there came back to stay for a while. The house had called her back, Gwen knew, and she decided to visit the girl. Perhaps she could persuade her to leave, while there was still time. But time was running fast these days, it seemed.

Fast and sideways.

You're just reaching for something that will make you feel useful, she tried to tell herself. But Gwen believed in her bones her story wasn't quite over yet.

CHAPTER 11

The next day, Gwen got up and made herself a breakfast of oatmeal and some strong coffee. She took a shower and put on some comfortable jeans and tennis shoes, and a light button-down shirt. She knew it would be hot, but she had always been cold-natured, plus she just didn't wear shorts anymore. She pinned her hair in a low bun and put on some jewelry. She looked at herself and smiled. She looked like a lady who was going to meet friends for lunch.

Bill Montgomery's father called and told her they would be releasing the body after an autopsy, and that they would notify her so she could make arrangements. Nothing to do but wait, so Gwen decided to visit the girl in the house.

Gwen drove in silence. She made a list in her mind of all the things she needed to do later. It was comforting to her to put things in order. It wasn't a far drive, about fifteen minutes, but she had not been out this way in a while, and she marveled at the beauty of the scenery: the lush green fields, the dense woods behind them, the farms and houses nestled back away from the highway.

She arrived at the house and parked behind a small, black sports car that was covered in dust. She got out, careful to have a firm grip on her cane, and looked at the house.

The evil was still here, she sensed. It wasn't just the spooky design of the gothic style; she would have sensed it if it had been a simple log cabin. The hairs on the back of her neck stood up as she walked closer to the house.

Gwen saw a window that looked shinier than the others and figured this was the window Jesse had gone out of. Someone sure had worked fast to fix it, she thought. She looked down and noticed a beautiful woman standing just outside the front door. Gwen felt her skin prickle in fear.

Progeny, she thought.

Gwen raised her hand in what she hoped was a friendly wave and tried to smile, to put the girl at ease, but she just couldn't do it. This house was awful. And the memories were coming, fast and heavy like someone throwing a heavy shroud over her. But Gwen was determined. She walked to the house and stepped carefully onto the rotting porch.

The girl's hair was dark blond, and she had a natural cascade of curls down almost to her waist. She had large amber eyes and chubby cheeks. Her delicate face seemed almost not to fit with her curvy figure. To Gwen, she had the face of a fairy on the body of a burlesque dancer.

"Hello," the girl said. She was looking at her curiously, and there was a brusqueness to her friendly greeting.

"Hello, I do apologize for coming by unannounced, but I had no way of contacting you beforehand," she stepped forward slightly, her hand extended.

"My name is Gwendolyn Mynatt. I'm Jesse's grandmother." Jacey's eyes widened, and she looked frightened and ashamed, but she shook Gwen's hand.

"I–" Jacey started.

Gwen gently patted Jacey's hand. "Please, I don't mean to cause you distress or alarm you, dear. Is your name Jacey?" she asked

Jacey nodded.

"Is it a family name? It's quite unusual," Gwen asked.

Jacey blinked and seemed to come back to the moment.

"Um, yes, it's actually short for something else. I heard it was a family name, but I don't really know," Jacey said.

"Oh, I see."

"Would you like to come in?" asked Jacey.

"It's such a nice morning, maybe we could sit on the porch?" Gwen said. She had no intention of going in that house.

Jacey was already sweating, but she nodded. "Sure. May I get you anything? I have tea or sparkling water."

"A sparkling water sounds wonderful," Gwen said.

Jacey dragged the two porch chairs closer together and wiped the seats, then went to get the drinks. Gwen sat down, took a linen handkerchief from her purse, and wiped her brow. She sighed and looked around. She noticed the sidewalk. There was a hose laying in the yard and a bucket filled with what Gwen assumed was cleaner. Someone, probably Jacey, had been scrubbing the sidewalk. That must have been where Jesse fell.

She jumped when the door creaked open. Jacey came out with two glasses filled with ice and two cans of sparkling lime water. She poured one for Gwen, who took a sip right away; her throat felt as dry and dusty as those windows.

"What is it short for?" Gwen asked. A bird sang sweetly in the distance.

"Ma'am?" asked Jacey.

"You mentioned Jacey is a shortened version of another name."

"Oh, yeah," Jacey's cheeks turned pink, and she looked away. "It's short for Jacinta, which means hyacinth, it's Greek I think, silly, really," Jacey said, swirling the glass and clinking the ice.

"Oh, no, it's a beautiful name, and you should be proud," Gwen said.

Jacey noticed the hose and the bucket. She cleared her throat. "Are you sure you don't want to sit inside? The parlor is actually nice," she said.

"I'm tougher than I look. I had to be in order to survive burying my daughter and then raise that disappointment of a grandson," she blurted out.

Jacey's eyes widened in surprise.

"Well, it's true, you and I know it, as did everyone in this town." She shook her head and took another sip of her water.

"Don't get me wrong, I did love him, but I did not like him," she said. She looked at Jacey. "You know what happened with his mother and father?"

Jacey set down her glass and leaned forward in her chair. "I remember his father killed himself, but his mother, she died not long after he was born?"

"When he was two years old. A car accident. My daughter, my only child," Gwen said.

"I'm so sorry."

"Yes, me, too. She was a sweet girl. Always wanted everyone around her to be happy, and she loved to have fun. She met Keith, Jesse's dad, when they were both just kids. She got pregnant, and he was so in love with her. She was fond of him, but it wasn't love, but she married him when she found out she was pregnant. Today, they might have just remained friends and shared custody of Jesse." She paused and took another drink. "I thought about moving away after Keith killed himself, but I never did."

"Why not?" asked Jacey.

"Oh, I don't know, scared I suppose. ... But really I think I just didn't want to leave my daughter. It just broke my heart even more to think about her being alone. I just could never leave her," she said softly. She looked at Jacey. "I know that sounds foolish."

"No, not at all, in fact it makes perfect sense," Jacey assured her.

"Anyway, I did the best I could, I think," Gwen said.

Jacey stared off into the distance, then set down her glass. "Do you think some people are cursed?"

"Yes," Gwen said without hesitation.

"Really?" Jacey was shocked.

"Without a doubt, I truly believe that," she said.

They watched a squirrel skitter up a tree.

"Most people are not cursed, they are merely products of their unfortunate circumstances. My Michelle was raised with love, and we were never cruel to her. My husband and I never argued in front of her. But for whatever reason, she made the wrong choices most of the time, and she had a child with a man who was weak and unstable," she said. "It may have been because her father died so young, but I don't think that was why. I sensed it in her from the time she was born."

Gwen set her glass down on the crate. The ice had almost melted.

"But she was cursed, and it was my fault," she said. "And I believe that families, people, can have generational spirits attached to them, through something a family member has done. Or through contact with evil people."

"What do you mean, what did you do to curse her?" asked Jacey.

Gwen was silent for a few moments.

"I knew your grandfather," Gwen said.

"I'm not surprised. It's a small town, we all pretty much know each other," Jacey said.

"Yes, but I knew him ... intimately. Michelle was his daughter," she said. Her voice shook slightly.

Jacey glared at her. "What are you talking about?"

"Michelle was his child. I never told him, or anyone. He was of course married to your grandmother, so I would have been a pariah if anyone found out, but more than that, if anyone found out the real nature of our relationship, well, it might have been so much worse," she said.

Gwen looked at her. "Can I tell you a story?"

Jacey said nothing. She stared straight ahead, and she was so still Gwen thought she looked like a statue.

Gwen settled into her chair.

"I know after I tell you the story, you will hate me," she said. "I'm sorry."

CHAPTER 12

Gwen's Story

I met your grandfather in this house. I developed a friendly acquaintance with your grandmother – we both worked at TVA. We would talk on our lunch breaks. Sometimes we would go outside and have a cigarette at the picnic tables when the weather was nice.

I was almost fifteen years younger than her, and it was my first job. I was a secretary in one of the civil engineering offices. I was a fast typist, and I was also good at keeping my boss's calendar and meetings in order.

She told me about this house and the land they had just bought. How they were building another house on the property for their daughter and her husband and their children. I can't tell you how surreal it is to be sitting here with you now and telling you this story. If someone had come from the future and told me this would happen.... I read a passage in a book once that ka is a wheel. Destiny, fate, it all means the same thing. Everything comes back around to where it is supposed to, no matter what we do to try to stop it.

One weekend I came over for a visit, and they are working on the house, working overtime to get it ready for move-in. One of the workers has a question, so your grandmother went to speak with them. Your grandfather came in and I was struck by his ... intensity. He was not a handsome man, and I tried for a few years to pin down what it was that was so magnetic about him. I realized later, after I found a man who was good and loved me, that all that magnetism was just a heightened sex drive; I was a young girl of nineteen, and my hormones were in full swing. He was an older man, and he knew what kind of attention to pay me.

We spoke while she was away, and he told me how beautiful I was. Yes, he worked that quickly. He put his hand on my waist and showed me around the house. He didn't take me upstairs but did show me the parlor.

He kissed me and told me I was the most beautiful girl he had ever seen. He told me his wife went to visit her mother on Saturdays and to come by during the afternoon.

When your grandmother came back in, I told her I had a horrible headache and needed to leave.

But the next weekend, I drove back here to see him. I couldn't help it, it's like I wasn't myself, and I felt a thrill at being pursued by an older man.

He was waiting at the door and smiled at me. "Gwen, my dear, I'm so glad you came," I remember he said, and then he kissed me passionately. He led me into the parlor. There were people in there! I thought we were going to be alone. The people were reading from a book and talking about how to get what you need, mostly in terms of financial means. They were powerful people, locally anyway.

THE DEAD BORN

I noticed there was a type of altar set up in the middle of the floor. He stood behind me and removed my dress, then my underclothes. I turned around and he naked, too. He laid me down on the floor and got on top of me. I was a virgin and cried out in pain at first, but I felt an underlying pleasure.

He had sex with me several times, and I forgot there were people watching us. I even get on top of him, and I ... sorry, I am trying not to get too graphic. But it was ecstasy and shame all at once, and I abandoned myself. It took me a long time to recover.

I had sex with the other men there, too. And he was having sex with the other women.

At one point, some of them began to chant, and he got behind me again. He was rough. He grabbed my hair, pulled my head back, and entered me. It hurt.

Then I felt something hot and sticky on my face and my back, and I opened my eyes and saw someone holding something over us.

I looked closely and realized it was blood. Then I saw that it was coming from an infant. They slit his throat, and his blood was dripping on us.

I screamed until I went hoarse.

Eventually one of the women took me to the bathroom and instructed me to wash in the shower, and then she dressed me. I was so sore I could barely stand and walk outside. I kept waiting for them to kill me; I was certain I was going to be the next sacrifice. I repeated the Lord's Prayer and asked for forgiveness. And they did nothing, just drove me home. I went to bed and slept. I think they drugged me, because I slept for almost fourteen hours.

A couple of days later, I called my employer and told him I quit. He was bewildered, but he didn't ask many questions, and he even offered to be a reference for me. I stayed with my parents for about a month, and then I found a job as a secretary at a legal office downtown. He was a criminal attorney, and I ended up working for him until I got married a couple of years later.

Unfortunately, TVA was also downtown, and sometimes I would see your grandmother on Market Square. She never spoke to me. I think she knew something had happened, but I don't believe she knew what her husband was. At least not back then.

I met my husband at an office barbecue. He was just starting law school, and by that time I knew I was pregnant. I didn't go to the doctor, I just knew. We talked for hours at the barbecue and went out later for a walk around downtown and a late movie. I told him right away that I was pregnant, and I would appreciate it if he let me tell everyone at the firm and endure the humiliation on my own time.

He asked what I was going to do. I told him I would have the baby, but after that I wasn't sure. I flirted with the idea of adoption. And I had heard women could get an operation to not be pregnant, but I didn't know where or how to even go about doing that. But honestly, I really wanted to keep the baby. I had always wanted to be a mother.

He asked me to marry him right then. I told him he was obviously crazy, but he kept asking, so we eloped, bought the house that I live in now, and seven months later, Michelle was born.

Anyway, I saw your grandfather right before we moved into our house. It was at the bank. I was going in and he was coming out. He saw me and smiled and said it was so good to see me, and he congratulated me on my marriage.

Then he put his hand on my belly. I froze. He said that the child in my belly was his, and that there were more. Not just with me or his wife, but many other women. All in his service, and when the time was right, we would be called back.

When Michelle was born, she was the sweetest baby, and we were happy. She grew up in the light, and my husband loved her like his own flesh and blood. When Michelle was two, we tried to have another baby; I wanted nothing more than to have this man's child, this man I loved so much. But each time they ended in a miscarriage. Exams showed we were both normal and healthy. After a while I was warned to stop trying to conceive, as my body might not recover.

I was devastated, but I had Michelle and Marty. I eventually stopped pressing him about moving, mainly because Michelle was in school and had friends, and we had our group of friends, too. And honestly, I didn't see your grandfather or grandmother much. It seemed like they stayed at the farm all the time.

I did see you two together one time. You were maybe eight years old. You were with him at the store, and I knew as soon as I saw him with you that he was hurting you. The way your face was pale and serious, the way you looked trapped. Your eyes were so sad. No one else seemed to notice, and I wondered how that could be.

I didn't know what to do to help you. And around this time my husband fell ill, and my attention turned to him. He died not long after, and I was absolutely devastated. Michelle was the only thing that kept me going. I really did love Martin; he was such a gentle and caring man. And Michelle was just like him. She looked like him, had his sweet eyes and smile.

At any rate, I had my hands full with Michelle, so I did not really have time to grieve for Martin. Michelle was inconsolable for a while and took up all my energy. She simply couldn't understand why her father wasn't there anymore.

I never remarried. I didn't really want to. I dated a couple of men, but I never loved anyone. But also, I felt guilty and protective of Michelle. The truth was, I did not trust any men around my young daughter. I knew that I would not take any chances with my daughter. What happened to me was something I didn't acknowledge consciously, but subconsciously my mind was alert, and my instincts never slept.

As I said, I managed to avoid seeing your grandfather, and I never saw any of the others who were there that night. In fact, what happened became more and more like a dream, a bad dream, and I almost had managed to convince myself it never happened.

But one day I took Michelle and her friend to the Friday night baseball game. It was a beautiful summer night. The sun was setting and the air was soft, and I felt like a teenager myself. I bought us all ice cream, and after a couple of innings, Michelle and her friend walked to her friend's house, which was only a few blocks down from the ballfield.

The sun was going down in a brilliant blaze of red, and it looked like the sky was on fire. I was so lost in the beauty that I forgot everything that was going on around me. I was so totally happy in that moment, and aside from Michelle being born, I had never experienced such bliss.

I was walking around a grassy area near the field when I heard a voice behind me. "Gwennie." I was so startled I nearly screamed. It was a woman, perhaps late forties, very pretty, but there was something about her that made my skin crawl. I stepped back, instinctively clutching my crucifix necklace.

"All grown up," she said. She was wearing jeans and a Poplar Hill Pioneers T-shirt, but I could tell she was a cultured and wealthy woman.

"Do I know you?" I asked. I felt like I needed to run away, and I forced myself to remain calm. It was then I knew who she was. I had looked up at her, crying, that night.

"We have never been properly introduced, and I'll just keep it that way. You don't need to know my name, dear," she said.

I stood frozen and wondered if she had come there to kill me. Would she use the same knife that she used on the infant?

"What do you want?" I asked in a whisper.

"I knew it was you, as soon as I saw the girls. The little one is your daughter," she said.

As soon as she mentioned Michelle, something in me snapped, and I was no longer afraid, I was furious. I've never been so angry

THE DEAD BORN

in my life. I think I could have ripped her head off and thrown it into the middle of the baseball diamond.

I got in her face. "Stay away from my daughter, or I will kill you," I said. My voice was shaking, not from fear, but rage.

She stepped back, and I could see she was wary but not scared. She smiled an icy disconnected smile.

"You should know something because it will help you later. She is not chosen," she said. "But she is marked." She said it like she was reading off a grocery list.

I shoved her as hard as I could, and she fell backward, right on to her scrawny behind. I had enough presence of mind to not go running out of there; I didn't want to draw attention to myself. I got in my car and drove to Michelle's friend's house and made sure they were okay. I was scared, but I didn't think anything would happen then.

That night I decided I would put the house up for sale and move away. It would be hard for Michelle, but she would adjust. I called on Monday and spoke to a real estate agent and began to look for houses in Knoxville. I mentioned it to Michelle one night and expected her to throw a fit. I was shocked when she said she would be okay with it. I told her I was surprised, and she shrugged and said, "I think we need a fresh start. There are a lot of bad memories here, don't you think?"

She seemed so wise and mature, and I felt that there was something unspoken between us; I felt then that somehow she knew something dark had happened to me. I cried and she held me.

Anyway, that never came to pass. Not a single person made an offer on the house, no matter how much I lowered the price. And then a couple of years later Michelle met her husband and had Jesse, and by then I had long taken down the for-sale sign. It was as if something was keeping us in Poplar Hill.

Now, I don't know the purpose of your grandfather's doings. But I do know that they have killed at least three children and two adults.

SHE STOPPED TELLING HER STORY AND LOOKED AT JACEY INTENTLY.

"I have a feeling your friend was killed to bring you back here because he marked you. His own blood. Michelle may very well have been his child, but you are his daughter's daughter, the blood is doubled, maybe even—"

"I don't understand what you are trying to tell me," Jacey said. "What do you want me to do? I would never hurt anyone, and I can assure you I don't worship the devil, I don't curse people, and I certainly don't partake in orgies that end with a baby's throat being slit open."

Jacey thought about some of the things she had done, though, thoughts she had … but no, she was not like him.

Gwen watched her. "I don't think you want to hurt anyone, not intentionally, and I know you are not like them. But Jesse is dead, and he's dead because you came back here. True, the path he was on was never going to end well for him, but who knows."

Jacey stood up and turned her back on Gwen. She bit her lip to keep herself from saying something she might regret later. She took a deep breath and turned back to Gwen.

"None of this is my fault. I didn't kill Crissy or Jesse. I didn't choose the family to which I was born, and I sure as hell didn't choose to get abused by that devil I share a bloodline with. How dare you suggest otherwise," Jacey said.

Gwen sighed and shook her head. She set down her glass and stood up.

"Your grandmother stayed married to him even after she suspected what he was. She wanted to maintain the comforts of money and land, a big house. She was not evil, but she was

THE DEAD BORN

an accomplice. She preferred to stay in her daydreams. Artistic creation was an escape for her, but by doing this, she only aided his plan. Evil loves nothing more than those who avoid suffering at all costs. She willfully ignored the suffering of innocents, even her own kin, to avoid facing the mess she had gotten herself into," Gwen said.

She took Jacey's hand.

"I suspect you know quite a bit about escape, about running away," Gwen said.

Jacey stared at Gwen and felt the thing inside her uncoil. Recently she had felt it was more like a snake, no longer a wounded mooncalf, but a serpent, molting and shedding. Now it hissed in anger. Jacey had a fleeting thought: What was one more body on the pile of fools who had come eagerly to their fate? Jacey shook her head. No, she was not that person. She would never hurt anyone.

"You're a good girl, I can see that about you, but there is darkness not only inside of you but all around you," Gwen said. She waved her hand and looked up. "This place, it's got whatever evil he seeded it with still inside the walls. I don't know if you can escape this curse, but your journey out of darkness starts here. By finding out the truth and shining the light on it. You're here for a reason, but don't turn it into the wrong reason. Don't continue it, Jacey. No matter how tempting."

Gwen stepped down from the porch and turned around, looking at Jacey. "I will pay for my sins, we all do, even if we had no intention of committing the sins. You won't see me again, I know that, but I will do what I can to help you. I want to make amends. Always remember to go toward the light," she said.

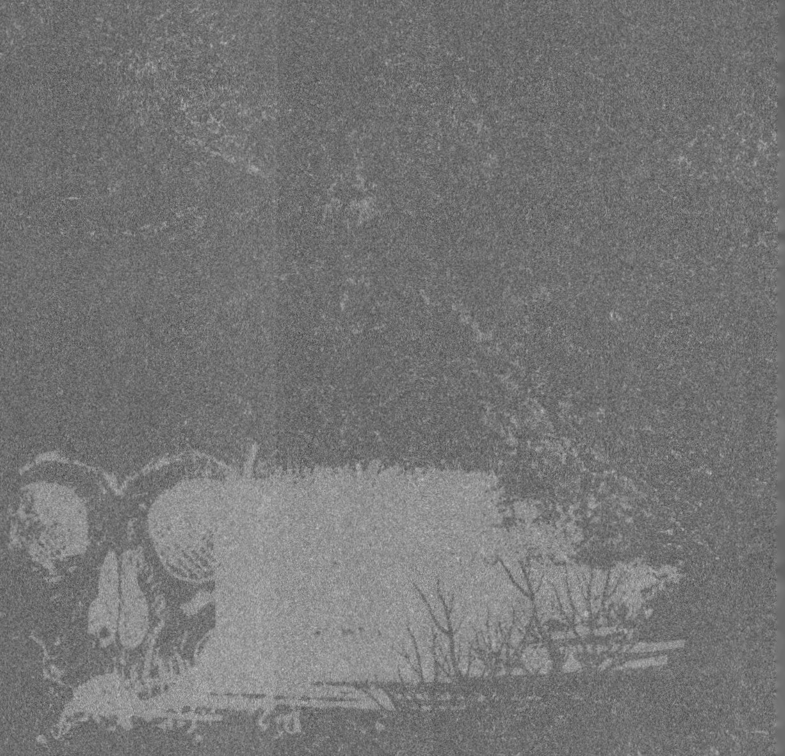

PART 2

THE WITCH

CHAPTER 13

After Gwen left, Jacey sat in the kitchen looking out the window. Moon paced beside her; she was restless, picking up on Jacey's distressed mood.

Jacey walked into the parlor and sat down cross-legged in the middle of the floor. Jacey thought of Morgan. He had sent the man to fix her window, but why had he not come to see her, to check and make sure she was okay?

Jacey closed her eyes and saw a woman, the same one she had seen her first night back in the house. Now Jacey remembered more. Jacey had carried the psychopomp in childhood. The Seer, yes, that was Jacey's name for her. The Seer had long golden hair and eyes the color of port.

Jacey didn't hear the thunder in the distance or notice the sky darkening to the color of a bruise. She saw:

The Seer was walking toward a tree. She was in the woods behind the house, and it was nighttime, a full moon shining down and illuminating her path to the tree. The Seer stood in front of the tree and held her hand up and pointed to the tree. Here is where you must go, you have been told, but you do not listen. You must dig, you must die to live, this is the only way. Through death, you will be reborn. By the blood of your ancestors, the ones who walked in His glory, through them you will find Him, you will be reborn. The Seer opened her gossamer gown, and Jacey saw her breasts were full and slightly leaking milk, and her belly was swollen with a child. Her bare feet walked on grass soaked with blood, making horrid squelching sounds.

A loud boom woke Jacey from her trance. She realized it was thunder when she saw lightning flash outside the window. The lights flickered off, then on. This happened three more times, then the power stayed off. Jacey sat and waited. She heard the front door blow open.

She ran to the door and had to push with her whole body to shut it. She stood, panting. She swore she had locked the door.

Suddenly a flash of lightning lit up the house. Jacey opened her mouth to scream, but all she could manage was a gasp.

It was him.

He was illuminated by the lightning for only half a second, but Jacey knew it was him. He was younger, but she recognized him. She took a step back and fell to the floor. Jacey whimpered and scooted backward, not taking her eyes off the shape in the gloomy darkness. In the blink of an eye, he was standing directly in front of her. His eyes were black, and they shone with an unearthly light.

He seemed to flicker in and out, then he spoke to her. Jacey's eyes flicked to the box that held the urn, her great-aunt's ashes.

"Jacinta," he said. She was hearing him in her mind. His voice was pure evil, but she couldn't look away or stop listening.

"I've waited for you to come back." He smiled at her.

"Why?" Jacey asked breathlessly.

"It is a beautiful house, isn't it? You always loved this house, didn't you?" He laughed. "You have ever since you were a small child. I would watch you, and I saw you loved my house. No one loved it like you and me."

"It's my house now," she told him.

"Yes, of course, your house now, but I am so happy that you're here."

"Why have you been waiting for me?"

"You were promised to me."

"What do you mean by that?"

"A deal was made," he said.

"By whom? What kind of deal?"

"By your mother. But you already know that, don't you?"

"No, I don't know what you're talking about," she said in a whisper.

He was getting stronger. It seemed like the more she looked at him and spoke to him, he grew more solid and lifelike.

"You do remember. Your mother spoke about it with you when you were a child."

Jacey knew. She remembered her mother talking about it. Years later Jacey asked her about it, but her mother had acted like she didn't know what she was talking about.

"Watch," he said, pointing toward the window.

The window became a bedroom. Jacey saw a dark-haired teenager sitting on the bed. It was her mother. She was talking to someone else, but she was alone. Then she saw she was whispering and looking down at something. Praying. When Jacey heard her mother's voice, she began to cry.

Then Jacey heard another voice. It was sexless and ancient, and she knew it had never been human. It was speaking to her mother, coming from some God-forsaken realm that only they could hear.

"Hello, Jane," it said.

Her mother sat still as a tree. Her mouth was frozen in a look of shock, and her eyes were wide, horrified. And there was something else. Regret, Jacey saw. It was a look that said *what have I done?*

"I'm here, as you prayed for me to be," it said.

"Go away, please!" her mother sobbed.

The thing laughed.

Her mother buried her head in her hands, rocking back and forth. She moaned, "No, no, no, please, God, I'm sorry, I take it back."

"God can't help you now, Jane."

"You will have what you asked for, and in return, I get your children's souls."

"I won't have any children!" she cried.

"You will, I see it."

"Take my soul instead, please!"

"No, it is done."

"I'm offering mine instead, why don't you take it?"

"There are rules, Jane, and I only follow the rules, rules that were set long ago. There is no other way."

Her mother continued to sob. Jacey felt her heart break, and at the same time, she felt rage building inside her. Her mother looked at her.

"I'm so sorry," she whispered.

"Momma, it's okay, you didn't mean to," Jacey said and wiped away tears.

The scene faded and Jacey found herself looking out the window at the rain coming down in torrents.

"No!" she yelled and put her hands over her face. She was crying so hard, her belly hurt. She finally took her hands away, hoping that all of this was a horrible dream.

But she saw the man in the room.

Jacey stared out the window, dazed. There's a demon in your home and he wants your soul – do something!

She thought about her mother. Her mother, who she had treated horribly until her tragic death. She thought about all the times her mother had held Jacey when she was sick, had cleaned up her shit and vomit, and held her as she cried hysterically. She thought of the time they had gotten into a physical fight. She thought of all the horrible things she had said, the judgment, the superior and condescending attitude. Jacey physically shuddered at all the times she had hurt her mother.

"You can make amends for your mistreatment of your mother," the thing said.

"What do you mean?" she asked.

"You know what you have to do for her."

Jacey wiped her nose and stood up to face the thing. "For her? This is not what she would want. She was tricked! You tricked her! She was a child."

"I don't trick. She made the deal on her own. Never any tricks," he said calmly, almost serenely.

Jacey exhaled. She turned away, looking out the window at the crazy storm. Jacey saw her reflection, then darkness. The juxtaposition scared her.

"What deal did she make? Why did she do it?"

"For this." He put his hands out, palms up, gesturing to the house. "For a birthright, for land and a home that will be standing one hundred more years."

"No, I don't believe you," she said and laughed. "It says in the Bible that you are the father of lies."

Moon came into the parlor and growled low and menacing. Jacey ran to her and picked her up, hoping to shield her.

"I am not the devil," he told her.

"A demon?"

"Call me whatever you want – it all comes to the same thing in the end, no matter what I am."

"Jacey, get out of here," a barely audible voice said.

Jacey turned around and saw her mother. She still appeared young, but a couple of years older than she was in the vision. She smiled at Jacey.

"Momma," she whispered. Her mother looked beautiful. Her hair was glossy and dark brown, almost black, and it hung straight and past her shoulder blades. She was slender and tall. Her face beamed with a calm but intense illumination. She looked like a goddess.

"Jacey, you need to leave this house right now." Her mother turned her attention to the demon standing in her old house.

Jacey walked toward her mother. She wanted to hold her hand, to hug her. She looked at her mother's shapely hands. They were smooth, not like the last time Jacey had seen them, when they had IVs in them and bruises ran along the tubing. Her mother stepped back and held up her hand.

Jacey looked behind her. The demon was gone. She looked back at her mother. She was smiling.

"I love you, Momma, and I'm so sorry for everything I did," Jacey said through tears.

"Me, too, and I love you, my sweet girl. I always will."

"I love you. I wish ... I wish I could take back all the bad things, I wish everything was different."

"I'll always be here. Now, go. Go, now!"

Jacey ran to the door but the thing was standing in front of it.

"There is nowhere to go, Jacey," it said.

"Run through him, Jacey," her mother's voice said in her mind.

The front door flew open, and without hesitation, Jacey ran through the demon.

She ran off the porch, and the rain and wind slammed into her. She almost slipped on the wet grass but made it to her car. She put Moon in the passenger seat, started the car, and peeled out, skidding in the mud and gravel.

Jacey drove to the only place she could think of. She just hoped he was home.

When she got to the gate, she pressed the buzzer and the gate opened immediately. She drove down the drive and parked next to Morgan's truck. She turned off the engine, and sat in the car, not getting out. She looked at Moon. She looked calm despite what had just happened.

"Should we go in?" she asked. Moon's tail slapped on the seat, and she meowed loudly.

She picked up Moon and got out of the car. The door to the house opened, and Morgan walked out with an umbrella. He smiled until he saw Jacey, and the smile was replaced by a look of concern.

"What the hell happened?" he asked her.

Jacey intended to lie to him, but she just started crying.

CHAPTER 14

Morgan brought Jacey a cup of tea. She had demanded a drink, but he told her later. She sipped the tea and sat back on the couch. She was wearing one of Morgan's shirts and a pair of pajama pants, cinched as tight as possible, but still almost comically too big for her. Moon lay in front of the fireplace, sleeping. Jacey had patted her dry with a towel, and she had gone immediately to the rug and slept.

"This is good," Jacey said, sipping the tea. "I never would have thought of you as a hot tea person."

"My mother always kept that kind of thing around," he said.

"She's …" Jacey began.

"Yes, about two years ago," Morgan said.

"I'm sorry."

Morgan nodded and sat back on the couch. "Are you going to tell me what happened?" he asked.

Jacey looked down at her cup. "Don't you already know?"

"I know what someone told me, about Jesse, committing suicide at your house, but I don't know anything else," he said.

"Who told you?" asked Jacey.

"One of my buddies. I was in Texas and couldn't come, I'm sorry. I just got back late last night. I wanted to see you, but I didn't know if you even wanted to see me," Morgan said.

You could have called, thought Jacey, but she kept quiet.

As if reading her mind, he said, "I tried to call, but I got no answer. I figured you were asleep, but I knew you were okay, and I planned on coming by, I promise."

"I never got a call from you," said Jacey, but she hadn't really looked at her phone.

"I sent Danny Bryant over to fix your window. I hope you don't mind," he said.

"No, of course I don't mind. What do you mean you knew I was okay?" asked Jacey.

Morgan shrugged. "I just felt you were okay. If I thought or knew you had been hurt, I would have come to you. I guess I was too worried that you were angry with me," he said.

"I'm not angry. I'm glad you did that to him – he might have hurt me," Jacey said.

"I won't let that happen. Ever," Morgan said. He paused before he asked, "Why would Jesse come to your house?"

"Maybe he was planning on confronting me because I asked about Crissy, and he …" Jacey couldn't finish her sentence. She was still spooked from earlier.

"And he what?" asked Morgan.

"He found what is in my house. There is evil there," Jacey began. She was about to cry, and she shook her head. "No more now. I promise I will tell you, I just can't right now."

"Maybe you should rest. You can sleep in my room, or this couch is incredibly comfortable," he said.

Jacey set her cup on the end table. She curled up under the soft throw blanket. Morgan got up.

"Where are you going?" she asked.

"Just going to sit over here and do some work. I'll be here, don't worry," he told her.

Jacey nodded. She laid back down, looking at him.

"What do you do?" she asked him.

"I'm an engineer," he said.

"What kind?"

"Aerospace engineer," he said.

"Damn," Jacey said.

"Rest for a while, then we will figure out what to do," he said. He took his laptop and sat in the chair across from the couch.

"I don't know anything about you," Jacey said. She closed her eyes.

Morgan looked up from his laptop. He stared at Jacey. He was struck again by her beauty, and the mystery of her. It was powerful but also dangerous. His instincts were screaming at him to put some distance between them, even before the incident with Randy. But here he was, and here she was. He checked to make sure he had a gun downstairs and that it was loaded.

Moon was staring at him, her eyes glowing in the light of the dancing flames.

"It's okay, I won't hurt you or her," he whispered.

Moon laid her head back down and closed her eyes.

Morgan saw the rain was letting up. The storm had come out of nowhere, violent and sudden. He was reminded of a mission. It had begun to storm as he was sighting his target. His gun was wet, and his fingers could have slid on the trigger. But he had hit his target. He always did.

He shook off the memory and put his laptop away. He stood guard.

Later, after Jacey had told him everything that had happened, she followed Morgan's truck back to her house. The rain had stopped, and the evening was excessively humid. Frogs croaked and teemed with intensity, and the whippoorwills were singing in the early dusk. Moon followed Jacey and Morgan to the porch.

"Wait here," Morgan said and went to check the house.

She sat on the porch and looked at the sunset. It was a deep burgundy, surrounded by hues of smoky violet. A few stars were out, and Jacey marveled at the beauty of the sunsets here. There was no other place like it.

Morgan came outside. "Come in, it's okay," he told her.

Jacey showered and put on fresh clothes. She gave Morgan's clothes back to him, folded. He took them and stood looking at her.

"Thank you for everything," she said.

"You're really leaving?" he asked. He was still holding the clothes in his hands, and Jacey felt sadder than she ever had in her life. She took the clothes and put them on the bottom step.

She took his hands. "I would have to be insane to stay. How many more times can I be given signs that I need to leave? If everything I told you happened to you, would you stay? I think if I stay here, it's going to end badly. Don't you?" she asked. She looked at his face, hoping he would tell her something profound so she could stay.

Morgan stood over her. Jacey took a step backward and bumped into the wall. Morgan moved closer. He seemed to tower over her. He put his hands against the wall, so each of his arms was on each side of her head.

Then he kissed her. He brought his hands down and cupped her face. Then she felt his hands circle her waist, and he pulled her into his body.

Jacey pulled away, breathing hard, and her legs felt weak.

"Jacey …" he said.

"I know," she said. "Hey, come visit me in Savannah, okay?" She handed him his clothes and guided him to the door.

"You don't need to be alone. Let me stay here; I'll sleep on the couch. Or stay with me," he said.

Jacey shook her head. "No, I'll be fine. I have some things I can do to put some protection around me," she said. She stood on her tiptoes and kissed him. Morgan said nothing, but he finally walked out the door.

Jacey went upstairs, murmuring the Lord's Prayer, and she stood in the bedroom listening, feeling. There was nothing here now. Maybe the energy needed time to build back up.

She opened the bedroom window, realizing she was sad to be leaving. Jacey began to pack but after a minute heard a car pull in and looked out the window. It was Morgan's truck.

Jacey stood at the open window. She heard the door shut, and after a few seconds the headlights shut off. The moon glowed in the starry night sky, and a light breeze rustled the leaves of the huge maple trees.

She heard Morgan knock at the front door. She didn't go down, just stood looking out the window. After a bit, Morgan came into her view and looked up at her. He could see her in the moon's eerily bright glow. A breeze kicked up, and it blew her long hair around her face and shoulders. She looked like a princess or some unnamed angel of the night. Still, she said nothing.

He walked back to the front door and found it unlocked. He went inside and saw Jacey standing at the top of the staircase.

"You shouldn't be here, Morgan," she whispered.

"I can't leave," he said.

Morgan walked up to her and put his hands on her face. He looked her up and down, lightly rubbing his hand up her arm. She tried to push him away, but he kissed her, pinning her hands against her sides. He kissed her neck and the tops of her breasts.

"Stop it," she said.

He stopped, looking into her eyes. They had a wild glow in them, and her lips were full and pink. Then she pressed against him, rubbing between his legs. She didn't want him to stop. He was here, he was real, and she clung to him and this moment, knowing it wouldn't last. He kissed her again. He did it slowly at first, giving her a chance to pull away. Knowing she wouldn't.

He wrapped his arms around her. He kissed her hard on the mouth again, her lips parted, and she felt his tongue and smelled his sweet breath. His beard scraped her face.

He picked her up and carried her to the bedroom. The moonlight spilled into the dark room, and a breeze blew through the open window. The leaves on the trees rustled, and it sounded like whispering. Morgan took off her shorts and turned on the lamp so he could see her.

"No, leave it off," said Jacey. She was suddenly self-conscious about the way she looked. Morgan paused, then he walked her over to the antique full-length mirror propped in the corner. He stood Jacey in front of it and he began to undress her. Jacey squirmed and turned her head away.

Morgan firmly turned her face to the mirror. "Look," he said. He pressed his body against her.

"See how beautiful you are. And how hard you make me. If you act like you're not, I'll do this every time until you believe it," he said.

Jacey watched as he slipped his hand between her legs, and she arched her back slightly. She kept her eyes open, watching as he touched her. She saw how hard her nipples were and brought his other hand up to her breasts. She moaned and let herself get lost in the touching.

Morgan picked her up and laid her down on the old bed and lay on top of her, kissing her. He sucked on her nipples and Jacey moaned. He stood up, pulling off his shirt and taking off his pants, then straddled her.

He kissed her stomach and moved his hands over her legs. He got on top of her and spread her legs apart. He went into her, and Jacey hissed in slight pain, but she was so wet, it only hurt for a brief second. He increased his speed and drove deeper into her. He grabbed her hips and held them as she cried out as he pushed into her again and again.

Jacey opened her eyes and saw a shadowy outline standing to her right. It was a man. She ignored him, too caught up in the bliss of the moment to care.

Again and again throughout the night, they made love. At one point, Jacey almost left her body to watch, but she didn't want to. She had never felt such a connection with anyone, and she wanted to relish every moment.

Finally, Morgan turned on his side and pulled her to his body. She turned and let him wrap his arms around her. Jacey pressed her body against his. He kissed her shoulders and rubbed his hand over her waist and hips.

"Keep your mouth on me," Jacey said.

Morgan kissed her deeply. Jacey fell asleep and didn't dream at all that night.

CHAPTER 15

Jacey woke up and turned over, intent on going back to sleep. She could tell it was morning, and she wanted to sleep until the afternoon. Then she remembered: Morgan. He wasn't in bed, but she heard a noise downstairs. She sat up. She smelled cinnamon. She checked her phone and groaned. It was ten a.m. She shuffled to the bathroom, noting the soreness in her body.

She took a hot shower, brushed her teeth, got dressed, and went downstairs. Morgan greeted her with a smile.

"Good morning," he said. She looked at her kitchen. He had made French toast and scrambled eggs. Her stomach rumbled. But she needed caffeine.

"Morning. That looks good," she told him, walking to the fridge to grab a bottle of water and a Diet Coke.

He pulled her to him and kissed her, and her knees almost buckled.

"Sit down, let's eat," he said.

She sat at the table, and he brought the food. She drenched her French toast in syrup and put pepper on her eggs. She wolfed it down, not caring what she looked like.

"This is really good," she said in between bites. Moon came and purred and rubbed against Jacey's ankles. Jacey gave her a piece of French toast.

Moon made her way to Morgan, meowing at him and rubbing her body against his leg. "I already fed you, miss," he said and chuckled. She raised her tail straight in the air and sauntered into the other room.

Jacey realized no man had ever made her breakfast before. She looked down, and her plate was almost empty. She felt embarrassed, not wanting to look at Morgan. Suddenly everything was uncomfortable.

Morgan looked at her. "I have to go, but can I see you later tonight?"

Jacey nodded. "Sure. Oh, wait, I can't – I forgot I'm supposed to have dinner with Shawnee." She frowned.

"So you're staying?" He stared at her.

Jacey nodded and smiled. "It might be late," she said.

"That's fine," he said.

"Okay, just text me later." She got up and put their plates in the sink. She looked at the dishes, wishing she had a dishwasher.

He walked to her and turned her around to face him. "Do you regret last night or something?"

"Are you for real?" she looked into his eyes.

"Yes," Morgan said.

"No, I don't regret anything," Jacey said. He touched her face and kissed her again.

He stared at Jacey. He wanted to say he loved her; he had almost since the moment he had first seen her. But he couldn't. *Coward*, he thought.

"I have to go. I cooked, so you do the dishes." He winked. "Or I'll just buy you a dishwasher. I have a feeling they will still be in the sink when I come back," he said, walking out.

"I resent that!" Jacey yelled. She smiled and finished her Diet Coke, then did the dishes.

When she was finished she went to the bathroom upstairs and looked at her face. She wanted to know if she looked different. Well, she was smiling like a loon. She leaned closer and saw a large mark on the side of her neck, near her earlobe.

"Oh, my gosh!" she said and laughed.

Well, it could be hidden, she just had to wear her hair down today. She yawned and decided to take a short nap. She felt raw and bruised and sore all over. She set her alarm for noon and fell into bed.

After her nap, she texted Shawnee: Still on for today? Shawnee immediately texted back: Yes, come over anytime.

Jacey stopped on the way and picked up a bottle of wine, mostly for herself, as Shawnee had never been much of a drinker. As she drove, she noted how nervous she was. She had always felt this way around her. Well, at first, she thought. They got along well even though they were different. Even later, as Jacey realized Shawnee had more stuff than her, it was okay. Jacey searched her memory for what had happened to change their dynamic. Then she remembered.

Somehow Shawnee had found out about her grandfather. More likely, Shawnee's mother had and then prompted Shawnee to try to get Jacey to talk about it. After that, Jacey and Shawnee slowly drifted apart. Shawnee dated a popular football player and joined the cheerleading squad, but Jacey's family couldn't afford the cheer uniforms, so the two began to hang out in different groups. Jacey got into dark-metal music, tarot cards, and horror books, and she adopted a goth persona.

During their senior year, Shawnee and Jacey had a class together, and they hung out a bit more. By then Shawnee was dating a guy who was in a band, popular with all the subgroups at school, and now Shawnee was hanging out with his friends who were in college and smoking weed and drinking. One of the guys in this group of friends named Brian became enamored of Jacey, and they dated for about a year. Jacey didn't really like him, but he kept coming around, and finally, Jacey caved.

After a few months, Brian began to get jealous when Jacey hung out with what few friends she had, and eventually Jacey just stopped going anywhere unless it was with Brian. Jacey was aware of how abnormal this was, but in a way, she was secretly happy about the fact that someone could be so in love with her that he wanted to spend all his time with her and keep her to himself.

When Jacey started taking classes at the community college, things went off the rails. Jacey had made a couple of friends at school, and she saw Brian less and less. After he attempted to rape Jacey, she broke up with him, and he attempted suicide by slashing one of his wrists. His parents put him in a mental hospital for a couple of months. She visited him once and it went badly, and she never contacted him again.

These memories ran through Jacey's mind as she drove to Shawnee's house, a neat two-story brick home. Now that she had remembered these things, she just wanted to visit for an hour, smile, then tell her she had a date. Which was true.

Jacey rang the doorbell and Shawnee answered quickly. The two stood awkwardly, then they briefly hugged.

"Come on in, I'm so glad you came," said Shawnee. Jacey followed her into her spotless kitchen. Shawnee was always very neat and orderly. Jacey handed Shawnee the wine.

"Oh, well, I don't know, but ..." Shawnee stammered.

Jacey smiled tightly. "It's for you, we don't have to drink it now, Shawnee."

"Ah, what the hell. After all, this is a celebration, right?" Shawnee got out two crystal wine glasses, then grabbed a corkscrew from a kitchen drawer.

Jacey leaned against the large island, looking at the granite surface. "Yeah, I suppose it is a celebration." She took a glass from Shawnee. "It's nice to have a break from all the morbid shit going on around here."

Shawnee sighed. "It's just awful about Crissy. I can't even believe it," she said and led them to the living room, where they sat on the sofa.

"I really like your house, Shawnee," Jacey said.

Shawnee's face brightened. "Mark and I just got it about a year ago." She looked around the room, smiling. "He knows the real estate agent, and we closed on it pretty quickly," she said, tucking her legs under her. Shawnee's blue eyes sparkled when she said her husband's name. Jacey studied Shawnee. Jacey felt the old jealousy try to boil up. Shawnee had her mother's eyes, but everything else was from her father, who was full-blooded Cherokee: the long, straight, glossy black hair, the olive complexion. Jacey had always felt like a lumpy potato in Shawnee's presence.

Jacey suddenly wanted to run out of the house. She finished off her wine.

"Here," said Shawnee, handing her the bottle. Jacey poured another glass.

"So, how did you meet Mark?" asked Jacey.

"Blind date, can you believe it?" Shawnee laughed.

"Seriously?" Jacey asked.

"Only one I've ever been on. Talk about luck, huh? I had just gotten out of a relationship, total asshole, and a friend from work set us up." Shawnee looked off, remembering the date. Then she said, "I heard you were married."

Jacey took a long sip of wine. She nodded. "For about five minutes. Colossal mistake."

"Sorry," Shawnee said. "You always had terrible taste in men. I guess we both did, huh?"

Jacey laughed. "Yeah, I can't deny that. But I didn't sleep with all my terrible men, unlike you." Jacey giggled.

Shawnee looked at her. She set down her wine glass. "Why do you always do that?"

"Do what?" Jacey asked, a smirk creeping across her face.

"Passive-aggressive comments, or just outright insults," Shawnee said.

Jacey sat down her glass, too. "Passive aggressive? You're the queen of passive-aggressive, as well as undermining and downright backstabbing!"

Shawnee rolled her eyes. "When did I backstab you?"

She stood up and pointed at her. "You went behind my back and told Brian I was just using him. What kind of friend does that?"

"I never said that!" Shawnee said, standing up to face Jacey.

"All my life, I never felt like I was good enough when I was around you. And you liked it that way. Whenever I tried to break out, tried not to be poor trash anymore, that's when you stopped talking to me!" yelled Jacey.

"Hey, you stopped talking to me, remember? The truth is, Jacey, you were a shitty friend, too. It's not my fault I was born with more money than you, and that I was more popular. It's not my fault your family was fucked up, and your grandfather messed with you. I even tried to help –"

Jacey slapped Shawnee across the face. Shawnee stumbled back, her hand on her cheek where Jacey had slapped her, her face etched with shock.

"You bitch!" Shawnee said. "You know what, you're right, I did tell Brian you were using him because you were, but I also wanted you away from him because he was crazy, and the guy you married was probably a lunatic like him. I was hoping you

THE DEAD BORN

had changed, but even though you're successful now, you're still broken, and you try to break everyone else around you," she said.

Jacey screamed and tackled Shawnee.

Jacey straddled Shawnee and punched her in the face. Shawnee kneed Jacey in the side and tried to sling Jacey off, who attempted to pin her arms down, but she was too strong. Shawnee boxed the side of Jacey's mouth.

"Ow!" yelled Jacey.

"Hey! Hey! What the hell?" A man's voice boomed behind them.

The man dragged Jacey away from Shawnee, who lunged at Jacey. The man, who Jacey assumed was Shawnee's husband, put his body in between the two women and held Shawnee back.

"What the hell is going on?" he asked.

Jacey stepped back. She was breathing hard, and she sat down on the edge of the couch. She felt her lip and looked at her fingers – blood.

Shawnee was breathing hard, too. Mark stood beside her, his hand on her shoulder.

"Do I need to call the cops?" he asked.

"No, she's leaving," Shawnee said.

"You bloodied my lip," Jacey said.

"You punched me in the face! My eye will probably swell up."

"I didn't punch you that hard. I held back," Jacey said.

"So did I," Shawnee said.

"I know."

Suddenly, Jacey caught a thought from Shawnee: *Only real friend I ever had.* Jacey saw that Shawnee looked like she was about to cry.

They looked at each other. Jacey went to Shawnee and hugged her. "I'm sorry," she said. Shawnee was sniffling, and both girls began to cry. Mark looked at the two friends, puzzled.

"I'll get some ice packs," he said.

Later, Shawnee and Jacey sat outside on Shawnee's back deck. The sun was just beginning to go down. Two melted ice packs sat next to the empty bottle of wine. Jacey's lip was a little puffy, and Shawnee had a welt under her eye. Somewhere between a fight, some takeout food, and wine, the two women had become friends again.

"Shawnee, do you remember seeing Crissy out with anyone who seemed ... suspicious?" Jacey asked.

"Everyone she hung out with was suspicious," Shawnee said.

"I know, but do you think any of them are capable of killing her?" asked Jacey.

"I don't know, I don't think so. But then again, it's always someone you never suspect," she said. She looked at the sunset and drifted off for a second.

"What?" Jacey asked.

"Well, she worked at that strip club for a while, maybe we should —" Shawnee stopped and looked at Jacey, as if she couldn't quite get out the sentence herself.

"You want to go question the people in the strip club?" Jacey laughed. She couldn't help it. She was picturing Shawnee, a refined lady, walking into a titty bar with her Kate Spade purse and her sensible haircut, demanding answers.

"Keep it up, I'll give you a black eye to go with your busted lip," Shawnee said, but she was grinning.

"I mean, why not?" Shawnee stood up.

Jacey thought about it. "Now?"

"Yes, before I lose my nerve."

CHAPTER 16

Shawnee drove, and Jacey stared out the passenger window. The silence was not uncomfortable; the two women were bruised and tired but exhilarated.

"So, are you going to tell me who gave you that hickey?" asked Shawnee.

Jacey's hand went guiltily up to her neck. She swept her hair over the mark.

Shawnee glanced at Jacey, grinning. "Even if you didn't have the evidence on your body, I would have known just from the look on your face," Shawnee said.

"What do you mean?" Jacey asked. She looked out the window, slightly alarmed but also amused to feel herself smiling.

"Please, it's so obvious you are in love – you're glowing," Shawnee said. "Truth time. I'm a little envious but mainly curious. So who is it?"

"Envious? You and Mark seem really happy."

"We are, but it's different when you have been together for a while. It's beautiful in a different way, but there is nothing like the beginning of a relationship, that intense excitement."

"I never experienced that before last night," Jacey said.

"Well, savor it, relish every second of it with …" Shawnee waved her hand in a come-out-with-it gesture.

Jacey sighed and put her hands over her face. "His name is Morgan," she said.

"Morgan … Morgan DeArmand?" Shawnee squealed with excitement.

"You know him?" asked Jacey.

"I do, not well, but he seems like a good guy. A little mysterious, but he has his shit together. Oh, don't mess this up–" Shawnee caught herself.

Jacey glared at Shawnee, seriously considering giving her another black eye.

"I'm sorry, I'm sorry. I can't stop being a judgmental bitch in the span of a few hours, but I'll do better," Shawnee said.

"Well, I don't have the best history, but yeah, you need to do better," Jacey replied. "What do you mean he's mysterious?"

"Well, he was in the military, some sort of black ops spy or assassin or something. No one really knows for certain."

"Honestly, I'm not surprised, he has that vibe," said Jacey.

"Vibe? He's a badass," Shawnee said.

"I shouldn't have slept with him, but I was … vulnerable."

"Sure, what happened to Crissy, and whatever happened at your house – which you still haven't told me much about."

"Can we finish talking about Morgan first?" Jacey said with a laugh. She looked at Shawnee. "I really like him."

Shawnee laughed and pulled into The Pink Pussy Cat. "We're here," she said.

There were only six cars in the lot, and Shawnee parked away from the other cars.

"Slow night," she said.

"It is the Lord's Day," Jacey said.

Shawnee unbuckled her seat belt and took a deep breath. "This is really dumb. What are we even going to find out here?" Her big blue eyes scanned the parking lot as if she were waiting for a SWAT team to descend on the strip club.

"I'm sure someone working here hung out with Crissy, and I bet they can tell us something, maybe some stuff they were too afraid to tell the police," Jacey said.

Shawnee nodded. "Okay, are you ready, then?" Shawnee looked terrified, and Jacey had to stifle a laugh.

"It's fine, Shawnee. Have you never been in one of these before?"

"No, why would I? Why? Have you?"

"Once, with some friends in college."

"Really? Why?" asked Shawnee.

"I can't remember, although I do remember it wasn't as fancy as this one," Jacey said and began to giggle.

Shawnee punched her arm. "You are the worst. Okay, let's get this over with."

"Oh, wait, do you have any money? I totally forgot," Jacey said as she began to dig in her purse.

"You didn't bring any? I thought you were the expert," said Shawnee.

"I have ... about a hundred bucks."

"I have sixty."

"I'm sure they have an ATM if we need more. All right, let's go," Jacey said.

They opened the club's door, and the guard at the entrance looked at them disinterestedly.

"Ladies get in free," he said. He stamped their hands for some reason, then he went back to his phone.

"Damn, do we look that old? He didn't ask for ID," Shawnee said.

It suddenly occurred to Jacey that Morgan had said he had been here before. She felt a ping of jealousy.

A goth metal song was playing, one Jacey was surprised she couldn't place.

The topless woman onstage glided over and bent down so a man could tip her, then took off her G-string and began to dance completely naked in front of him. The woman was attractive, but she looked about Jacey's age, which, she thought, was too old to be a stripper. Jacey saw another young woman dancing on the other side of the stage. She was young and pretty, but her face looked too mature, as if she had been through a lot. Jacey felt another pang of jealousy, strangely mixed with desire. She wondered if that one had been here when Morgan had been in. Then Jacey thought of Crissy doing this, and she got a sinking feeling.

Jacey looked around the club. A few of the men there looked at them with interest. They might think we're about to audition, Jacey thought and giggled.

Jacey and Shawnee sat down at the bar.

"How are you ladies doing tonight?" asked the bartender, who was young and had multiple piercings on his face, and tattoos covering his arms. The bartender peered at their faces oddly for a second, then Jacey remembered that her lip was swollen and Shawnee had a swollen eye.

"Good, how about you?" said Jacey.

"Amazing. What can I get you ladies?" he asked.

"Jack and Coke, please," Jacey said.

"Um, same, thank you," Shawnee said.

The bartender mixed their drinks and then set them on coasters shaped like a cat's head. Jacey took a sip; it was strong. Jacey paid for the drinks and stuck some bills in his tip jar.

THE DEAD BORN

A young woman with a neon-pink wig walked up to them and asked if they wanted a private dance.

"Maybe later, honey. Is that lady free, the one with the black hair?" Jacey asked.

"Go ask her yourself, bitch," the young woman said and walked away.

"Don't pay attention to Layla, she isn't an evolved soul yet," the bartender said from behind them and then set down two more drinks. "From Eddie. He's a regular." He gestured to a man in a John Deere hat. He was approximately fifty, and wearing a chambray shirt and work boots. He waved to them. Jacey waved back.

Shawnee leaned over and whispered, "If that guy's a regular, shouldn't we talk to him?"

Jacey shook her head and nodded toward the black-haired woman walking toward them.

She had hair down to her waist and a lean, muscular body. She had boobs that she definitely was not born with, and a scar across her face. She looked dangerous up close, and Jacey felt the hairs on the back of her neck stand at attention.

"You wanted a private dance with me?" she said.

Jacey picked up a thought in the woman's head: blood magic.

"We would," Jacey said. *I know blood magic, too,* Jacey thought.

"Follow me," she said.

Shawnee and Jacey took their drinks and followed the woman to a back corner room separated by string lights. Jacey and Shawnee sat on the sofa, and the woman stood in front of them.

"It's fifty for a private dance," she said and held out her hand. Jacey handed her one hundred bucks.

The woman looked at it. "I said a dance, that's it. If you want some pussy, you can talk to one of the other girls," she said.

"I just want to talk," Jacey said.

The woman sat in the chair across from her. "Talk, huh?" she asked.

"About Crissy Freeman. You knew her." Jacey did not know this woman, but she felt that this dancer had known Crissy. The woman stared, saying nothing.

"We aren't cops or anything. I was her friend, we both were, and we just want to know if you can tell us anything that could help us find out who killed her," Jacey said.

The woman stared at Jacey, and a creepy, icy grin spread across her face. The woman looked at the money and stuffed it in her black lace top. She stood up. "I'm gonna keep this money, but you two are gonna walk out of here and not come back," she said.

Jacey looked at Shawnee.

"I don't think so, you know something, and I'm not leaving until you tell me," Jacey said.

The woman stared at Jacey. Part of her couldn't believe Jacey had the balls to confront someone like her, and the other part of her wanted to slice Jacey's throat. But there also was a trace of fear on her face, and suddenly Jacey had what she needed.

"See, we're not cops, but my friend here, she has some family that is, and I'm sure the owner and you don't want any unnecessary attention from the law," Jacey said. "And you do know Crissy had a son, and I bet as a mother you know how hard it can be to raise a kid alone."

The woman's black eyes were glinting with rage, but at the mention of a child, her face softened ever so slightly.

"We weren't friends, none of us here are friends," she said and paused, then continued. "We went after work one night to get some pills. Some guy named Jesse, her baby daddy, hooked us up."

"Jesse Vineyard, I knew him," Jacey said.

"Some other guy was with him, a big biker-looking guy, long hair and a beard, looked like some sort of eighties metal video reject. We went to his house out on Ridge Road, got high, stayed all night, and fucked both of them. That was about a year ago. Crissy quit a few months later, and I never talked to her again," the woman said.

"The other guy, do you remember his name?" asked Jacey.

"Ricky ...No, Randy maybe," she said. "I don't mess with that shit anymore, so I don't talk to anyone in that world. I keep clear of it the best I can."

"Did they say anything suspicious?" Jacey asked.

"Everything they say is suspicious," she said wryly. "I remember they were talking about some other dude ... Wade. They said he was gonna have to have a talk with Wade. He did something that pissed the big dude off. And when I drove Crissy home the next morning, she said this Wade guy was a really bad dude, and she wasn't going anywhere near those guys again if she had to be around Wade."

Jacey was silent. At the mention of Wade, she suddenly had memories wash over her, and she felt like throwing up.

The dancer smiled. "That's all I know. That, and you got a blackness surrounding you. Don't come around here again, or you'll be sorry," she said.

"Thank you for your time," Jacey said. Shawnee and Jacey walked through the string lights. Jacey paused, looking back at the dancer.

"That darkness you saw should be a warning to you. I come from a family of real witches, so don't try any of your black magic on me or you'll be the one who's sorry," Jacey said. It was the first time she had admitted it out loud.

Jacey and Shawnee were silent for a few minutes after they left the strip club.

"I think that went well, considering the circumstances," Jacey said.

"I saw your face when she said Wade. Who is he?" asked Shawnee.

Jacey looked out the window, making her face stay neutral. "Wade, the bootlegger. You've heard of him. Everyone usually calls him Bad Eye."

"Oh, yeah! But wait, he must be about a hundred years old by now. He's still dealing?" Shawnee asked.

"I guess so," Shawnee said.

"Well, we can't talk to Jesse, so this other guy she mentioned …" Shawnee began.

"Randy. I know him, he's an Outlaw."

"How do you know him?"

"I met him at The End of The Line. He knows Morgan," Jacey said.

"So Morgan could talk to him?" Shawnee said.

"I don't think so."

"Well, you need to let Morgan do it. Some of those bikers are shady."

Jacey started to zone out and only heard part of what Shawnee was saying.

"Jacey?" asked Shawnee.

"What?"

"What was that stuff about black magic?"

"That skank had an evil eye tattoo on her arm, and she wore a Baphomet ring. Not too hard to figure out she's into witchcraft," Jacey said.

"Yeah, but you felt something from her, too. Even I did, and I'm no witchy person," Shawnee said.

"I think she got Crissy into it, and something scared her off."

They pulled into Shawnee's manicured subdivision.

"Shawnee, have you ever heard any stories about devil worship or anything going on in our town?" Jacey asked.

Shawnee turned off the engine, and they sat in the car, listening to the engine make ticking metallic sounds as it began to settle and cool off.

"No. Why, what does that have to do with any of this?" she asked.

"Never mind, another time. It's getting late, and Morgan has texted me three times already," Jacey said as she opened her door.

Shawnee opened her mouth to say something, and her smooth forehead crinkled with concern.

"I promise, just … not right now, okay?" said Jacey.

Shawnee sighed and shook her head. She walked with Jacey to her car.

"Be careful," Shawnee said.

Jacey nodded. She hugged Shawnee.

"Does this mean we are friends … again?" Jacey asked.

Shawnee smiled. "Yes, I hope so. I think we are the same, but different in the ways that matter," she said.

"Better wash that off," Jacey said.

"Huh?" asked Shawnee.

Jacey held up her own hand that had the Pink Pussy stamp on it.

Shawnee laughed. Jacey picked up Shawnee's thought: *I intend to take a very hot shower to wash all of that off me.*

"Me, too, scalding hot," Jacey said. Shawnee opened her mouth in surprise. Jacey waved and got in her car before Shawnee could ask her questions.

Jacey saw Morgan's truck when she pulled up to her house. He was sitting on the bed of his truck in a T-shirt and jeans. She saw Moon's white fur next to him. Jacey got out and couldn't help but smile. A thought came to her mind: *family*.

Morgan patted the cat and hopped off the truck bed and walked over. He didn't say anything, just kissed her. Jacey winced and he looked at her lip in alarm.

"I got in a fight with my ex-best friend, but it's okay, you should see her. Plus, we're friends again now, so it's fine," she said.

"Shawnee?" he asked.

Jacey nodded. "Kiss me again."

He pulled her close and kissed her deeply. She couldn't imagine him doing it any other way. She wrapped her arms around his neck, then moved her hands to his shoulders. Morgan pulled her even closer, his hands circling her waist. She didn't fight it; she gave herself totally to the moment, his hands and his hot skin, and his smell that reminded her of a forest after rain – gritty but sensual, rocky, and soft.

For the second time, she felt him. She saw his skeleton beneath the flesh, she saw him, she saw him as a child, and then as an old man, and she wasn't scared. She felt what he was. His soul was light coming through the darkness. He was a light-bringer. He was too good for her.

But for now, he was here. And she could feel the doubt, the hunger, the longing, the fear, the hope, the lust, the love. Jacey suddenly saw an image in her mind: blackness, nighttime, a man falling from the sky. The only sound was a whooshing noise as he fell, the wind softly rippling the black clothing on his body. Then a white mushroom shape appeared above his body. A parachute. He floats like a ghost in eerie silence to the ground.

The image disappeared and Jacey knew she had just seen Morgan in the past. He was some sort of military operative. She felt pushback from him. *Don't go there.*

Jacey suddenly wanted to give him something. Food, she thought, I can cook for you.

"That sounds good," Morgan said. Jacey was certain she had not said that out loud, but she was not surprised.

Later Jacey and Morgan sat outside watching the lightning bugs dance, and they saw at least five shooting stars.

"I have to leave tomorrow," Morgan said. "It's for work, but I feel like I should be here. Or better yet, you can come with me."

Jacey didn't look at him. If she did, she was afraid she would give in to anything he wanted.

"I can't leave my cat," she said.

THE DEAD BORN

"I think she would be fine. That's the thing about cats, they're self-sufficient. What's the real reason?" asked Morgan.

"Where are you going?"

"Houston. I'll be gone for a week," he said. Jacey didn't reply. "We could stay somewhere luxurious, and you could get back to writing."

"I need to stay here. I have some things I have to do," Jacey said.

"Like what? Get into more trouble?"

"Maybe, but it has to be done."

"What are you talking about now?" he asked.

"I don't want to tell you," she said. "Not because I don't trust you, or that I think you can't handle it, but it's something I have to do myself. And you must be okay with that for now."

"I don't have to be okay with any of this, Jacey," he said. He stood up and leaned against the column, one leg forward.

"What am I to you, anyway? You think we could ever be anything normal? Are we going to get married? Huh? You going to fix me? Am I going to fix you? We know nothing about each other," Jacey said.

Morgan looked at her and shook his head.

"I feel sorry for you right now, Jacey," he said.

"Sorry for me?" she replied. "I feel sorry for you, you're the poor fool who let himself catch feelings for a white-trash woman who made good on her ability to create fantasy worlds and sell them to people who are more comfortable in an alternate reality.

"You act like you're so much more evolved, but you're just as stunted as I am. The only reason you are even pursuing me is that you know it won't really go anywhere."

Morgan pushed open the front door and practically threw Jacey onto the parlor floor. He straddled her, ripped off her panties, and tore open her dress. Then he flipped her onto her stomach and began to fuck her. Jacey moaned with pleasure and humiliation. *This is what you wanted, wasn't it*, she thought.

The orgasm flooded up through her body and she cried out. Morgan turned her over. "Don't move," he said.

He sucked on her tits and spread her legs apart, then drove hard into her. She put her arms above her head. He pulled her hips closer to him while holding her legs apart, watching as he went into her, harder and deeper. *Do it, give me your worst*, she thought. Jacey needed this brutality from him because it was balm for her own conscience. He was one of Jacey's characters, playing the part she had written for him.

"Come inside me again," she said. She screamed inside her mind, *Do it, I want it from you, and only you.*

He did.

CHAPTER 17

Morgan fell asleep on the private plane to Houston, and he had the dream again. It was four years ago and his mother was dying in the hospital, and Morgan couldn't get to her in time to say goodbye. In reality, Morgan had been with her, along with his father. But he had always felt that he let her down, that he should have done something else to help her. If only he had told her to go to the doctor sooner, maybe she would be alive today.

Morgan woke and looked out the window as they began to make their descent. He wanted to think of something – anything – else, but he replayed the day again.

His mother had just died, and he and his father had come home from the hospital. The house was the same, but it wasn't. No mother. No wife. Just father and son. Neither Morgan nor his father spoke. They both stood in the house looking around as if they were trying to remember how to be people.

His dad cleared his throat and went into the kitchen. Morgan sat on the couch, looking at his mother's favorite chair where she would read books and drink her hot tea. Morgan walked over to the book sitting on the end table. *Tinker, Tailor, Soldier, Spy* by John le Carre. His mother had read every one of le Carre's books, but this was her favorite. Ever since Morgan had gone into the military, she devoured spy novels. It was as if she was trying to formulate her son's new identity since Morgan could not tell her anything about what he did. Morgan thought it was sweet. Morgan picked up another book, a Nora Roberts book, *Carolina Moon*. She had loved Roberts, too.

She loved the arts, but mostly, she loved books. All of them, but mostly romance novels. After she married Morgan's dad, she went to college and got a bachelor of arts in English literature. Morgan remembered her telling him when he was young that she wanted to be a writer. When Morgan asked her why she didn't, she said she wanted to be a mother more. Morgan didn't know what to think of that, but it comforted him and made him sad at the same time. It was the first time he had an inkling that his mother was a woman and not just his mother.

Morgan put the books down and walked into the kitchen. His dad was heating leftovers for them. Some casserole either a relative or friend brought over.

"Come on, Morg, let's try to eat something," his dad said.

Morgan felt his heart well up. His father still wanted to look out for him, to feed him. Morgan sat down, and he and his father ate in silence. They didn't talk about the future, or the grief, or the fear, or the guilt. It's just too hard. This was a time for silence.

Morgan watched as the plane hovered over the ground and prepared to land. He always watched at this point. Since he was a child he had loved planes and anything mechanical, especially engines, but he was most passionate about aircraft. His parents encouraged him in this, and they enrolled him in a private high school in Dallas after he tested way above average in his science classes.

As the plane landed, Morgan remembered the incident that changed his life.

A few days before high school graduation, he was at a party on a classmate's farm. A guy who had not been invited had been bothering one of the girls. Then he became belligerent and ripped off the girl's bikini top. She slapped him and tried to cover up her naked breasts, and the guy grabbed her and pulled her to him.

Morgan saw it happen and grabbed the guy around the neck and twisted his arm behind his back. Morgan pushed him to the ground, face down, and told him to leave. The guy said he would go, and Morgan let him up and turned to ask the girl if she was okay. That was when the guy socked Morgan on the side of the head. It wasn't too hard of a punch, but it didn't matter – it was a punch. So Morgan hooked the guy in the jaw, knocking him down, and got on top of him and pummeled the guy's face. Suddenly he knew the guy was a predator, that he had molested his younger sister. Morgan had no idea how he knew this, but he did.

Eventually, his friends pulled him off and he came back to reality. The guy was unconscious, and Morgan realized he had beaten him almost to death.

His parents were upset at what happened, but Morgan could sense his father was secretly proud that Morgan had defended himself. His mother was worried about lawsuits from the parents, but Morgan told them there was no need to worry.

"Why do you say that?" she asked.

"He's over eighteen, plus he's a bad guy. He ... did things to his own sister. I don't think he wants the law involved," Morgan said.

"I thought you didn't know him," his mother said. Morgan knew she was worried about his temper and him resorting to violence. Morgan wanted to tell her that sometimes, violence was the only way. But he kept quiet.

"I don't know him," he answered.

"Then how do you know? Did your friends tell you?"

"I just know. The way I know things about people sometimes," Morgan said.

His mother's brow furrowed, and she looked at Morgan's dad. He was standing with his arms crossed, closed off. Morgan always had trouble reading his father.

"Go to your room," his mother said.

Morgan knew his mother was thinking about the time when he was twelve and he told her that his grandmother was dead and that she had visited him in a dream. And the time Morgan told her he knew his mother was going to give him a baby brother.

But after his mother's miscarriage, Morgan suppressed his knack for seeing and knowing things. He didn't want it anyway if he couldn't use the information for good.

Later, Morgan's father knocked on his door. Morgan was watching a baseball game on TV. He muted it and sat up on his bed. His dad sat beside him.

"I know your mother's upset right now, but give her some time and she'll get over it," said his dad.

"You're not mad," Morgan said.

His dad turned and faced him. "Don't ever turn your back on anyone in a situation like that, Morgan – that guy could have killed you. People are capable of immense evil," he said. His dad looked down, lost in thought for a second. He had been a Green Beret, and though he told Morgan he had not been in much combat, Morgan never really believed him or understood why he wouldn't talk about it.

"You'll be eighteen soon, and I can't tell you what to do for much longer, but I hope you will continue to take advice from me. I want you to take some martial arts classes; I think it would be good for you. Teach you to defend yourself properly, but also to channel and harness that temper of yours. What do you think?" his dad asked.

Morgan had agreed and taken to the martial arts classes like a duck to water. He continued to take them throughout college. Morgan majored in aerospace engineering, and after he graduated, he joined the Air Force against his parents' wishes and eventually qualified for special forces training, which he immersed himself in. It was grueling but exciting, and he felt more alive than he ever had.

Now he was a security consultant for companies, and he liked his career. But he missed the military: the preparation, the training, the danger, the thrill of being called away on a moment's notice.

Morgan got off the private plane and walked into the airbase. He showed his credentials and walked to a waiting black SUV. He rode in silence. He was lost in thought about his past and about Jacey. He felt shame and desire when he thought of that last night with her. But mostly he felt intense longing and a need to be with her. He had never loved anyone, and he didn't know how to handle it.

Morgan looked out the tinted window, which made the bright afternoon look like night.

CHAPTER 18

Even Corey's beast of a truck couldn't cushion all the assaults from the back road. These were not potholes, they were gulches, random washouts from all the rain the day before. The sky was a striking blue, and the rain had turned the grass into a brilliant and fragrant green blanket. Jacey took out her flask and took a sip. Her stomach lurched and sent up bile into her throat at each bump and bounce. She hoped the bourbon would settle it.

It had been a little more than fifteen years since she had been on this backroad, but it looked basically the same, it just gave her a bigger sense of foreboding. She recognized every shack and rusty trailer that was somehow still standing.

The last time she had driven up this road was with her brother. His old Camaro had slid around every sharp corner, and Jacey had been sure they would skid into one of the fields or a tree. But he had not been scared. Jacey felt her eyes well up with tears at the memory of her brother. She took another sip of the bourbon.

Corey was saying something, but Jacey had tuned him out. She sat up, craning her neck and leaning forward to look out the window. The two-story farmhouse had probably been charming fifty or sixty years ago. The white paint was almost completely chipped off on one side. Tires were strewn in the front yard, though *yard* was not the right word. It was a bog of weeds and brownish-black puddles. And there was a medium-sized brown dog with matted brown fur that unleashed a series of barks that made her ears hurt. He was chained to a steel rod that had been stuck into the ground, and he bucked and lurched back as he barked, trying to get free and rip their faces off.

Jacey grimaced. This was a graveyard of old appliances and rusted-out cars. On the front porch was a sofa that had once been beige or tan perhaps, but now it was the color of dirty dishwater. Corey parked and turned off the engine.

She saw a curtain part, and the outline of a face peered out at her. She was startled when Corey asked, "Ready?" She nodded.

"Stay behind me," he commanded.

Jacey looked at the dog again, who was barking in between gasps of breath. He would choke on the leash, then fall back. She felt a deep disgust mixed with an almost drowning sadness. The dog's eyes looked lost and hopeless. She knew what he was thinking: *How did I get here? I could leave, but I don't know how.*

They walked up the porch steps, which sagged and creaked with each footstep. Jacey saw the curtain fall back into place behind the grimy window. Corey knocked: "Wade, it's Corey!"

She heard a thumping sound behind the front door. The door opened a few inches. "Corey?"

"Yeah, man, it's me." He stepped forward. Half of a craggy face peered out at them.

"Who you got with ya?"

THE DEAD BORN

"Just a friend, man, went to high school with her," Corey said.

"You ain't coming at a good time." The bastard sounded ancient. Jacey wondered how old he was now. He had seemed so old when she was a teenager.

"Hell, Wade, this won't take long. Come on, it's hot as hell out here," Corey said.

The door opened, and the past washed over Jacey.

July, sixteen years ago

TWO GIRLS CREPT PAST THE GUARD DOG RESTING ON A POLYESTER couch. He looked up, then made a circle on the couch and laid his head on his paws with a sigh. The mom is in the bedroom snoring. She will not wake tonight: hers is the exhausted sleep of a working single mother.

It's late, but the moon is so high and bright that it almost looked like day. A car idled at the end of a gravel driveway. Jacey and Crissy walked quietly but quickly to the waiting car, muffling giggles behind their hands, trying not to wake anyone.

Jacey was wearing a black sundress that had delicate prints of cherries. The dress was short, and with her cork wedges, which added almost two inches to her height, it almost came up to her ass when she sat down. She had placed little-girl hair clips strategically throughout her blond hair. Both girls had also used liberal amounts of glitter body spray on their cleavage, shoulders, and legs. Crissy and Jacey got into the waiting car. Stevie Baker climbed in and stared at Jacey's legs. Crissy sat in the front since her boyfriend Patrick was driving.

"We've been waiting like twenty minutes, Crissy, what the hell?" Patrick said.

"Sorry," said Crissy. "We had to wait for my mom to fall asleep."

"So, are we going to go, or what?" asked Jacey. She saw Patrick look at her in the rearview mirror.

"Yeah, Patrick," Stevie said, "we need alcohol!"

When the car pulled away from the house, Patrick turned on the Toyota's headlights. "Stevie, get that J going," he said. Jacey squirmed in the backseat. She had never smoked pot. Stevie produced a rolled joint from his shirt pocket.

"Where are we gonna get alcohol from?" Crissy asked. "None of us has a fake ID."

"Wade," Patrick said as Stevie handed him the joint.

"The drug dealer?" Crissy gave Patrick a slightly panicked look.

"He ain't a drug dealer. Well, not really. He deals some pot, but he's a bootlegger," Patrick told her. He exhaled a cloud of smoke, passing the joint to Crissy. She took a small hit and passed it to Jacey.

"It's true, Crissy, I've been up there with my brother before – he has all kinds of stuff," Jacey said. She turned her head to the side and took a small puff, not really inhaling. She passed it to Stevie.

"Wait, you like, know him?" asked Stevie.

"Um, no, my brother always goes in," Jacey said.

"You ever seen him before?" Patrick asked.

"No, why?" asked Jacey.

Patrick laughed. "He's a weird motherfucker."

"I heard he and his brother used to fuck their own mom," Stevie said. He licked his fingers and extinguished the roach, putting it in the small ashtray on the side of the door.

"Did he tell you that?" Jacey said.

Stevie and Patrick laughed. "No, just one of the rumors going around," Patrick said. "But I would totally believe it."

Wade was sitting in a ripped black-leather recliner smoking a Camel cigarette and drinking coffee that he had spiked with liquor. Jacey and Crissy were sitting on an ugly and quite smelly

THE DEAD BORN

green couch. The couch was tiny, and the girls were forced to sit so close that their shoulders touched.

Two men stood in a circle with Patrick and Stevie. One was old, maybe thirty, and the other was not much older than Jacey. They somehow knew Patrick, and they were passing around another joint, talking about cars. Wade looked at the girls. He had black eyes, and he squinted through them like a hillbilly pirate. He was wearing a white T-shirt that was stained with what Jacey hoped was chili and mustard.

"How old are you two?" asked Wade.

Jacey and Crissy looked at each other.

"Fifteen," Jacey said.

"Yeah, fifteen," Crissy echoed.

"Fifteen, fifteen," croaked Wade. "Patrick, why do you have these beauties out so late?"

He didn't wait for a reply. Wade passed them a bottle of clear liquid in a mason jar. Crissy looked at Jacey, then took the jar. She looked at it.

"Is this moonshine?" she asked.

Wade chuckled. "It won't hurt ya. Go on, turn it up."

Crissy took a sip. She exhaled sharply and coughed. Her whole body shivered, and her face immediately turned red. She handed the jar to Jacey, who took a big sip and swallowed. It was like drinking liquid fire, and it burned all the way down to her stomach. Someone passed a joint to her, and she took a hit off it. She passed it to Crissy, and Crissy took a huge hit and began to cough again. The guys laughed.

After that, most of the night was a blur. Jacey remembered Stevie trying to have sex with her in the back of Patrick's car. "You're fifteen, what are you waiting for?" was the best argument he could come up with. Jacey pushed him off, but he kept trying. His pimples brushed against her cheeks as they tongued for a few minutes, and his breath smelled like weed and stale beer. She was disgusted, and she hated him. This guy used to tease her in middle school. She was late-developing, and she had not grown into her face. It was only after graduation that she would be what many people described as beautiful. But she had started to develop big but firm breasts, and his hands sought them out like a greedy infant.

"Get offa meee," Jacey said in a slightly slurred voice. She wormed her way out of the car, intent on going back into the house. She would grab Crissy and make Patrick take them home. She stopped and looked up at the sky, blinking away the tears that had welled up in her eyes. The moon was so bright and full, she could barely see the stars. Stevie was already halfway nodded off; he had taken pills, too. She walked to the house but stopped at the living room window.

She could see Crissy passed out on the couch, and one of the men, Jacey couldn't remember his name – Donnie or Ronnie – was raping Crissy. Her new dress was pulled up to her belly button, and the top part had been pulled down, her boobs exposed. The other one, the black-haired one with the beard, stood over them, taking pictures with a small camera.

Patrick was standing with his pants down in front of Wade, who was still in his chair, his arm on the top of the chair, to steady himself, Jacey supposed. Wade was sucking Patrick's cock.

Jacey ran from the window. She looked in the car. Stevie was passed out in the backseat, his mouth open and his head lolled back, snoring.

Jacey sat down next to the car, squatting and rocking back and forth, her hands over her head as if to protect it. She realized she was moaning and made herself stop. Run. Just run. If you go in there and try to stop what is happening to your friend, you'll get raped, too. Or worse. She wasn't even that good of a friend though. Jacey knew for a fact that Crissy had stolen some CDs and makeup from her. And once in middle school, she had cut off three inches of Jacey's hair while she was sleeping.

"Help," Jacey whispered to the sky. The moon looked down at her, beautiful and uncaring. Jacey reached up to the sky. Her hand appeared to be cupping the moon in her palm, and she felt a surge of energy enter her.

Jacey stood up. She didn't have a plan. One of the men, she couldn't tell which one, walked onto the porch and lit a cigarette. Jacey ducked down and crept along the side of the yard out of view until she made it to the road.

Jacey started walking, the wedge shoes making her feet scream with pain. She finally just took them off and walked barefoot, every now and then small rocks digging into her feet. The moon lit her way, so she walked and walked. When possible, she walked through fields, the grass dewy and cool on her feet. She heard animals rustling and running through the woods on either side of her.

She saw headlights in front of her. Jacey jumped off the road and ran up the slight embankment on her right. She waited, sweating and panting. She closed her eyes. The car sped by, spraying dust and gravel into the air. She waited a few minutes and got up and kept walking.

Finally, she made it to the main road. There was a store with a pay phone about a half mile up ahead. She saw no traffic and walked in the middle of the road. She realized she was humming *Walking After Midnight* as she walked on the yellow line. She heard a car and sidled over to the side like a drunk. She thought about hiding but was too tired to care. The car slowed down, stopping beside her, and the window rolled down. It was a woman in a minivan, so Jacey got in. The lady chatted some, but Jacey didn't remember what their conversation was about. She dropped Jacey off at her house. Jacey snuck in through her bedroom window. She got ready for bed and then tiptoed into the kitchen with her dress and shoes balled up in her arms. She put them in a plastic bag and put them in the garbage.

    She crept back to her bed and passed out, but she woke up every couple of hours, picturing Crissy, and wondering if she made it home. Jacey felt like she would go to hell for leaving her friend there. But more than anything, she felt a secret, perverse relief that it had not been her being raped. She saw the moon shining through her window. It judged her. Jacey cried and pulled the sheet over her head.

    The whippoorwills were outside her window. She remembered her mother telling her the whippoorwills were lost souls, and Jacey believed her. Especially now. Lost souls trying to get back home. Either that or they knew where their fellow lost ones abided, waiting for their permanent home, their home of dark woods and lonely dirt roads at night.

"Jacey?" Corey was holding her arm and lightly shaking her. "Hey, you all right?" He was speaking into her ear. "You look pale, you gonna pass out?"

    "Fine, I'm just … I didn't eat, and I feel dizzy," she said.

    "This was a bad idea," Corey whispered.

    Jacey grabbed Corey's muscular bicep and held her breath. The air was muggy and it felt like they were standing in a bowl of hot soup, yet Jacey shivered.

    Wade's right eye was covered by a grimy black eye patch. He stared at them with this good eye, which was as black as a marble.

    "Get in if you're gettin'," he croaked. "I ain't standing here all fuckin' day trying to let out the cool air!" He hacked up a ball of phlegm and spat. It whizzed by Corey's face and landed with a plop on the concrete step.

    Corey gently tugged on Jacey, and they squeezed past Bad Eye. Jacey was sure she would scream if any part of her touched him.

"Shut up!" he screamed at the dog. Jacey and Corey both jumped. The dog stopped his barking but began to pace around, whimpering. Bad Eye's voice didn't sound old. There was a strength to it, and he would probably be able to yell like that on his deathbed. Her grandfather was like that. It seemed the gift of strength was a special gift bestowed upon mean old cocksuckers and satanic killers.

Wade slammed the door shut. "Kitchen," he said, clumping past them on his cane, not looking at them.

The kitchen smelled worse than the living room. A cloud of cigarette smoke hung just below the ceiling, and the stench of old grease clung to the walls. It was the accumulation of years of bad cooking and even worse housekeeping. There was a lone plastic kitchen table littered with envelopes and several ashtrays and soda bottles. The kitchen floor was a dingy white and light-green print, and it rolled up at the corners.

A woman came into the kitchen. Jacey recognized the long, straight, black hair and the scar on her face. She looked at Jacey, and her black eyes glinted with anger.

"I'm not surprised you're here," Jacey said.

"You know her, Angie?" asked Wade.

"She came down to the club asking questions about Crissy," said the dancer.

Angie came closer to Jacey. "Guess you aren't gonna threaten me with the cops right now, are you?" she asked, her eyes lively with amusement and anger.

"You brought Crissy here, didn't you, even though you knew what happened to her here, what he did to her," said Jacey, pointing at Wade.

Jacey stepped back from Angie. She could feel anger coming in waves off her body. She saw Angie's fists clenched with rage.

"You sold Crissy out to get out of whatever sick arrangement you made with them, some of the bikers. You passed yourself off as a witch to protect them with a spell. But it didn't work, because you ain't shit, and now you're keeping yourself from being killed by running drugs for them," Jacey said.

Jacey saw a flash of an image: Angie in Wade's bedroom, sitting on his face, dope sick, needing what Wade had.

Jacey shook off the image and came to just as Angie charged at her. She grabbed Jacey's hair and jerked her across the kitchen. Jacey slipped and fell, but Corey pulled Angie off of her. Angie was flailing and snarling.

"I'm gonna kill you, you fucking cunt!" Angie screamed. She was about to bust out of Corey's grip, she was flailing so violently.

Jacey was so angry she could barely see straight. Her scalp hurt from where the wild bitch had tried to yank out her hair. Jacey grabbed the woman's dyed hair and tilted her head back, then punched her as hard as she could, her fist connecting with the woman's nose, and she heard a crunching sound. Blood immediately poured from the woman's nose. Jacey grabbed a couple of dirty washrags from the counter and smashed them onto her nose. She then stuffed one in her back pocket.

She heard a click behind her and turned. Wade was leveling a pistol at them. Jacey stepped back from Angie.

"Corey is gonna let you go, Angie, but you ain't gonna do nothing but go sit in this chair like a good girl. Let her go, Corey, or I'll shoot all three of ya," Wade said.

Corey did, and she sat in the chair as instructed, holding her busted nose.

"You two get out of here, and if you ever come back here, or talk about me again, I'll send some boys to take care of you both," Wade said.

Corey walked slowly over to Jacey, his eyes on Wade's gun. "Let's go," Corey said.

"You forgetting something, Corey?" asked Wade.

Corey dug some cash out of his wallet and handed it to Wade. Wade reached into a sugar bowl and brought out some pills wrapped in cellophane from a cigarette pack and tossed them to Corey.

"Now that there's a transaction, you won't be so prone to talk. Now get the fuck outta here and don't ever come back," Wade said.

Jacey and Corey walked out, and from behind her, Jacey heard him say, "Crissy was just one of many. She ain't the last one either."

When Jacey got home, she fed Moon and went into the parlor. She sat with the Book of Shadows in front of her. She took the rag with Angie's blood on it and put it next to the book.

Jacey looked at the spot where the woman had been found. Jacey felt odd. Why think of her now? Then something clicked. The woman had something to do with all of this. She was the reason Jacey was here, and for Crissy, Jacey understood.

Jacey suddenly felt like she had strings tied around her; she was being played, and so was Morgan. She got a sick feeling in her guts, and she feared she might vomit.

Jacey calmed herself and took out the picture she had kept all these years, the one of her and Crissy in high school, dressed up to go to the football game. Jacey took the picture and sat down on the floor of the parlor with it.

She studied the picture, then laid it down in front of her. She closed her eyes and kept Crissy's face in her mind. *Take me to the night you were killed, Crissy*. Jacey had never done this with someone who was no longer here, but she tried anyway. At first, Jacey saw only Crissy's face, then she got a flash of something, small dots of light in the darkness. It went away, and only blackness remained. Jacey conjured her Seer, and immediately Jacey saw the Seer's long golden hair and garnet eyes, and Jacey repeated the name *Crissy* in her mind.

Jacey saw the small flashes again, intermittent dots of light flickering off and on in the dark. Jacey realized they were lightning bugs, and suddenly she smelled the night air: the honeysuckle, the grass, and the waft of cigarette smoke hanging in the thick, humid air of a summer night. Jacey saw what she asked for.

CHAPTER 19

Crissy Freeman sat in her living room. The lighter flicked a few times, then the orange flame lit up the darkness. She liked the dark. You cannot see what's there, but that was the beauty of it. And the shadows didn't worry Crissy anymore.

She touched the flame to the pipe. There was a crackling sound, and the contents of the pipe glowed like a pretty campfire. Crissy hit it hard and held her breath for as long as she could, then exhaled the huge plume of smoke. She felt it hit her right away, and she sat back, the shadows falling around her like a soft blanket a mother would lay over her infant.

Crissy stretched out on the lumpy sofa, her backside falling into the sagging middle of the stained couch. Her feet no longer hurt from the ten-hour shift at the Get-N-Go. This was good weed, Crissy marveled. Wade always had the best. Better than the Percocets she had taken at work for her back. She reached over and gently passed her hand above the coffee table beside the couch.

Someone looking at her hands – dainty and pretty hands – would have thought she was conducting an imaginary symphony. Her hand found the glass, and she took a long swallow of the whisky, relishing the pleasant burn when it hit the back of her throat.

Crissy rarely felt good, but right now she did. She clung to the feeling.

SOMETIMES CRISSY MISSED BEING A DANCER. THE HOURS WERE LATE, but Crissy had never minded; she had always been a night owl. And the pay was good. She came home with no less than one hundred dollars most nights, but usually more, depending on who came into the club. Her feet hurt her worse then. She had thought dancing in high heels would be the worst part, and at first, it was hard to get used to it, but she practiced at home – when she was alone – and she found she was surprisingly good at it. The worst part actually was the time spent just standing, talking to the customers. When she finally did her last dance of the night and changed into her jeans and tank top and flip-flops, she would sometimes almost limp out to her car, her feet hurt so much. She would soak her feet when she got home, then have a glass of wine or beer and a big pull off her pipe.

Crissy had saved up a sizable stash of money. And even though she was ashamed of being a dancer, it was the only thing she could think of besides selling drugs or being a prostitute that would make her a lot of money. She had saved up almost eight thousand dollars, and she had already picked out where she was going to move: New Orleans. Crissy had found a book that her old friend Jacey had loaned her in high school. Jacey had fallen in love with Anne Rice books, and Crissy had read the witch ones. She liked it, but she especially liked the idea of being in a city like New Orleans; it seemed like the kind of place to start over, where people could reinvent themselves.

THE DEAD BORN

Every day when she came home from work, she put her night's money in her underwear drawer in the small dresser she had owned since she was a teenager. It was wobbly and the white paint was chipping off it. Crissy worried about it in the underwear drawer, so she moved it into a shoebox in her small closet. But one night, her ex had come over, and he had gone looking for a jacket he swore he had left. Crissy stood behind him, sweating, terrified he would look in the shoebox and see her wad of cash. He didn't, but she moved the money again. She walked into the bathroom and pulled the small top drawer of the sink out. She put the money in a Ziplock bag behind the drawer, then slid it back into place. It closed almost all the way, and it was only noticeable if one looked closely. Crissy didn't think anyone would notice, and if they did, they wouldn't bother to investigate. But eventually, the stack of money got too bulky for the drawer.

A few nights later, she had come home in the early morning and knew as soon as she walked in that her money was gone. The front door was unlocked, and she knew. She saw the hefty baggie laying on the floor. Her ex had taken all of it, not even leaving a few bills for her to buy a bottle to get drunk on.

Crissy sat on the floor and cried. She cried so much and so hard that she fell asleep for an hour. She woke up on the floor, the sun streaming in through the window, and she winced and squinted against the glare. She dug in her purse and found her wad of tips from the previous night and went to the liquor store. She thought about driving her car into the side of the brick building of the liquor store, but she couldn't do it.

She opened the bottle of Jack when she got home, stripped off her clothes, and ran a steaming hot bath. While the water ran, she sat on the floor naked, lit a cigarette, and drank. She paused, got up, and looked under the sink. Next to her tampons and half-full bottles of various shampoos and lotions, she saw the bottle of Percocets. They were expired, but Crissy popped two immediately, washing them down with the Jack. She looked over at her jeans in a heap on the floor. She leaned over, looking in the pockets until she found the small pocket knife. She opened it and gently placed the blade on her wrist. The blade felt cool against her skin, and she marveled at how it looked.

She tossed her cigarette butt in the toilet and climbed into the tub. The water was so hot, steam rose off the water, and she hissed at the temperature. But Crissy got all the way in, her skin already bright red, relishing the pain. The tub was small, and she had to bend her knees up to her chest.

She laid her head back, staring at the ceiling. Her right hand draped off the side of the tub, holding the knife. Crissy downed the rest of the drink and let the empty glass fall to the floor.

She poised the knife over her wrists, ready to cut. Her arm was sore from holding the knife, and she finally lowered her arm. She could not do it. She kept seeing her son's face. And even though she knew she would never have a relationship with him, Crissy felt that offing herself would be the ultimate betrayal to her boy. As much as she had already failed him, she could at least keep herself alive for him. He didn't need a mother who had committed suicide. Look at what happened to Jesse. She could spare him that shame, at least. Crissy tossed the knife on the sink and sat back in the tub and cried.

These thoughts raced through her mind as Crissy looked out the small window of her trailer. She saw a lightning bug flash. It was May, and she had seen her first lightning bug. She thought about that night for just a minute, then pushed it away. She didn't know, well, anything really, but she did know how to keep unwelcome thoughts away.

Summers were hard for Crissy sometimes. The warm weather made her restless and a little panicked. Brief images of that night out with Jacey and the boys, the moon looking bloated and menacing. She shook herself out of it. Another flash from the lightning bug. It was so pretty because it was so brief. Tonight, everything seemed so pretty and inviting.

She got up and opened the door, and the air rushed into her living room and over her. She lifted her arms and the summer breeze caressed her breasts through the thin tank top. Crissy smiled. She was grateful for the breeze. It was not officially summer yet, but it was already hot and humid. She rubbed a hand along her belly, which pooched out, and felt the Cesarean scar, and looked at the stretch marks that crisscrossed her belly. They had faded, and the scar was not so big, but Crissy was self-conscious about them. This made her think of her son, but she shook the memories away so she wouldn't cry.

Instead, Crissy thought about how her boyfriend constantly remarked about her belly. Lately, he had mentioned it so much that she kept a shirt on every time they had sex, and even then, he still said something to upset her. She never enjoyed having sex. And now he made fun of her for being so dry down there. Crissy was glad that his use of pills was beginning to affect his sex drive.

Crissy made a drink and grabbed her smokes and walked outside into her small backyard. The breeze felt nice. She sat in the grass and lit a cigarette. Crissy began to think about Angie, the other dancer who she thought of as her friend.

Crissy realized how desperate she was just to have a friend; it constantly got her drawn into doing things she didn't want to do. But one night after a slow night at work, as they were sitting in the club waiting to be walked out, Angie pulled out some tarot cards. "Ask something," she said.

"Will I get a new boyfriend?" asked Crissy.

Angie shuffled the cards, which didn't look like any tarot cards Crissy had seen. They were glossy black and had strange symbols drawn on them.

Angie laid out three cards. She shook her head. "No boyfriend coming anytime soon, sorry, honey," Angie said.

"Yeah, I didn't think so," Crissy said.

"You will have a visitor, though, someone you don't expect," Angie said.

"You know what, I don't want to know anymore."

"Come on, hang out with me. I can't promise a boyfriend, but I do have a guy you can be with tonight. He's cute."

Angie took Crissy to the biker clubhouse, and Crissy wasn't pleased because Jesse had been hanging around there lately. She told Angie on the drive she didn't want to see Jesse because he would get mad at her, not for seeing other guys, but because he tried to act like a big shot around them, and he thought Crissy would tarnish his image.

"He's not there, trust me. I talked to Randy, and it's just him and a couple other guys. You know, if you hit it off with one of them, you may not have to dance as much – these guys have money," Angie said.

The music was blasting at the clubhouse, and five men were sitting around a table smoking and drinking and playing poker. Crissy and Angie went into the back room with Randy and a guy named Doug, and Randy cut up lines of cocaine for all of them.

They drank and snorted more lines, and at some point, Crissy got up to pee. She asked where the bathroom was and walked into the wrong room, where she saw two shapes sleeping on bunk beds. She walked over and looked at them. They were young girls, no more than fourteen or fifteen, and Crissy felt a wave of horror rush through her body.

She quietly closed the door and used the bathroom. She walked back into what Randy had called the Party Room and sat beside Angie on the couch. Crissy tried her best to cover her worry and disgust.

Randy sat between Crissy and Angie. "Why don't you pop those titties out," he said.

Angie giggled and took off her top. Randy began to rub Angie's breast, and his other hand rubbed Crissy's thighs.

"Your turn, honey," Randy said.

Doug sat next to Crissy and kissed her neck and rubbed her breasts, his hand sliding clumsily up her shirt. He guided her to a bed, and Crissy took off her clothes. She wanted out of here, and she knew this was the fastest way out. Angie was naked now, too, and she laid down on the bed and pulled Crissy to her. She kissed her and caressed her body.

"Hell, yeah," one of the men said.

Angie spread Crissy's legs and went down on her. Crissy closed her eyes and moaned. She had never experienced it like this from any man. Then she remembered the sleeping girls in the other room and prayed. She had not prayed in years, but now she prayed for this to end so she could get out of there.

Randy laid Angie on her stomach and had sex with her. Crissy gave Doug a blowjob, but he couldn't get off because of the drugs. It went on for too long, but finally, they passed out in a sweaty heap on the bed. Crissy woke up not long after and quietly dressed and slipped out of the room. She walked down the road and onto the highway and hitched a ride home.

The next time she worked, Angie came up to her and put her arm around her in the dressing room. "You ran off the other day. What was that about?" Angie asked. Crissy only now noticed how evil Angie's eyes were.

"I didn't feel so good. That was not what I had in mind," she said.

"Seemed to have a good time to me," Angie said. "I know I did, and I'd like to do it again, just us two."

"I'm not into girls," Crissy said.

"Could have fooled me."

Crissy felt disgusted, and she shook out of Angie's grip.

"Who were those girls in the other room? They were very young," Crissy said.

The smile left Angie's face, and she grabbed Crissy's arm and twisted it behind her back. Crissy wanted to cry out in pain, but she bit her lip.

"I'd forget about that if I were you. Otherwise, it's serious trouble for both of us, understand?" Angie asked. Crissy nodded. "Good girl."

Crissy came back to the moment, happy to push those thoughts away.

The trailer park was quiet at this time in the early morning. The park was noisy during the day. Lots of families. The kids would be right outside Crissy's window, screaming and playing, often waking her up. But Crissy didn't really mind; she just put on earplugs. Sometimes she would think about her son and cry, wondering if he was outside playing, too.

Her Aunt Marla bought the trailer and a small lot for Crissy. Ten years ago, when she had given her custody of her son. Crissy had saved up money to get an abortion, but her aunt and her aunt's pastor had talked her out of it. Crissy remembered the pastor's face looking over her body as he explained how she must not murder her baby. It was a sin, especially when there were good, Christian people like her Aunt Marla who never got the chance to be mothers and would take care of and love her baby.

Crissy wanted to ask him why God didn't perform a miracle for her aunt and let her be able to have a baby. And how they could call this baby a miracle when she had not even wanted it. How could a man forcing himself on her be considered miraculous?

Her son's birth was a blur. She remembered Aunt Marla being with her at the hospital and telling her she would be fine. She remembered a strong feeling of pressure when they cut him out, but no pain.

THE DEAD BORN

When they handed Crissy the baby, she only held him for about a minute. He was red and crying, his face bunched up in what Crissy thought was anger. He was bald and squirmy, like he was a tiny alien that would slide out of her grip and slither across the cold hospital floor. Crissy bent closer to his face, trying to see if she could find any resemblance to her, or even to his father. But he didn't look like anyone she knew. Crissy felt tired and she was starting to hurt, so she handed the baby to the nurse.

Later, when she was finally in a room, a nurse came with some paperwork. She had to tell them the baby's name was Benjamin. She told them the father's name, but she decided not to give the baby his last name. Crissy had called him and told him she was in labor, but he never showed up. Crissy watched as they took Ben's hand and footprints, and finalized the birth certificate.

Aunt Marla was angry that Crissy had named the boy; her aunt had a list of names she had been saving for months. But Crissy had been firm. In fact, it was one of the few times she had ever stood up for herself.

She stayed with her aunt for a couple of years, but she got tired of being bitched at for staying out late and drinking. Aunt Marla eventually bought her the trailer. She liked it better this way, and she knew her aunt did, too. Crissy knew she just wanted her baby.

Her aunt's house reminded her of the past as well, when Aunt Marla's husband, Steve, molested Crissy when she was thirteen. They had taken her to the drive-in, and when her aunt went to get drinks and popcorn, he had told Crissy to sit up front so she could see better. He had felt her breasts and shoved his hand down her pants and stuck his finger inside her. Crissy was frozen with fear. Her aunt gave her weird looks when she said she didn't want any popcorn. She looked at Crissy like she wanted to ask if she was okay, but then she grew uncharacteristically quiet.

After she had given up Ben, Crissy told her aunt she didn't want Steve around Ben. And that if her aunt didn't keep him away, she would make trouble for her. In the end, her aunt sighed and said she loved Ben and would not let anyone hurt him. Crissy believed her; she knew her aunt loved Ben. Crissy wanted to ask her aunt why she had never loved her, but she never did. She didn't have to, really. She knew that when her aunt looked at her, she saw a child that had caused her sister's death. An illegitimate child, fathered by a loathsome man who had been twenty years older, and married, to boot.

Aunt Marla paid for the funeral expenses; she always made sure she looked good. Crissy remembered sitting on the sagging brown sofa after the funeral. Women had fluttered around her aunt, her belly shaking like a giant blob of Jello as she heaved and cried. The women told her she had a new angel watching over them, and it took Crissy a minute to realize they were talking about her mother.

The women brought lots of casseroles and desserts. One of her aunt's oldest friends guided the line of women with their dishes into the kitchen after Aunt Marla received their hugs and wet kisses. Only a couple of the ladies talked to Crissy, and she couldn't remember what they said to her. At one point, her aunt looked at Crissy, and there was a gleam of suspicion glinting through her muddy eyes. Crissy realized that she must have been making a knowing face, and she looked down immediately, not wanting to stir up her aunt. Crissy instinctively knew to keep herself quiet and innocuous, only visible when it was necessary.

Crissy shook herself out of the unpleasant memories and took another sip of her drink.

She lay back on the grass, looking up at the moon. It was almost full, and the light was so bright it illuminated the tiny backyard. Crissy suddenly felt lonely. She wished she had a guy there to enjoy this big full moon with. A guy who could sit outside with her and just be happy to be with her. Crissy pictured what she wanted him to look like: nice soulful eyes, cute grin, tall, muscular. Maybe a tattoo, but one he never showed to anybody except her, and he would tell her the story behind it. Then he would take her for rides on his motorcycle, a nice one, not a sputtering bike like her ex had. Her ex had only taken her for a ride on his motorcycle twice, and the second time it had broken down. He left it parked outside, and when he was drunk or high, he would go out and walk around the bike, looking at it, sometimes squatting down and looking at the guts of it, but never actually trying to fix it.

One night some of his friends came over, and they teased him about still not getting the bike running. Two days later, he had sold it, and when Crissy asked where it was, he told her to shut her mouth and shoved her into the stove.

Crissy saw headlights come up the long gravel hill. She closed her eyes and waited. Soon someone knocked on her front door. She wanted to ignore it, but she didn't want to be alone. For some reason, the shadows suddenly seemed scary. She went inside and walked to the door.

She knew from the outline who it was: Jesse. Crissy sighed. He knocked again, louder. "Cris! Open up!" Crissy could tell by his voice that he was high. If she didn't open the door, he would start yelling and piss off the neighbors. She had already been warned by the landlord that she would kick Crissy out if she had any more raucous visitors.

"Crissy!"

Crissy looked at the table and saw the book she had been trying to read. It was one of Jacey's books, *Hellbound Heart*. Crissy quickly hid the book under a pile of magazines. She wasn't sure why. Then she opened the door.

"Jesus, okay, wake the dead, why don't you," she said, looking around to make sure no neighbors' lights had come on. She closed the door behind him. "What are you doing here?"

Jesse sat on her couch, lit a cigarette, and turned on the TV, flipping through the many channels of static.

"Thought you had cable." Jesse was keyed up and bouncing his leg.

Crissy put her hands in her pockets. "Can't afford it," she said. Some fucker stole a bunch of money from me, she thought.

"If you hadn't quit dancing, you'd have money for cable." Jesse craned his neck and looked up at her. "Did you quit or did they fire you?" He reached out his hand and jiggled a roll of fat on her belly.

Crissy lurched back from him, smacking his hand away. He laughed and shook his head. "I'm kidding, you look better than some of them, fucking gross bitches," he said.

Crissy watched as he put his feet up on her coffee table.

"Can you grab me a beer, babe?" he said.

"Get your feet off my table," she said. She was suddenly furious.

"What?" he asked.

Crissy walked to the couch. She noticed her fists were clenched. She tightened them.

"I said, get your feet off my table." She was so mad her voice trembled.

His eyes darkened. He stood in front of her. "What did you say?" He had a look of dumb surprise on his face.

"You heard me. And what are you even doing here?" Crissy stepped closer to him.

He laughed and slapped his knees. "Oh, shit, oh, shit, look who finally grew some balls!" He giggled like a little boy.

Crissy shoved him. Jesse stumbled back and his feet got tangled. He fell onto the floor, knocking over an end table with a plant on it.

"You fucking stupid bitch! What the hell's your problem?" His voice squeaked on the last word, and she saw fear in his

THE DEAD BORN

eyes. Crissy stood over him, her hands balled into fists. She was breathing hard, and her eyes blazed. She looked down at him and grinned, practically baring her teeth.

"If I had any balls, I would kill you. You stole my money!" Crissy wiped the tears from her cheeks. She kicked him as hard as she could in his side, hoping she would crack a rib. "You stole my money! You stole my money!" she chanted. She alternated feet to kick him, but he was scooting away. He got to his knees and stood up. He held his hands out.

"Crissy, I'm warning you – stop it," he said warily.

Crissy picked up the unopened beer can and hurled it at him. The can missed him and landed with a light thump on the carpet. She immediately picked up a paperweight and tossed it at him. He ducked and it went crashing into the sink, breaking dishes.

Crissy was weeping, "What did you spend it on? Pills? Buy everyone drinks at the bar? Did your boys hang out with you for a few days since you had some money? I bet you let them bleed you dry after about a week," she said. She sat on the couch and put her head in her hands. Her rage had burned out and transitioned into despair, her default state.

"I was going to start over," she said. She looked at him and saw how little he cared. "I was going to leave here, I was going to finally get away from this place. Now I'm stuck."

He sidled around her, wary of getting something else thrown at him.

Crissy looked at him. "You have anything to say? Anything at all?" She hadn't realized how wormy-looking he was until now. He was shorter than her, and skinnier. His jeans hung so low on his hips they were almost falling off. His eyes were gray, but not a pretty shade, instead a gray the color of a cloudy puddle on a grimy city street. His hair was his only redeeming feature, but lately, he wore it in a buzz cut and covered it with a ballcap. His skin was sallow, and he squinted at her.

"I wish I had never met you," she whispered. "I wish I had never been born. I never would have met any of you or had a baby. And moving away was the closest thing I had to being someone else."

Jesse shrugged, grabbed his hat off her couch, and walked out the door.

Crissy locked the door behind him. She stood with her head against the glass peephole. If she weren't so damn sad right now, she would be proud of herself – she had never stood up for herself like that. She let a thought inhabit her: What else could I do?

Crissy suddenly thought about her aunt and uncle. It occurred to her where she had gotten the idea of hoarding her money in different spots around the house: her aunt. Crissy remembered looking through hat boxes in her aunt's closet. Crissy found a beautiful wide-brimmed hat with flowers and a velvet ribbon and lifted it out of the pink and white hat box, and she saw stacks of money in the box. She heard her aunt's voice from downstairs and quickly put the hat and box away and ran downstairs.

Crissy decided she was going to steal it. Well, it's not stealing if you are owed it, she thought. She took a shot and paced the house. She chided herself for not thinking of it sooner. She could go now. No, her aunt and uncle would be home now. Bad idea. Plus, Crissy was fairly certain there was a gun somewhere.

Tomorrow was Sunday. They would be gone most of the day. Church service in the morning, out to eat for lunch, socializing, then back at church in the evening.

When Crissy got up the next day, she called into work and drove to her aunt's street, parked the car where she could see the house, and waited.

Crissy watched as her aunt ushered Ben into the car. He had gotten so big, and Crissy choked up looking at him. He was a handsome boy, despite who his father was.

THE DEAD BORN

She bit her nails, worried she had not seen her uncle yet. Surely Aunt Marla would not let him skip church. Crissy waited, then sighed with relief when she saw him hobble out on his walker. Aunt Marla had gotten fatter, and she eclipsed his scrawny frame as she impatiently hustled him down the porch and into the car. Crissy slid down lower in her car, praying they wouldn't see her. But her uncle was focused on not falling, and her aunt was focused on him. She finally got him in the front seat, and she waddled to the driver's side.

Her aunt took forever backing out of the driveway, but they finally left. Crissy watched as the brake lights went on and off, her aunt pumping the brakes for some reason.

Crissy laughed and sighed, her hand on her chest. She got out of her car and walked right up to the door, not worried about anyone seeing her. Crissy took the key from under the big potted plant on the porch and opened the door. She replaced it under the plant and walked in. The house was dark and stuffy. Crissy bounded up the steps to her aunt and uncle's room.

She began in the closet, grabbing the four hat boxes. She uncovered the first, marveling at how ugly the hat was. It suddenly occurred to Crissy that these were the only pretty "feminine" items her aunt owned. And actually, it was damn strange that her aunt even had these, because all her aunt's clothing consisted of big shapeless skirts and house dresses, and monster-sized shoes. It made no sense. Why would her aunt keep these pretty hats in their lovely hat boxes?

Crissy checked the second box. No money there either. She wiped her forehead; it was sweltering in the bedroom. And it smelled like old people. Crissy opened the third box. Nothing. She glanced at her aunt's nightstand. There was a Bible and a Danielle Steel novel, as well as a picture of Ben.

Crissy replaced the lid on the third box and looked at the fourth one. She was unconsciously biting her lip. What would she do if she couldn't find the money?

"No," Crissy whispered, "it's here, I know it is." She looked in the box. This hat was the most elaborate and actually was pretty. She felt like she was looking at something brought back from Paris during the Gatsby era. It was a blood-red hat with a wide brim, and the top was adorned with a huge flower, and feathers waved around it.

She lifted the hat. No money, but there were pictures. But first, she took the hat to the mirror and tried it on. She adjusted the hat to where it was slightly cocked to one side and pulled down the delicate red veil over her face. She looked in the mirror and marveled at how she looked.

Crissy carefully took it off and set it down, then flipped through the pictures in the box. She saw pictures of her aunt as a teenage girl, wearing one of the hats. She was at a horse race, and people around her were dressed up, too, drinks in their hands, toasting the camera. Crissy looked at the back of the pictures. Each one with the hats was labeled *Kentucky Derby*. Crissy was puzzled; she had never known her aunt to go to a race, or even be interested in horses.

Crissy began to go through drawers, looking carefully, pulling each one out all the way, looking behind, looking for false bottoms. Nothing. She looked around the room, willing herself not to cry. She studied the uncle's bed. It looked like a hospital bed; it was raised, and it had a full-size mattress on a rollaway base so it could be moved around easily. Crissy walked around it.

She squatted down, looking underneath the bed. No dust. She lifted the blankets, her skin crawling at having to touch what her aunt had always called bedclothes. She lifted the fitted sheets and saw the mattress liner zipper. She unzipped it, stuck her hand inside, and felt around. She heard something crinkle before she felt it, but she grabbed it and yanked it out. A plastic zipper bag full of money. It was packed with twenties and hundreds. She stripped the bed and unzipped it the rest of the way. She found another plastic bag and put it on the floor. She flipped the mattress off the bed and inhaled sharply. On the box spring was a garment bag. It lay almost flat, its light plastic material shining cheaply. Crissy unzipped it and looked inside. It was full of money, too. Crissy placed all the money items on the floor and put everything back as she had found it, setting aside the hat box with the pretty hat.

She hesitated, then walked around until she found Ben's room. She stood with her hands clasped in front of her. She felt like she was not good enough to stand in his little room, and she was careful not to touch anything. She looked around. His bed was shaped like a car, and it had blue *Toy Story* blankets and sheets. It was made up, but it was clear Ben was in charge of that because the corners were crooked. Crissy looked on his dresser. There were awards, one for baseball and a Boy Scout medal. She saw a picture as well. It was Ben with his kindergarten class. She picked him out right away. He was standing toward the back, smiling broadly, and she could see he had lost a front tooth. Crissy took the picture and put it in her purse.

She wanted to look around some more. She knew the old biddy had stashed more. But Crissy looked at her pile of treasures and thought, *Do not get too greedy*. It was enough, more than that asshole had stolen from her, and she would be able to move away and start over.

She grabbed everything and walked calmly to her car, not looking around. She drove home following the speed limit.

When she got to her trailer, she locked her doors, closed the curtains, and pushed her couch against the door. She took a butcher knife and put it next to her bed. She wished she had a gun. Then she started a load of laundry. She wasn't in a hurry. She figured her aunt would not be home until night. Crissy had time to pack, clean her house, and maybe take a nap.

She put the money in a duffel bag, saving a couple of bills for her purse. Crissy estimated the haul was about five thousand dollars.

She packed and made herself a peanut butter and jelly sandwich and waited for her clothes to dry. It was almost one p.m. Plenty of time. She took a quick shower and dried her hair, then looked outside. No one was around. She quickly put her suitcase in the trunk of her car and went back inside. She locked the door back and sat on the couch. She turned on the TV, then immediately turned it off. She couldn't sit still.

I should leave now, she thought. *So why am I stalling?*

Now that the moment was here, Crissy was choking, like she always did.

No, Crissy told herself, *not this time*. She got up and made herself grab the duffel bag. She turned off all her lights and shut off the TV. She was digging out her keys to leave on the table when she heard a knock. She almost screamed.

"Crissy?" said a woman's voice that Crissy recognized. It was her neighbor, Mrs. Fischer, an older woman whose husband had recently died. Mrs. Fischer was one of the few nice ones in the park. Crissy put the duffel bag in her bedroom and shut the door. She ran to the door.

"Hi, Emma," Crissy said and made herself smile.

"Hey, there, sorry to bother you, but I saw your car here, and I took a chance. I was wondering if you could jump my car."

"I don't have jumper cables," Crissy said.

"Oh, I have some. It will only take a minute," she said.

Crissy nodded. "Okay, sure, no problem," she said. It occurred to Crissy then that she didn't even know if her car would make it to Louisiana, but she decided she would walk if she had to.

THE DEAD BORN

Crissy drove her car to Mrs. Fischer's trailer and waited while she rooted around in her trunk looking for the cables. Thankfully the car started, but Crissy had to endure another fifteen minutes of chatter. She tried to smile and look interested, trying not to keep darting her eyes to her trailer. Finally, she said she had to run to the post office.

"Got the day off then?" Mrs. Fischer asked.

"No, I work tonight, so I need to go run my errands before work. See you later, Mrs. Fischer." Crissy waved and drove off before Mrs. Fischer could get going again. Crissy felt terrible. She hoped she hadn't offended her neighbor. She really was the only one of the neighbors who had always been nice to her.

Crissy stopped at her trailer, and her phone buzzed. It was Barb, her friend from work. *You want anything?* the message read. *Shit. I should stock up before I leave town*, she thought.

Yes, be over in about fifteen, she typed back.

Crissy went over to Barb's and bought weed and pain pills for her back, about double what she usually did. Barb peered at her. "Damn, you win the lottery?" she asked Barb.

Crissy laughed. "I wish. It's from all that overtime," she said and got up to go, but Barb stopped her.

"You have to try this," Barb said. She fired up a bowl, and Crissy took a couple of hits. They chatted for a while, and before Crissy knew it, it was almost five o'clock.

She hugged Barb goodbye and drove home. She was extra careful, and she resisted the urge to speed. When she got to her trailer, she went directly to the bedroom and sighed with relief when she saw the duffel bag. Crissy decided to nap for about an hour to sober up, then she would leave.

Crissy jerked awake. She had been dreaming she was on the road, driving to New Orleans. In the dream, she had pulled over on the shoulder, gotten out, and laid down beside an alligator that was sunning itself. She wanted a picture with it, and she pulled out her phone to snap a picture, and the alligator clamped his huge jaws on her head.

The dream still clung to her as she stood up, trying to come back to reality. She had set her phone alarm, but it hadn't awakened her. She picked it up and looked at it. She had set it for a.m., not p.m. "Fuck!" she hissed.

She heard a jingling and rattling, and looked at her door and saw a shadow. Then the door slowly creaked open and her aunt came in.

Aunt Marla saw Crissy, and her brow furrowed. She shut the door behind her and stood in front of the door. She looked enormous in Crissy's tiny trailer, and Crissy was concerned she might actually fall through the thin foundation. Crissy prayed it would happen. Aunt Marla was studying her, a look of curiosity turned to knowing disappointment.

"Hmm, sleepin', or more like passed out. I went by that place you work, they said you called out sick," said Aunt Marla as she leaned on her cane and pursed her lips. She looked around the trailer as she spoke to Crissy.

"I told the man working there that you were sick, all right, have an allergy to actual work, and odds are you were laid up in some guy's place or he was laid up with you getting high," she said, shaking her head. "I see I was halfway right."

She walked closer, and Crissy shrank back, sitting down on the couch.

"I guess at this point you have gone through all the men, and they all left you after you let them use you up," she said, pretending to be sad for Crissy and shaking her head in pity.

"You don't know anything about me anymore," Crissy whispered. She thought she might cry, so she turned away from her aunt.

"I do, though," Aunt Marla said. "More than I want to. You can't hide from me, little girl."

Crissy sniffled, not able to look up at her aunt.

"Just give it back to me and I'll go. It's not too late ... not yet."

Crissy looked at her finally. "You didn't call the cops?"

Her aunt shook her head. "No, like I said, girl, it's not too late."

"Where did you get all those nice hats?" asked Crissy.

Her aunt was startled by the question. "What?"

"I took one of them, it looks good on me. I was just wondering why you have them. And why are you saving up all that money?" asked Crissy.

Aunt Marla looked at Crissy with utter contempt.

"None of your goddamn business," she hissed.

Crissy's mouth dropped open. She couldn't believe her aunt had taken the Lord's name in vain.

"I figure I'm owed that money," Crissy said. "After all, you let that old fucker get after me."

"Shut your mouth! He never did, he is a decent man. You were a wayward girl, always were. I tried to help you, but you turned away from me and the help I tried to give you," she said.

Crissy shook her head. "No, you knew about it, but you didn't care. You used me, you let him do those things, and you did nothing. I was a kid, and you treated me like I was a whore." Crissy began sobbing.

"I would take Ben with me, but I know you've already turned him against me," she continued. "And I know that money is mine. I'm leaving, and if you want to call the police on me, well, go ahead. I'll tell them a few things about the home life I had with you and him. And since there's a small boy around him, they will have to investigate. What do you think your nice church friends will think about that?"

Aunt Marla hit Crissy across her head with the cane. It made a light thunk sound, and Aunt Marla held it up in the air as if she had expected it to make a louder sound.

Crissy staggered back for a second, her hand going to her temple. She leaned against a wall, made a surprised sound, and slumped to her knees.

Aunt Marla walked over to Crissy. "No, no you won't, you troublesome bitch," she whispered. Crissy looked up at her, a blank look etched on her face; she was still stunned. Aunt Marla held up the cane and aimed for the top of Crissy's head, then struck her again and again. Blood droplets spattered the walls, and Aunt Marla felt some of the drops hit her face. She kept swinging until she was out of breath. She stepped back and dropped the cane, sitting down, not even sure if there was a chair behind her.

She was breathing hard, and she was sweating profusely. She closed her eyes until her breathing returned to normal and her heart wasn't thudding so hard in her chest.

She got up and staggered to Crissy's bathroom. She splashed water on her face and wiped off the blood. She went to retrieve her cane, willing herself not to look at Crissy. Not yet.

She scrubbed her cane off in the sink. She cleaned the sink, wiped off all the surfaces that she remembered touching, and put everything in a plastic garbage bag. She found the duffel bag of her money and set it by the door.

She looked at Crissy. She was still breathing, maybe. Aunt Marla stood over her niece, wondering if she should call one of the others. She decided to get home first. Later, after the sun went down, she would call one of the others. They could make it look like a robbery or something, or even take her body away.

Marla turned off the lights in the trailer. She peeped out the window, saw no one around, walked to her car, and drove home without incident.

CHAPTER 20

Back in her parlor, Jacey came back into her present. She sat up and saw Crissy's soul standing in front of her. Crissy looked just as she did the last time Jacey had seen her: younger and a little less sad.

"Your aunt killed you," Jacey said. It seemed stupid to say, as if Crissy didn't already know this, but for some reason, Jacey suspected that Crissy didn't know. No, it was more the feeling that Crissy had forgotten. But the trauma still surrounded Crissy; Jacey could feel it like a weight on her whole body. It was awful. She felt the confusion and disorientation, the horror of knowing something was wrong but not what it was. Crissy only looked at Jacey.

"Crissy, I'm so sorry. I should have said something that night when we snuck out. Maybe if I had this never would have happened to you," Jacey said.

Crissy's soul said nothing, but Jacey could hear her.

You seek to redeem yourself, but you have nothing to redeem. You are the guide. That is why you are here now.

"But Crissy, you are not here, you have been gone for two weeks," Jacey said.

I was told to wait for you. It's why you're here. You are the—

Crissy stopped. She couldn't remember the word, but Jacey knew.

"My psychopomp, the Seer, but she is not me," Jacey said.

It's you, she is you, the Seer, it is why you are here, yet you don't see. But you can, for me, for everyone, for Ben. They want to use him for their evil. I want to go now. I've stayed longer than I should have. I hope I can still go.

Jacey conjured up the image of the Seer. She saw her long, golden hair, her burgundy eyes, her translucent skin, and sharp teeth against full, pink lips.

The Seer took Crissy's hand, and they turned and walked into the stars.

Jacey had many questions, but she fell into blackness. Soon Crissy's voice floated to her. *You have to make it right; she was not alone. Goodbye, Jacey.*

Jacey woke up in the woods. She had no memory of getting there. She sat up, looking around. Moon walked to Jacey and stood up on her hind legs, her front paws on Jacey's arm, her little face forward, smelling Jacey. Jacey held her close, nuzzling her soft fur. A bobcat screamed in the distance, then the frogs began to sing again, an owl hooted, and a whippoorwill joined in.

Jacey picked up Moon and walked to the house. She thought about calling the sheriff, but she knew she would not. Jacey was the one who had to make it right. But what? Should she kill Marla and orphan Crissy's child? Jacey sat down at the table where she had talked and laughed with Morgan only last night.

So you'll leave the child with a murderer? Jacey felt shame at her doubt and sudden lack of conviction. Where would he go? What would happen to him? Marla was a murderer, and her husband molested Crissy. What are you going to do? Jacey picked up the phone. She called Shawnee first.

"This is beyond insane. I could be fired," Evans said. He was pacing while Jacey, Shawnee, and Ashley talked to him about Marla. The only reason he was still listening was because of Shawnee, his first girlfriend and the only woman he ever really loved.

"Josh, it won't hurt to question her," Shawnee said.

Evans rubbed his hair, and he sat down in the chair opposite the three women.

"Sheriff, this is highly unusual, but I think you are, well, obligated to question this Marla. You have a witness to the murder," Ashley said.

Evans shook his head and smirked. "Witness? She saw the murder in a vision. How the hell is that not going to be laughed out of court when the time comes?" he asked.

"Well, we can leave that part out, of course, but you have a valid reason to question Marla: Ben's father was Jesse, so how do you know that Jesse didn't try to see Ben before he went to Jacey's that night?" Ashley asked.

"Why do you believe her?" he asked. He was looking at Shawnee.

Shawnee leaned forward. "Josh, I've known Jacey since we were in kindergarten, the same age as Ben, and she has always had a gift to see things that other people can't. She would have dreams …" Shawnee stopped and looked at Jacey, who nodded, indicating Shawnee should keep talking.

"Once she told me that she had a dream that my grandfather died but that I shouldn't be worried because he said–" Shawnee paused, trying not to cry. "Because he said 'I'm somewhere else, somewhere just fine, Teacup,' that was his nickname for me. No one knew about it, not even my mother, and I know I never told Jacey."

"All right, I'll take a ride over to Marla's, see what she says, but first I want to go talk to Randy," Evans said.

"No, that won't do any good, you have to go to Wade's. Somehow he's more important in this, I know it," Jacey said.

"Wade? What does Marla have to do with him?" asked Evans.

"Because Marla was going to call the others to make it seem like a robbery, but something happened. I feel he's connected, like somehow he's running things. There's this woman named Angie, a stripper, she worked with Crissy. I know they got drugs from Wade," Jacey said. "I just feel like you need to talk to him first."

"He's like two hundred years old," Evans said. "What the hell is he gonna do? Besides, if kids are being trafficked, I have to tend to that first."

"That would alert him – and whoever else he's involved with," Jacey said.

"It wouldn't hurt to start with Wade, would it?" asked Shawnee.

"Okay, fine, but no one knows about what we talked about, got it?" Evans said. The women nodded.

"Thank you, Josh," Shawnee said.

"We'll come with you," Jacey said.

"No," he said. "Go on, now. I have some work to do before I go over there."

Jacey went home and paced around. She had a bad feeling that she couldn't shake. Something wasn't right. No shit, she thought to herself. But that wasn't it. She had a feeling that she had sent Evans into a trap.

Jacey grabbed the Book of Shadows and sat cross-legged on her bed and flipped through it. Besides the letter to her in the front, there were no other notes about her family or herself. There were spells, though. Jacey saw one for commanding lower entities, one for conjuring spirits, and one called Transference. Jacey noticed a piece of yellowed paper stuck between two pages near the end of the book. She pulled it out and unfolded it. She read: *Bound by the witch of fire, locked by the magician, you will be released only to the unholy sire.* Jacey also saw a name she didn't know. She folded the paper and without thinking put it in her pocket.

Jacey realized Marla and her friends were low-level practitioners. They either couldn't perform high magic, or they simply didn't know about it. Jacey got off the bed and walked downstairs.

This is all wrong, thought Jacey.

She fed Moon, then paused and put out extra food and water. She left the window open so Moon could climb in and out to use the bathroom.

"I'll be back. If I'm not back for a while, someone will come to look in on you," Jacey said. Moon stared at her, her tail swishing back and forth. She knew Jacey would be back, but that she would be hurt because she was going to see more bad people. But Moon knew Jacey would be okay. Moon heard the things in the woods; they were waiting, holding back. Moon waited, too.

JACEY THOUGHT ABOUT GOING TO SEE GWEN. WHAT IF THEY KNEW she had warned Jacey? What if they tried to hurt her? But Jacey thought better of it. She realized people were better off when she avoided them.

Jacey parked her car down the street from Wade's, hidden in a spot behind some trees. She walked through the brambles and high grass until she could see Wade's house. Jacey saw Evans come out the front door and leave in his patrol car.

Jacey realized she had forgotten about the dog, who was not chained up outside at the moment. She hoped he was in the house.

As if on cue, Wade came out and whistled, and the dog came running out. He stood with his head in the air, looking around.

Wade grabbed him by his collar and tied him up to the metal spike in the yard. The dog immediately began to bark, looking in the direction where Jacey was hiding.

"Shut up, you dumbass!" yelled Wade.

Wade walked back inside and slammed the door.

Jacey sidled along the side of the house, peering through the windows. It was no good. Even if the windows had not been covered with years of dust, thick curtains were shielding the glass on the inside. One window even had cardboard covering it.

Jacey wiped the sweat off of her face. She was suddenly nauseated from the oppressive heat and the musty smell of Wade's place and took a knee.

She heard a noise behind her, but before she could turn, she felt something heavy pressed against the back of her head. Jacey gasped and felt fear flood through her body.

"Get up." Jacey recognized the voice.

Jacey slowly stood up and turned around. Randy lowered the gun. He grinned and looked her up and down.

"Blondie, I swear you turn up in the funniest places." Randy chuckled and grabbed her arm. Jacey tried to wriggle away, but he tightened his grip and Jacey cried out in pain. He pulled her close to him.

He was right in her face. "If you do something dumb like that again, you won't walk out of here," he said. She smelled whisky and cigarettes on his breath, and she felt her stomach turn again.

"Let's go inside. Then I want some alone time with you," Randy said. His eyes were glazed, but he looked excited.

Morgan, Jacey thought. She sent the thought out to him, wherever he was. Jacey almost started crying.

Randy pushed her into the house. There was no air conditioning, but fans were blowing in all corners of the room, which made the heat slightly bearable.

"Keep walking to that door down the hall," Randy ordered.

Jacey arrived at a small door between the kitchen and a bedroom, and Randy told her to open it. She saw wooden stairs leading down to the basement.

"Walk, or I'll throw you down," Randy said.

Jacey carefully walked down the creaky, unstable steps. *Morgan, Morgan I need help*, Jacey screamed in her mind.

Jacey thought she heard a voice answer her back. It could be Morgan. Or it could be her desperation and fear. But in her mind she said, *I'm at Wade's, I think they'll kill me. Send someone.* Jacey smelled blood, dirt, and sweat. She looked around and saw an altar in the middle of the basement, which was surprisingly large in length and width. The altar was decorated with a pentagram and other symbols. There were unlit candles surrounding the altar, and in another corner was a dirty mattress on the cold dirt floor. Jacey went to the altar, studying the symbols on it. She saw dried blood on it.

"Take off your clothes," Randy said.

Jacey looked at him and shook her head.

"One way or another, you're getting naked. If I have to do it, then you'll probably get a broken nose or arm," he threatened.

Jacey looked at the gun he still held.

"Then I guess I get some broken bones," she said.

"I like it when they fight a little," Randy said.

He tucked the gun into his small holster and walked to Jacey and hit her hard across her face. She saw stars, but before she could fall, Randy threw her on the mattress. He tore at her shorts and got them unzipped and off with creepy speed.

Jacey felt herself going away, like she used to do. She could just float up and out of the room. But she stopped herself. No. Not this time.

"Morgan's going to kill you," she said.

Randy paused, then laughed. "Morgan ain't here, blondie, it's just you and me, for now," he said.

Jacey heard a loud bang and felt something hot spray against her face. Randy fell forward on top of her. She looked at him. His face was gone.

MORGAN EXCUSED HIMSELF FROM THE MEETING HE WAS IN AND stepped out into the hallway. He had heard Jacey's voice in his mind. He called her number, but it went straight to voicemail, and the recording told him the mailbox was full.

Morgan looked inside at the men in the office. Morgan's father got up and came out into the hallway.

He seemed upset, but the look on Morgan's face made his expression change to concern.

"Is everything okay?" asked William.

"I don't know. ... Well, no, everything is not okay, Dad," Morgan said.

"What is it?"

"I have to go, I have to go help someone, a woman, she's, well, I guess she's my girlfriend," he said. He wanted to laugh. A girlfriend – is that what she was? But as soon as he said the word, he realized how much he wanted it to be true.

William looked at him intensely. His voice was icy calm as he said, "Morgan, whatever is going on with your girlfriend can be handled after this meeting, I'm certain of that."

"No, it can't, she's in trouble, and I need to get on a plane right now. I'm so sorry, but I know you can handle it by yourself," Morgan said.

"A plane to where?" asked William.

"Home. She's from Poplar Hill."

William looked back into the room. The two men inside were waiting impatiently, looking at them through the office's glass doors.

"You know how I can feel things," Morgan said. "I'm telling you I have to go. Please understand."

"I don't like this. I have a bad feeling," William said.

"Me, too, but I have to go."

William planned to keep talking until he persuaded Morgan to come back inside, but he realized it was useless. Aside from himself, Morgan was the most stubborn person he had ever known.

"What can I do to help you?" he asked with a sigh.

Morgan thought about it. "It's best if I try to handle it alone," he replied.

William nodded. "Be safe, son."

Morgan walked back into the room with his father. "Gentlemen, my apologies, but an emergency has come up. My father will take it from here," Morgan said.

Morgan boarded a private plane on his way back to Knoxville, praying he wasn't too late.

Jacey finally squirmed out from under Randy. She was screaming and wiping blood off of her face.

Jacey scuttled across the basement floor. Randy's body was still, but he wasn't dead. It finally occurred to her that he had been shot. That's what the loud noise had been. Jacey's ears were still ringing.

She looked around to see who had shot Randy and saw Angie standing across the room at the bottom of the stairs.

Angie was staring at Randy as if she couldn't believe what she was seeing. Her mouth was open as if she was about to scream, but she could only moan as her chest heaved.

Jacey saw Randy's spirit leave his body. A strange grayish orb zig-zagged across the room, then a seam appeared in the fabric of the air in the room. The orb zigged and darted away from the rip in dimensions but was sucked in. Jacey looked away from it; she didn't want to see where he went.

The gun, a voice said in her mind.

Jacey crawled across the floor toward it.

"Don't do it, I'll shoot you," a man's voice said.

Jacey looked and saw Wade standing next to Angie. And there were two more men and an older woman standing behind Wade and Angie.

Jacey froze and watched as one of the men came over and got the gun out of Randy's pocket. Then he grabbed Jacey's arm and dragged her to the middle of the floor. She was sitting on the pentagram drawn into the concrete.

Wade slowly walked to Jacey and stood over her. He suddenly seemed so much stronger. Jacey was afraid, but she sensed it was more than that. The death of Randy, of Crissy, of her fear, it fueled them.

Jacey tried to calm herself. She didn't want them feeding off her like vampires. *They*, she realized. She looked at the people standing behind Wade. She recognized Marla among them. She had never seen the others, or maybe she had when she was a child but had forgotten, but she knew they were the ones from Gwen's story. Jacey prayed that Gwen was okay, then tried to stop thinking of her, lest one of these devils picked up on Jacey's thoughts.

Jacey looked up at Wade. "What are you going to do?" she asked.

"After dark, we will start the ritual," he replied.

"What ritual?"

"You'll know then. You already know, you just don't see – not yet, anyway," he said.

"See what?" Jacey asked. She was crying. She couldn't help it.

"Your purpose," Wade said. He sounded stronger and more cultured, too. His accent was barely detectable.

Jacey looked at Angie. "You think it will stop with me? They will come after you and then your child, you stupid bitch," Jacey said.

Angie kneeled in front of Jacey. "I'm a little disappointed you didn't recognize your own blood," Angie said.

"What are you talking about?" screamed Jacey. But suddenly she knew. The eyes, her eyes. Jacey had known, but as the old devil said, she had refused to see.

"We met last in the parlor of the beautiful house, the home my relative – your grandfather – lived in, that your lineage came from. I needed a body on short notice, and she was easy. I'll have another soon enough," Angie said.

"That's enough, we still have to prepare," Wade said.

Angie looked at Wade, clearly ready to go now, but she deferred. Wade motioned, and the two men wrapped a blanket around Randy's head and dragged his body out of the basement into a room.

Angie's eyes flashed with momentary disappointment. "Angie enjoyed their carnal interactions, but he was stupid," she said and left with the others.

Jacey was alone in the dark basement. She tried the door where they had dragged Randy, but it was locked. She sat down on the floor, pulling her knees to her chest. She looked and saw a small window well. She would never fit through it. Jacey's eyes adjusted to the darkness, and she stared at the symbol drawn on the floor. Then she realized she had a lighter in her pocket.

She used the flame to study the symbols. She had never seen them, but she knew what they were used for: to call up lower-level entities and demons.

Jacey took her thumb off the lighter and sat in the darkness again.

They were low-level dabblers, but she knew her great-aunt was not. She would know this was child's play, that no real magic could be summoned through them, so she was helping them. Why? Why would she need to be here now? Why had she gone into Angie and not Jacey? *Because I'm too strong*, thought Jacey. *And now I'm the sacrifice, but for what?* Jacey realized the reasons didn't matter right now – she had to get out.

Jacey looked to her left and saw a shape move out of the shadows. Jacey flicked her lighter. It was a hound. But it looked stunted and malformed, like a dinosaur that had not survived its gestation. Its head was enormous, and its body was squat and had matted black fur. The eyes were two black marbles, shining with dumb malice. Jacey closed her eyes and waited.

CHAPTER 21

As soon as Morgan got off the plane, he rushed to his car and sped out of the garage at breakneck speed.

As he got on the interstate, the sun was going down in an enormous mass of red fire. Morgan normally would have taken time to admire such a thing, but he was too focused on smoothly weaving in and out of lanes to keep his speed.

When he got into Poplar Hill, he made a stop at his house, quickly changing clothes and grabbing his weapons. He stopped to listen for Jacey, to connect with her as he had in Houston, but he didn't hear or feel anything. Morgan felt panic trying to overtake him, but he shoved it aside.

He drove to Jacey's house and parked. He sat for a moment, listening. Morgan knew she wasn't here, but he felt that by being here, he could somehow find a way to tap into where she was.

Moon came bounding down the staircase as Morgan walked in. She meowed shrilly and pawed at Morgan's legs. He picked her up and tried to soothe her.

She looked into Morgan's eyes and yowled again, then leaped out of his arms and raced into the parlor. Morgan followed, and she jumped up on the small table at the foot of the velvet sofa. Moon pawed at a picture, looking desperately at Morgan. Morgan picked up the picture and saw it was a photo of Jacey and Crissy when they were teenagers. Jacey looked different. Her hair was cut in a bob, she had bangs, and there were clips placed throughout her hair. Morgan remembered Jacey telling him about how one night Crissy and Jacey had gone with two boys to Wade's to buy alcohol and weed, but she had not told the whole story, and Morgan remembered how Jacey's face had gotten sad and her whole body seemed to be shrinking from the memory.

Morgan placed the picture back where it had been. Then he bent down and petted Moon's fur. "Good girl," he said. "I'll be back. With her."

Moon was happy the man, her human father, had come back to save her mother. Moon raced back up the stairs to the open window. Moon heard her mother – she was in pain and afraid – but Moon also felt the stirring. Her mother's power was getting stronger, and soon she would know what to do. Moon watched out the open bedroom window and heard the things in the forest speak. Moon watched as her father's heavenly night descended, and unseen evil things ascended.

JACEY WATCHED AS THE HELLHOUND APPROACHED HER. HER FIRST instinct was to banish it, but she realized she could use it to her advantage. The thing appeared to be almost blind, its enormous head bobbing up and down as it moved toward her.

"By my hand, yield until such time as called upon," Jacey said.

THE DEAD BORN

The hound paused and began to look around the room. Jacey felt the presences waiting, waiting to be called forth.

Suddenly she heard the basement door open, and a shaft of light from above the stairs made Jacey squint.

"I command these entities to be staved by my hand until I call upon you to serve," Jacey whispered.

The hound disappeared, and the shadows retreated as the people came down the stairs. Jacey saw Wade, Angie, Marla, another man and woman, the woman who had accosted Gwen, and two more young men and women that Jacey did not know.

The two younger women came toward Jacey and tried to drag her out of her corner. Jacey initially struggled against them, but a voice told her to go limp and appear docile.

They dragged her to the symbol drawn into the middle of the floor. Jacey lay there, staring up as they lit candles and stood in a circle around her. She suddenly noticed they were wearing robes, and as if on cue, they took off the black robes and stood naked around Jacey.

Jacey saw they had drawn symbols on themselves. *For protection, from you,* she heard her voice whisper to her in her mind.

"No infants to sacrifice this time, you sick fucks?" asked Jacey.

"We finally have what we need," Angie said.

"What are you talking about? Me? I'm not that powerful," Jacey said.

"You are, you are my blood, and now our blood has finally mixed with someone just as powerful. It's fate, and now here we are, he can finally come through," Angie said.

"Who can come through? Why?"

"Your grandfather, newly born in dark blood as Baphomet, who is in essence a combination of different souls. He has been many people, and now he comes here tonight," Angie said.

"But why?" Jacey asked.

"To rule over this Earth, as has always been the goal since time immemorial, to usher in a new age, an age where there is total dominion," Angie said.

"Enough talking, we have to do this now," Wade interrupted.

"So you would kill your own blood?" Jacey asked, ignoring him.

"You were meant for this, and so was your baby," Angie said.

"I don't have a baby—" Jacey said, then realized how stupid she had been. Of course: Morgan. The times they had been together they hadn't used protection, and Jacey wasn't on birth control. She was pregnant. The voice in her mind, the sensing of her powers being magnified. Once again, Jacey had seen but had not seen.

"There's no way you can do anything – I can't be more than a few weeks along. She's not even formed, really, no soul to take," Jacey said. Jacey began to cry at her slip. The mass of cells was a girl, she knew it.

"And what are you but a formation of cells, connected by DNA sequence? A soul imbued into you, as all living things. And the child is powerful already, and yes, she has a soul, which belongs to us now. She is the portal, created by the merging of light and dark," Angie said.

"I'll kill her before I let you take her. At least that way she will go to heaven," Jacey said.

"No, you won't, you love her too much. And you love him too much to destroy what you created with him," Angie said.

Two men knelt and held her arms while the others took off the rest of her clothes. Jacey screamed and struggled. Someone slapped her in the face, and she stopped yelling. They stripped her naked and bound her wrists and ankles to the stakes driven into the floor.

Angie came forward and began to whisper in a language Jacey did not know.

They surrounded Jacey, their hands placed upon her belly, chanting the incantations. Jacey felt her body begin to tingle. Then she watched in horror as her stomach began to swell, ever so slightly at first. Jacey watched in amazed horror as her stomach began expanding even more. She felt pain, but more than anything, part of her was fascinated.

She felt hands rubbing her breasts, and hands rubbing between her legs. She cried out and tried not to let the sensations overwhelm her. Suddenly a thought brought her out of the disgusting pleasure of the ritual: They will do this to your daughter, then they will kill her.

Jacey quieted her mind and said: "Now, by my hand come forth, entities of hell, bound spirits, hounds of demons, lost and vengeful souls, departed ancestors. Kill these who try to harm me, by the power of my bloodline, do my bidding."

The air turned static, and Jacey watched as they stood and looked around, angered over being interrupted.

"She has called on lower entities," Angie said.

Jacey watched as the hellhound appeared and latched onto a man's throat, tore it open, and lapped at his blood.

Demonic shadow figures shrieked and flew around the room. They were chaotic and not of much help; the symbols the people had painted on their bodies had blocked their power.

"Demon spirit, invigorate dead bones," Jacey commanded. She heard the corpse of Randy, reanimated through her power, banging against the door, trying to get through.

Jacey whispered in her mind to her unborn child, who she already had named after a heroine from her book: "Adelaide, if you can, help, use your power," Jacey said.

Jacey looked down at her belly. She appeared to be about five months pregnant. She felt movement, and a nimbus hovered over her belly where Adelaide collected her power.

Angie was standing over Jacey, looking at the nimbus. Jacey could tell her great-aunt had left her body, and she saw the terror in the real Angie's eyes. She watched as the hellhound fed on the one man, and saw the others were backed into a corner, watching as the demons encroached on them.

"Loosen my bonds," Jacey said. Jacey watched as some of the shadows began to hover over the ropes binding her hands. Nothing happened. Apparently, they couldn't do something as simple as untie ropes.

"Angie, untie me before she comes back in you. It's the only way out for you," Jacey said.

Jacey saw the shadows and the hellhounds disappear, and suddenly Wade was standing over her.

"You have more power than I thought, but you are amateur; you don't know how to keep them bound," he said.

Wade brought the knife to Jacey's belly. Jacey screamed and her fear blotted out everything, he was going to slice her open and take Adelaide. Angie tried to grab the knife from Wade and almost got it, but he slipped out of her clumsy grip. Wade sliced Angie across the throat, and Angie fell over, gurgling and writhing.

The rest of the group looked at Angie and then formed another circle around Jacey, chanting, and Jacey watched as Wade prepared to slice open her stomach.

Suddenly a hole appeared in Wade's forehead. He dropped the knife and fell over.

Jacey turned her head as far as she could toward the stairs and saw Morgan coming down, his gun firing. One by one he shot the cult members, and they crumpled to the floor.

He came silently down the steps and found the light switch. After he cleared the room, he turned his attention to Jacey. His eyes were wide and stunned as he looked at her on the altar. Morgan stared at her belly in disbelief. Then he mechanically walked to her and untied the ropes.

Morgan found a discarded robe and was about to put it over Jacey's naked body, then thought better of it. He took off his button-up shirt, lifted Jacey, and helped her put on the shirt.

"I think she's dying," Jacey said tearfully.

Morgan put his hand on Jacey's belly. He saw blood on her thighs.

"I'll take you to a hospital," he said.

"No, we have to go home," Jacey said.

Morgan almost protested, but he knew there was no way a baby could survive after such a short term in utero. Despite any God-forsaken magic that was going on here. He glanced at the people he had killed and wished he could kill them again, except slowly. Take out their insides and cram them down their disgusting throats.

"She's already going, I can feel it," Jacey said. "Please, Morgan, we may be able to help her there, trust me."

Morgan picked up his woman, who was carrying his dying daughter inside her, and carried them both up the steps.

PART 3

THE DEAD BORN

CHAPTER 22

Morgan carried Jacey down to the tree as she had asked. He felt blood coming from between her legs.

Morgan positioned Jacey so she was propped against the tree. She was as pale as a ghost, and Morgan felt fear shoot through his body.

"Whatever you're gonna do, do it now. I won't wait much longer. I can't, Jacey, you're losing too much blood," he said.

Jacey looked at him. Her eyes were too big in her pale face. "I love you," she said.

Morgan took her face in his hands and kissed her. He fought back tears. He had never felt love for anyone, not really, not like this. But this was something more than love; it was as if his very soul had been ripped apart and put back together by her.

"I love you," he told her.

Jacey braced herself as the cramp clenched her abdomen. Her belly felt like it was made of cement. Then the cramp cascaded down and she felt more blood gush from between her legs. Jacey put her hand between her legs. The blood was dark red, and it smelled like pennies. She turned her head and vomited into the corner. She wiped her mouth, forgetting she had blood on her hands.

Blood on her hands. No denying that.

Jacey sat down, riding the waves of the cramps. She curled her legs into her body, laying down in a fetal position.

Jacey rolled over on her back, staring up at the stars. She whispered to the trees, to the sky, to the forces she felt coalescing around her.

"Adelaide, please hold on. I will try something to help you, please don't go," Jacey said.

A cramp gripped her whole body, and she screamed into the darkness, then made herself sit back up and leaned against the tree. She bent forward, looking at the red puddle between her legs.

"Oh, my God," Morgan said. He reached between Jacey's legs and cupped their daughter. The moonlight shone down on Adelaide, who was no bigger than Morgan's hand. He held her gently, crying, and he held her close to his face and kissed her.

"Give her to me," Jacey said. Morgan placed Adelaide in Jacey's cupped hands. Jacey saw an outline of formed eyes, a mouth, and the beginning formations of hands clasped together. Jacey howled in pain and rage.

She looked at the man figure standing above her. He looked impossibly neat and dapper in his wool suit. He was not handsome or ugly – his face seemed to be constantly melting and morphing into different people as if it was trying to decide on just the right face to torture her with.

She closed her eyes and waited a few seconds. She opened them. He was still there.

"You see now that you can't run? That for some, their destiny is determined before they are even born." It spoke clearly and softly, but his voice was melodically sinister. "You were doomed the moment you were born, and nothing can change that."

Morgan couldn't see the man, but he felt a presence, a presence of pure evil.

"You're a liar," Jacey said.

"Does it look like you have escaped your fate?" it asked. "You're bleeding to death in the dirt, your dead child in the dirt with you. That is your punishment for keeping her from me."

"I watched you die," Jacey told it. "I watched you get put in the ground, I made sure you were dead."

He stared at her, a deep relentless, hungry stare, and his black eyes seemed to glow from his seamless face.

Jacey kissed Adelaide and cupped her in her hands. "I'm so sorry, my sweet girl," she said.

Jacey saw Moon sitting in the grass beside her. Jacey watched as a strange glowing circle of light appeared around her, Morgan, and the cat. She saw a young girl standing in the middle of the circle, facing them. The girl had Morgan's features, his good bone structure, and his big, strange hazel-gold eyes that seemed to change color. Her hair was the same wavy dark blond as Jacey's. She looked to be about ten years old.

"Adelaide," Jacey whispered.

As Jacey looked, Adelaide dissolved, then reappeared as a toddler. Then she transformed into a teenager, tall and lithe, then she was around Jacey's age. Then she was an old woman, but still beautiful. Jacey was weeping, begging her to stop. She couldn't watch her own daughter grow up like that. Jacey closed her eyes and wailed in pain.

"Mommy, look at me, we don't have much time," said the voice, soft and feminine.

Jacey looked up and saw Adelaide was a small child again, as if she knew Jacey would be happy with that version.

Adelaide beckoned her parents forward.

Jacey felt another cramp and looked down. There was more blood dripping from between her legs, and it splattered on her bare feet.

Adelaide looked down, but only for a second. She pointed and began to walk, taking Jacey's hand. Jacey followed, Morgan holding her up, his arms around her. Moon streaked across their path and stood aside looking at them, her eyes glowing in the darkness, then followed alongside them.

Jacey and Morgan followed Adelaide past the garden, then past the barn and old servant's quarters. They went over the first swell of the hill and past the pond. The moonlight lit their path, and it was almost as bright as daylight.

They came to the persimmon tree and stopped.

Adelaide said nothing, just stared at the tree. Jacey knelt next to her, touching her hair and her face. Adelaide let her, but she only looked at her, not menacing or happy, just patiently enduring her mother's affections.

Adelaide's eyes were so beautiful, intense, and enchanting, just like Morgan's. Jacey swooned and almost fell over; she pitched her hand forward to steady herself. Adelaide looked at her like someone who was watching fish swim around in a tank.

"Adelaide, why are we here?" Jacey asked her.

"This is where they are, the other children," she said.

"What?" Jacey asked.

"The others that your visitor Gwen told you about, they are here, they buried them next to the consecrated ground as a cruel joke. You need their help," she said.

"They're demons. Why would I want their help?"

"No, they are only lost souls, like me, and you must help them and they will help you. They must be banished," Adelaide said.

"I don't care anymore. I just want to be with you. I don't care about anything else. Just take me with you," Jacey said through tears.

"It doesn't work like that, Mommy," she said.

"What do you mean?" Jacey screamed. She beat her hands against the ground. "Let them have the damned place, they can have it all. I don't want it! Let them keep killing and raping and slaughtering until the ground is soaked with blood, and God finally has enough and casts them all back into darkness!"

She looked at Adelaide, pleading. "Just take me with you," Jacey whispered. She fell to her knees and hugged her.

"No, Mommy, it's not your time yet. If you go now, we will not be together. I have been sent back to make sure that you do what you are meant to do," her daughter said. "You must be reborn, you must not live in darkness anymore. There is a power greater than anything you can comprehend. You must break the chains."

Jacey saw ten small figures standing under the tree. She watched as they moved toward her and slowly formed a circle around her. The haze of humidity had formed a ground fog, and Jacey struggled to make out what she was seeing. They were about the same height as toddlers, and their bodies were misshapen and their arms elongated. Their heads were bulbous, and they lurched forward. She saw one of them open its mouth to reveal needle-like fangs. Their eyes glowed the color of milky quartz with a horrible yellowish glint glowing from behind.

"Adelaide?" Jacey could barely manage a whisper. She heard Moon yowl into the night, and it broke Jacey's heart.

"Mommy," Adelaide said.

Jacey looked up and saw Adelaide standing above her. Next to Adelaide was Jacey's mother.

"Momma," Jacey said.

"You will be all right, Mommy. But you have to see and hear," Adelaide said.

Jacey saw them surround her, the poroniecs, the unborn who had become devils through no fault of their own. The hideous things loomed over Jacey, looking with ferocity and hunger. Their bodies twisted and their eyes glowed.

"No!" Jacey said, her voice cracking. She tried to push herself up. To try to reason with them. They didn't know how scared she was.

"Mommy, please," Adelaide said. Adelaide looked at her grandmother with pleading eyes.

"Jacey, you must do this, to save us and yourself. Lie quietly. It's not fair that this falls on you, but it's how it must be," Jacey's mother said.

Three generations of women here, all dead but me, thought Jacey.

She laid still, as her mother had said.

Soon she was lifted off the ground. At first, she thought it was her soul lifting out of her physical form, but she turned her head and looked down at the spot where she had been lying. She saw a puddle of blood, and she was not there. Her mother and Adelaide were still there, this time looking up at her. Moon had stopped yowling and also was watching Jacey float.

Jacey realized her arms were stretched out on either side, so she was in the shape of a cross, and she felt herself being pushed down. She couldn't describe it any other way.

She went away, that was all she could comprehend. She felt herself being hurled to a place that was dark on the ground and above filled with stars, comets, and unknown planets. She saw her mother's soul, and then the demon, and she knew this was their battle. The poroniecs would help her fight, they were part of her.

Jacey looked around. It was indescribable. It was once a beautiful place, but now it was absent of any real light. There was no noise, only a silence that was in itself so profound that it was deafening. It was at the end of the universe, the wastelands. There was no sense of placement or up or down, or gravity, or matter.

Jacey watched as she was surrounded by demons. Her mother was near, and she struggled to keep the connection. She felt her mother's anguish, though. It hurt her to be here. But Jacey felt the poroniecs tell her she was needed right now.

The spirits gathered, and a humming sound reverberated around them. The spirits were not monstrous, as she thought they would be. Instead, they looked like they were past-their-prime beautiful beings, former angels.

As if to prove her wrong, Jacey saw more emerge from all corners, and these were the grunts, the bottom-dwelling demons. They resembled aliens more than any gothic artist's rendering. Their eyes glowed red and orange, and some were a sickly green.

Adelaide was in the middle of the circle they had formed. Her soul was being pulled by the demons who fought to keep her and Jacey, who was trying to help her daughter get out of there. Anywhere was better than here, because she would only be turned into one of the demons cursed to do the bidding of evil people.

Everything went dark. Then Jacey realized her eyes were closed, too. She opened them. It was dark out, and the moon was higher in the night sky. She saw Morgan digging a hole to bury Adelaide.

The ritual, a voice spoke to her. *You are a soul guide, a between-worlds wanderer. It is your destiny. These rituals are imbued in your blood by the ancestors who were good and pure, but you must choose them, they cannot help if you do not ask.*

Jacey kissed Adelaide and began to hum.

She realized it was an old hymn from childhood. She began to recite the words, which came from the deepest part of her memory.

> *Abide with me, fast falls the eventide*
>   *The darkness deepens, Lord, with me abide*
>   *When other helpers fail and comforts flee*
>   *Help of the helpless, oh, abide with me*

Swift to its close ebbs out life's little day
  Earth's joys grow dim, its glories pass away
  Change and decay in all around I see
  O Thou who changest not, abide with me

Jacey laid Adelaide next to the grave.

Behold, this soul. Release from the darkness, release from the dark angel. Behold this child's soul. Take it into your kingdom, Father. All the faithful departed, aid her on the journey.

Release these souls, I pray, release from the fallen ones, beckon them into the light, and enfold them.

"Morgan, you have to bury her, I can't do it. Please …" Jacey's voice reached him through his fog of grief, and he got up and placed Adelaide in the grave. He didn't look in the grave, didn't hear the dirt piling over his daughter. Instead, he focused on the task until he finished, then patted down the dirt.

Morgan gripped his head with both of his hands. *I'm going to go insane*, he thought. He felt like his soul and his heart were ripped out of him. Part of him wanted to remain here with Adelaide, to kill Jacey and then himself so they could all be together.

Moon meowed shrilly at him.

Morgan looked up and saw Jacey. She's unconscious again. He scooped her up and looked at Moon. "Come on, honey," he said.

CHAPTER 23

The sunshine felt good on Jacey's face. It was October, and it was still relatively warm. She had a light blanket over her legs and feet, and she sat cross-legged in the chair. She looked out into the yard and saw Morgan's motorcycle. He wanted to take her on a drive later. She felt well enough to go. She no longer felt soreness and aching from the miscarriage. Morgan still called it an accident, and Jacey let it go for now. He was healing, too.

Shawnee had just left. She visited Jacey almost every day now. Shawnee had brought Ben with her this time, and Ben seemed to be a happy, normal child, despite everything that happened. Mark and Shawnee were going through the process of adopting Ben, and Jacey knew they would be wonderful parents. The old Jacey would have felt jealous of Shawnee's new family, but now she felt only contentment for her old friend. It was meant to be, after all.

Jacey tried to be thankful. *Yes, a new me*, she thought. She almost believed it this time.

After Morgan and Jacey had buried Adelaide, Morgan took Jacey to the hospital. Jacey was physically fine, and when she went to a follow-up appointment with the OB/GYN, the doctor told her she was healing normally and could even try to have more children in a couple of months if she wanted.

Jacey had said nothing back to the doctor, only thanked her and went home, not telling Morgan about the appointment.

Morgan had kept the events as quiet as possible. His father had gone a long way to ensure that, but Jacey knew Morgan had a hand in that as well. She still didn't know who and what he was capable of, but she trusted him.

Not long after everything, Morgan burned down Wade's place and everything in it. The last things to burn had been Jacey's great-aunt's ashes and the wretched Book of Shadows when he tossed them into the embers.

Jacey sent a glad thought out to him. A fire burned in her, too, a cleansing fire. *Come, Holy Spirit, enkindle in me the fire of your love.*

Moon patted her hand with her paw, then nimbly leaped onto Jacey's lap. She nuzzled Jacey's face, then circled and lay down.

The other day, Jacey visited Adelaide's grave. Moon was sitting in front of it, her ears perked and staring at the spot. Jacey had found out from Morgan that Moon visited it every day. Jacey knew he went every day, too, usually right before sunset. Morgan had even ordered a marker for Adelaide's spot. He had asked Jacey about it, but Jacey had walked away without answering.

Jacey lightly petted Moon as she slept. Jacey didn't know what to do with this knowledge, but like most things lately, she stored it away, not wanting to deal with any of it just yet. Jacey fell asleep, grateful for the sun.

On Halloween, Jacey bought a load of pumpkins and hauled them back in Morgan's truck. She and Shawnee and Ben carved the pumpkins, going for happy faces instead of scary ones. Jacey usually loved Halloween, but she felt a sense of dread at the thought

THE DEAD BORN

of celebrating it after what she had seen. She kept thinking about how she would never be able to make a costume for Adelaide, or how her daughter would never be able to trick or treat, or run through a pumpkin patch, or dance as the leaves fell from the trees in a blaze of technicolor reds and yellows.

It also was Jacey's birthday, and she declined the offer to go trick-or-treating with Shawnee, Mark, and Ben, then a late dinner after. As Shawnee was leaving, she gave Jacey a gift box wrapped with a large satin ribbon. After Shawnee was gone, Jacey opened it. It was a picture of Jacey and Shawnee. The girls had their arms around each other, smiling and posing, a moment of childhood joy and happiness captured. Jacey suddenly remembered that her mother had snapped the picture on Jacey's tenth birthday. The picture had been blown up and corrected for clarity, and it was in a beautiful frame. Jacey touched the picture and smiled. She would hang it later, next to the large window across from her desk.

She felt Morgan walk into the room. "Beautiful picture," he said.

"Yes. I thought I would hang it next to the window – what do you think?" she asked.

"I'll hang it for you," he said.

He walked to Jacey, and she thought he was going to take the picture, but he knelt and held out a box. Jacey took it mechanically and opened it. It was the most beautiful engagement ring she had ever seen. Jacey let Morgan slip the ring on her left hand.

"I hope you … I love you, Jacey. Will you marry me?" Morgan asked. He looked up at her, studying her face. He didn't seem surprised at Jacey's blank face and the heavy silence.

"Where will we live?" she asked.

"Wherever you want."

"I don't know," Jacey said. She paused. "I feel like I've been trying to fix the past, and somehow do things over, and I feel like maybe I'm fooling myself. I'm not the same person I was this summer. I feel like I'm finally ready to be what I was supposed to be."

She looked at him.

"Does that make any sense?" she asked.

"I don't know," Morgan replied.

"What do you want?" Jacey asked.

"I want a normal life," he said.

"You won't get that with me."

"And what do you want?" he asked.

Jacey glanced at the engagement ring. She thought about the question. "Please, stand up now," she said as gently as she could manage.

"For as long as I can remember, I have felt like I was a product of something. Reacting to events and people. I feel like I'm supposed to be the creator of ... something. I don't know what yet, but I do know I need to be alone to figure it out." She looked away. She couldn't look at him right now. She felt sad. But the more dominant emotion she felt was resolve. For once, a determination, a knowing that she was right.

"Alone?" he asked.

"I love you. I will never stop loving you, ever," she said. She took his hand. "I want to be with you, I do want to marry you, and–" She wanted to say *have children with you*, but was that even possible?

"I just need to be alone, here," she continued. "For a while. I don't even know if I will keep the farm. Maybe it's time to let it go. ... I need to be alone because when I see you, I see her. I see things that won't ever be. I see all the things that were taken away. I see all that I had wrapped up in you, in this fantasy, this dream, this ideal person." She paused. "I want all that you represent, but I also feel ... anger toward you. I pinned all my hopes on you, and that was wrong."

THE DEAD BORN

Jacey stopped talking. She wanted to tell him that it was more than anger, that part of her hated him. For the child that was lost, for getting her hopes up, for making her believe she could have a normal life.

The silence hung like a heavy stone, and then Morgan walked away. He paused after a few steps.

"You're wrong about one thing: Your purpose isn't to be with them, to die with them. I hope you see that soon," he said.

Jacey went to him. He wouldn't make eye contact with her, and she touched his face. She felt love for him, but it was deep down, buried like her daughter.

"I'm so sorry," she said.

"Me, too," he said. "She was my daughter, too, you know. I feel what you're feeling, maybe not the same, but I will never forgive myself for not protecting you, for not protecting her."

Morgan finally looked at Jacey. "And now you want me to leave you again."

"Yes," Jacey said.

Morgan nodded. Jacey tried to kiss him, but he pulled away. "I'm going to London for business. I had put it off, now I think I'm going to go," he said.

"That will be good for you, I think," she said. Morgan went to the door. "Morgan?"

"Yes?" said Morgan, turning to her.

"What is my purpose? What's yours? Do you know?" she asked.

Morgan thought about it.

"To change … to become … I don't know what. But I know it's not over, and I know you were born here for a reason, that we came together for a reason. This place …" Morgan paused and looked around the house. "This house, this land, it's part of it, part of us both now. Maybe my part is done, God only knows."

Jacey grabbed his arm. She looked into his strange eyes. "Tonight is a vigil for souls. She is in heaven. Ask her to pray for us, and for me, for mine, for all of us," Jacey said.

"I know she is, but what do you mean pray for 'mine'?" he asked.

"I don't know, I can't explain it," she said and turned away.

Morgan stared at her for a beat. "I've never met someone so hell-bent on destroying herself. I hope you find the answers. Maybe they are in that Bible of yours. Be safe, Jacey." And then he was gone.

"Only God knows," she whispered to the empty house.

Jacey walked outside, looking at her pumpkins lining the sidewalk. The leaves were blowing about in the blustery wind, and a full moon shone its haunting beauty on the land. Jacey sat down, wrapping the sweater around her and sinking her bare feet into the grass. She listened as the wind and trees sang to her, as the voices of souls spoke to her. They were so loud that she wondered how God could stand it. But she held vigil anyway.

CHAPTER 24

Et Verbum caro factum est. Et habitavit in nobis

Jacey sat at her laptop. She typed "The End" and saved the file. She had been working on the book since Morgan had left. She had not seen him since then, making sure she was gone on one of her walks when he came to get some of his things before he left for his trip. Thanksgiving had come and gone. Jacey had turned down invitations for Thanksgiving dinner from Shawnee, Ashley, and Corey. They all accepted her answer with no arguments. They understood she was healing and wanted to grieve alone. Shawnee dropped off a plate of food for her on Thanksgiving night. Jacey ate it on her couch, staring at the fire she had built, sharing bites of turkey and potatoes with Moon.

As December came, she had a schedule down: Get up, bundle up in a hat and warm clothes, go for a long walk in the woods behind her house, shower, and write. When it got dark, she would let Moon in and feed her and build a fire. Jacey would work until ten, then sit by the fire to unwind, and then go to bed. She was always so tired, she rarely dreamed. But she had begun to pray before she went to sleep. Sometimes the words came, but usually, she sat in silence. Waiting to feel or hear something from Him. But nothing.

She stopped drinking and smoking; she didn't want them now. And she had no visions or visitors. It was as if the universe was leaving her alone to finish her book.

Her book. It was unlike anything she had ever written. She knew it came from her, but sometimes she felt she was a vessel for some being that was using her hands to type words she had never even thought of before.

Now and then the Seer would pop up unexplainably. Not to help her see, but to show herself to Jacey. Jacey noticed that she was happy to look at her, but she didn't need her right now. The mewling thing inside no longer stirred because it was gone. Maybe it had somehow been ripped out of her, like her daughter. Maybe Adelaide had taken the thing with her as a consolation gift to Jacey. Only God knew. And this angered Jacey.

Jacey looked at the file saved on her laptop, then reopened it. She knew the name of the book. Jacey typed: *Blood Saints*. She emailed the book to her agent, with a page of notes about the book. She also emailed the file to herself as a backup.

There was a knock at the door. Jacey opened it and saw Bill Montgomery on her porch. He wore a thick jacket and a gray wool hat. He smiled nervously at Jacey.

"It's Christmas Eve, I should have called first," he said.

"No, please, come in, Bill," Jacey said.

Jacey hung up his coat and hat and motioned him to sit in the parlor. Bill and Jacey sat on the new couch, a deep-blue velvet sofa that Jacey had ordered.

"I was just going to make some tea – would you like some?" asked Jacey.

"No, thank you," Bill said. "Look, Jacey, I just wanted to come by and tell you that I ... well, that I missed you. I came by once before, not long after all that happened, but Morgan was here, I didn't want to cause any problems."

"You're a friend, Bill. I don't see how that would cause any problems," Jacey said.

"I thought we were more than that, or at least I hoped we would be, but I guess I can live with being a friend," he said. He noticed Jacey's left hand. Jacey saw he was looking at the engagement ring.

"It's complicated," Jacey said.

"Morgan isn't here with you?"

"No, he left. I wanted him to. ... I needed to be alone."

"You're engaged, but you want to be alone?" he asked.

"Like I said, it's complicated," Jacey said.

"What the hell happened this summer? I heard some things, mostly from Josh. I heard about Wade's house. That Wade and this other lady and Crissy's aunt were in some weird satanic cult, and that Wade killed them, then himself, in a ritual gone bad. Do you know anything?"

"I know as much as you do, Bill," she said.

"Yeah, right." He stood up and looked at the parlor fireplace. "You know, I saw the bones in the fireplace that day, when we came to get Ella. They were human. Infant bones, actually."

"I know that now," Jacey said.

"Then it's true – your family was involved in ritual abuse, witchcraft," he said.

"Only the two of them, I'm pretty certain of that."

"What about your brother? Did this have anything to do with what happened to him?" asked Bill.

"Yes and no. Yes in terms of the cycle of abuse and evil influencing everything and everyone around him, but no in regards to actual satanic rituals, but I don't know for sure. I don't remember, but maybe he saw something ..." Jacey trailed off as she had a flash of a memory: kneeling behind a shed, peering at their grandfather and a group of men standing in a circle, a knife, a lamb. Blood pooling around the lamb's white fur.

Bill stared at Jacey, then walked back and sat next to her. He took her hand. "Jacey, I think you need to get away from here, leave and go somewhere, a vacation, or maybe not even come back."

Again, Jacey found herself almost drunk with the affection Bill had for her. She felt it wash over her, and she knew he was almost powerless when he was around her. That deep-down sinister drive bubbled up in her: How far could she make him go for her?

"You want me to go?" she asked.

Bill looked down. "No, I want you to stay, more than anything. But I know you are not safe here," he said. He met her eyes again. "I would never have left you here alone."

Jacey had a flash of an image, a knife going across Bill's throat; another lamb being slaughtered. She pictured taking Bill upstairs, getting on top of him, fucking him, controlling him, locking him in a spell of lust until he was a servile heap of desire and helplessness.

Jacey stood up. "I'm tired, Bill, I need a nap," she said. "Thank you for everything you have done. I want you to go now, please."

Bill got his coat and hat. "Did you ever wonder if there were more of them doing this?"

"I know there are more. Goodnight, Bill," she said.

"Merry Christmas, Jacey," he said.

JACEY VISITED ADELAIDE'S GRAVE AS IT WAS BEGINNING TO SNOW. SHE watched as the flakes touched the cold ground, already creating a thin carpet of white. She looked up at the sky. The gray was merging with the cold and damp air, becoming a swirling cosmos of white. The snowflakes landed in her eyes until she had to close them. She pictured lifeless eyes, snow falling into them until they filled up with tiny drifts of snow. Unmoving and still.

She wiped away the tears. She couldn't see Adelaide's spot anymore. It was already covered by the snow, which was falling harder than ever. She shifted the pack on her back and began to walk to the woods. The only sounds were her breathing and her footsteps crunching through the snow.

She found a copse of small pine trees. She walked to the one she liked. It stood almost exactly her height and was just full enough. She dropped the bag she carried and stood close to the tree, breathing in the scent of the pine needles. She gathered up some pinecones that had fallen from the larger trees, her hands cold and fumbling with them as she filled her bag. Then she put on her gloves and got out the small ax and began to chop at the base of her tree. She swung and missed her mark a few times, but finally, she got the hang of it.

She smelled the open wound of the bark and the meat of the wood; it was almost minty and mixed with a sweet aroma, probably what woodland spirits smelled like. Finally, she cut almost through, then pushed with her foot until the tree fell. She put away the ax and grabbed the tree by the cut end and dragged it through the snow.

She had to stop and rest. The air was so cold it burned her throat, and the snow was falling faster. She went on. The wind moaned and swept the new-fallen snow up into white bursts. She heard a scream behind her. She stopped and looked around. She saw only white. Jacey thought about staying out here in the cold and the endless white. "These are my woods," she said aloud, then whispered, "Adelaide."

When Jacey got home with the tree, she kicked the snow off it, dragged it onto the porch, and propped it against the house.

She opened the front door and Moon streaked out to greet her, pawing her pants and sniffing her. She walked to the tree and sniffed it.

"It's our tree," Jacey told her.

She changed into a thick sweater, fleece leggings, and wool socks and padded back downstairs. She saw the wood stacked next to the fireplace. Morgan had chopped it. She remembered him telling her he wanted to build fires all winter. She felt a twinge of guilt. Mostly at the fact that she was happy to be alone.

She placed some logs into the fireplace and made sure the vent was open. She added kindling and scraps of paper and started the fire with a long match. Moon sauntered in and lay on the rug beside the fire and went to sleep.

Jacey realized she was starving. She went into the kitchen and made pasta and heated some marinara sauce, then grated some Parmesan cheese. She found a bottle of wine and poured herself a glass. Then she filled Moon's bowl with cat food and refilled the water dish. Shawnee texted her asking if she was okay and to extend a final invite to a Christmas Eve dinner at her house. Jacey declined, saying she wanted to be alone, but thank you and merry Christmas.

Jacey took her plate and glass and sat down in front of the fire. She ate two servings, and after the second helping, left the plate out for Moon. She loved Italian food and licked the plate clean.

Jacey put more logs on the fire, then got the boxes of ornaments and lights she had bought. She found the tree stand and took it outside to make sure it fit the end of the tree, then dragged it all inside and set it up.

Jacey filled the stand with water and strung some clear lights through the branches. Moon's eyes glowed as she watched Jacey hang the lights. Jacey smiled at her. "Isn't it pretty?" She put up more lights, this time a strand of green and red ones. They mixed well with the clear strand. Jacey tore open the ornament boxes and placed them strategically in the tree. She found the two ornaments – a snow fairy and a carriage being pulled by two horses – and the angel tree topper she had brought from Savannah.

Jacey stood on her tiptoes and put the angel on top of the tree. She stood back and marveled at the angel's beauty. She was tired and wanted to curl up on the couch under the thick throw, and look at the fire and the tree with Moon curled up next to her. But she wanted to finish decorating. She found a pack of silver icicles and hung them on some branches. Now the tree looked like it had been bathed in magical water.

She looked at Moon, who was watching intently, wanting to attack the icicles. Jacey threw some on the floor, and Moon twisted and rolled with the icicles, biting them ferociously. Jacey smiled. Moon had curtailed her ferocity as of late, and Jacey was touched to see her play.

Jacey slid the empty boxes aside, then put more logs on the fire. She sat near the fire, watching it blaze brightly, until the heat soaked into her, making her face feel like she was glowing like a hot coal.

She got up and lay down on the couch, covering up with the thick throw blanket. Moon jumped up, curling up between Jacey's belly and knees. Jacey picked out shreds of icicles from her whiskers and petted her until her eyes closed. Jacey closed her eyes, too, listening to the fire pop and hiss. It was soothing, and soon she fell asleep.

CHAPTER 25

Jacey woke up and realized the blanket was gone. Moon was not on the couch either, but she heard him growling.

Jacey sat up quickly and saw her grandfather in front of the fireplace. He was wearing the suit he had been buried in. Jacey felt an almost comical sense of calm. She realized she had been waiting for him.

Suddenly he changed again, and he was younger, the way he had looked when Jacey was little. She stood up, and her legs shook slightly. She realized she was backing up, moving the couch behind her. He was in front of her, so close she could touch him. Moon howled and lunged at him, but he disappeared and she stopped short, yowling with fury. Her eyes glowed in the dim light.

Without thinking, Jacey grabbed Moon, then leaped to the fireplace and grabbed a half-burned log, and tossed it on the rug. Immediately the rug began to smoke.

She ran to the door, but she couldn't turn the handle. She pulled and even pushed, but the door wouldn't budge. She ran to the back door, but it wouldn't open either. They were trapped. She ran back into the living room to get to the stairs, but he blocked her way.

The rug was smoldering even more, and smoke was starting to fill up the room. Moon squirmed in her arms, wanting to leap at the evil thing.

She held her tighter. "Be still," she said.

Jacey looked at him. "It's going to burn down. Then where will you go?" she asked.

How did he get back here? she wondered. She looked at the tree she had dragged in, and everything clicked into place. She had brought in part of the woods; there was something about the woods, the trees. He was tied to not only the place where the poroniecs were buried, but somehow he was tied to the forest spirits.

He disappeared and Moon jumped out of her arms, screeching while she looked for him. Jacey dragged the tree to the fireplace and threw as much of it as she could into the flames. The angel topper landed at her feet; Jacey grabbed it and held it close to her chest. Suddenly she was thrown backward, landing on her back on the hard floor.

Moon yowled and Jacey saw her body slam into the wall.

"No!" Jacey screamed. She tried to get up, but he was suddenly hovering over her.

Jacey smelled the tree burning. She could just go up with it all. It was what she deserved anyway. A voice whispered to her: *Now, remember who you are. Remember those who fought so hard for you.*

"In the name of God, by God's power, send your most fierce angels, loose burning destruction on them, and banish the demons from this house. I ask the saints to help me, to intercede, "she yelled.

THE DEAD BORN

He disappeared, and Jacey got up. The tree was almost engulfed in flames, and the rug was on fire, too.

"Moon!" she screamed and ran to her. The cat was trying to get up, but her back leg was hurt, maybe broken.

Jacey put the angel in her sweater pocket and picked up Moon as gently as she could and tried the door. This time it opened, and she walked outside into the snow.

The snow was still falling in fat, wet dollops from the hazy sky. There was probably about six inches of snow by now, and the wind whipped the snow into a blizzard. As Jacey stumbled in a drift, she realized she didn't have shoes on.

The snow was so bright, it illuminated the night. Jacey went to her car and opened the driver's-side door. She placed Moon on the passenger seat, and she cried out in pain. She looked at Jacey as if for help. "I'm so sorry. Wait here – I'll come back for you," she said and kissed the cat's head.

Jacey went back into the snow. The wind howled and blew powdery clouds of snow into her face. She had to get her purse so she could drive away; she knew it was on the kitchen table. Jacey ran to the house and saw smoke coming from the open door.

She hesitated, then peeked in through the door. The fire had not spread to the kitchen, so she sprinted to the table, grabbing her purse. She turned, and he was in front of her. She slipped in her wet socks and fell on her ass. She gasped in pain and inhaled a lungful of smoke. A coughing fit overtook her, but she managed to crawl away. She took off her sweater and held it in front of her nose and mouth. She got up and made her way into the sunroom and was almost to the door. He stood in front of it. Jacey stopped but then went forward, intending to walk through him. His presence held her in place.

"Die, you fuck! Die! You fucker!" she screamed, then broke out coughing again.

Then she heard a voice in her mind. It was her own voice, but from when she was a child.

"Face the monster," her voice told her. "The power is you, and the trees, the dark woods."

Jacey remembered now. She saw herself in the woods at night; the trees were alive, and she spoke to the spirits in them, and in the water, and in the flames of the small fires she built under the night sky. The woods were magic. The spirits imbued in the woods and the air and the water and the fire were from one source, the divine that she never even knew to recognize. The divine source of God was the most powerful magic; nothing else could stand a chance. All she had to do was invoke it.

Come, Holy Spirit.

Jacey suddenly stood still. She went out of herself and felt compelled to go to the moment her mother made a deal with the devil. She was in the room with her mother. She walked closer. Her mother was so young. She had been eighteen when she had Jacey, and now Jacey knew that her mother had desperately tried to make a deal for her unborn baby. To get away, to escape the evil. But in doing so, she had unknowingly sealed a tragic fate.

Jacey was taken to the hospital room where her mother was giving birth. Jacey watched as she came out of her mother. Newborn Jacey was not breathing. She was stillborn. She watched as the doctor pulled her out from between her mother's legs. Jacey looked normal, but she wasn't moving or breathing. Her mother screamed. The doctor took Jacey to a gleaming steel table and began to massage her tiny chest. Her mother was no longer screaming, just whispering a prayer. The doctor kept massaging Jacey's chest, and Jacey saw her newborn self finally take a deep breath and begin to cry.

Jacey came back to the moment. She felt something – roots, she saw – wrap around her ankles, and smelled the pine trees, the snow, the ice, the dirt. The roots crisscrossed her body like veins.

THE DEAD BORN

She soaked up everything around her and saw everything. The pulse of the universe, the subatomic and atomic particles colliding to become swelling balls of gasses and exploding into galaxies.

Send forth your spirit, and they shall be created.

She began to float up and out of the house. She heard a voice, a voice that made her want to fall on her knees and wail with praise. Such love poured forth from the being. How could a being this beautiful and good love her, love any vile human? *The things you see are from Me, this gift is Me, I have allowed you to manifest this for a reason. No soul can be sold, for all souls belong to Me. Ho diabolos, the scatterer, the rapist, confuses and lies, defiles. The things on your land are of him, not Me. The others succumbed to him, perverted their gifts. What will you do? Which way will you go?*

Suddenly hands were on her, and she was outside, back in the snow. She saw shapes: Adelaide, her mother, the poroniecs, which she now knew were the damned souls of some of her ancestors that had shown themselves as the sacrificed babies. To scatter and confuse, they did their master's bidding.

Someone was carrying her and speaking to her, but she couldn't make out what he was saying. She tried to talk, to tell him what she had seen, to tell him to help Moon.

Jacey looked at the house. She expected to see the house consumed by fire, smoke billowing to the sky. But there was only a little bit of smoke. The tree she had cut down and dragged into the house was laying in the yard. There was sap oozing from the bark, and even over the smoke, Jacey could smell its pungent and somehow alluring acridly sweet smell.

And You shall renew the face of the Earth.

Jacey saw men going into the house. They were dressed in hats and carrying hoses, and she watched them spray the water inside the house, then walk inside.

One of the men helped her inside a truck. She relished the heat and warmth. He put a coat over her.

"My cat, she's inside my car, her leg is hurt, maybe broken …" Her throat was sore, and her voice sounded froggy. She was still clutching the sweater, and she took the angel out of her pocket and kissed it.

The fireman shut the door. She watched him run toward the car, but she couldn't make out his shape. The snow was coming down harder. How would she get Moon to a vet?

The door opened and the man placed Moon in Jacey's lap. Moon looked up at Jacey and gave out a weak meow, then licked Jacey's hand.

"Hold on, I'll get you help," she told Moon.

The fireman was looking at Jacey.

"Please, we have to help her, she's hurt," Jacey said.

"I'll call someone. I know a veterinarian, we can take her there," he said. He reached out and petted Moon gently on her head. He put a small blanket over the cat.

"The snow … the roads," Jacey said.

"I'll get us there, don't worry," he said. "Take off your wet socks and put your feet under the heater." Jacey did as she was told.

As they drove off, Jacey looked at the house. Still standing. She saw Adelaide in front of the house. Then Jacey saw other figures standing and watching with her. The saints, the ones who would help guide her; they were her blood, the good blood, the pure and virtuous, and now they would guide her to the place she needed to be. Jacey got an image: an ancient, gnarled driftwood tree backlit by the sunset on a beach at night.

Jacey looked down at her hands. They were covered with scratches. She smelled the scent of pine needles, of bark and dirt. Still here, she thought. Jacey smiled and caught her reflection in the window. Her eyes were now a deep garnet color.

"How did you know to come here?" Jacey asked the fireman.

"Got a call from a man who said he saw smoke coming from your house. How the hell he saw smoke in this weather is beyond me, but we came over straight away. Lucky you're not too far from the fire department," he said. "Here, this was laying beside you when we pulled you out. Thought you might want it with you."

The man handed Jacey her Bible. It had been upstairs in the bedroom the last time she had seen it, but here it was. Jacey looked at the house.

"Is it going to burn down?" she asked.

"No, not even close. They have it contained, ma'am," he said.

Jacey started laughing. She couldn't help it. She saw the fireman look at her, concerned. She looked at him, and he ever so slightly shrank back.

"Contained. ... Yes, that's very true," she said. "Is it still Christmas Eve?"

He glanced at her. The man had noticed the woman's eyes again. They had appeared red at first, but he assumed it was his imagination, from the flames. But he saw her eyes clearly now, and they were a deep burgundy color.

"Technically, it's Christmas Day, since it's just after midnight," he said.

Christmas Day, Jacey thought.

Rebirth had been inevitable.

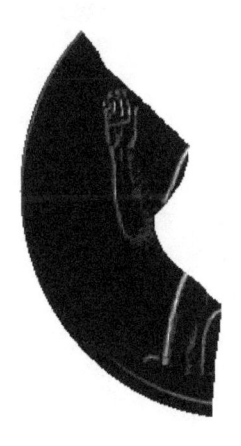

End.

CPSIA information can be obtained
at www.ICGtesting.com
Printed in the USA
BVHW041744131222
654112BV00006B/266